"I...wasn't sure whether to come inside, whether you wanted others to know, or..."

Heart pounding, she gave a lopsided smile. "You were protecting my honor?"

"Um. Yes. I suppose."

Sharon stepped closer to him, a small step. Because despite the need she saw in him, he looked like he might bolt at any second. "Or were you protecting yours?"

"What?" His head jerked back a little and Sharon swore at herself. *Don't do that, you idiot. Don't. Not tonight. Not with him so close.*

"I'm kidding," she said and smiled.

He visibly relaxed. "So...I have my car just..." He pointed vaguely back down the block towards Hastings Street.

"Okay." She smiled again, packing her own fears away. This was like coaxing a skittish tiger. You yourself had to be totally in control.

TERRI DARLING

Second Chances

fiero
PUBLISHING

Published in electronic form 2011 by Fiero Publishing
Published in trade paper 2013 by Fiero Publsihing
www.fieropublishing.com
Book and cover design copyright © 2013 by Fiero Publishing
Cover design by Terry Hayman/Fiero Publishing
Cover art copyright © archive/istock and krosseel/morguephoto

ISBN-13: 978-1927920091

ISBN-10: 1927920094

First Print Edition: December 2013

For the lost of East Hastings.
May they someday be found.

Second Chances

1

A LMOST FIVE P.M. She was going to lose her job if she was late many more times. And still she was here. Back in the stench of urine in the stairwells, the itchy paranoia of the guys you passed on the second floor.

It was too much like coming home.

"Third floor. C'mon." Micky waved her long, ruby red fingernails at her to hurry up.

Sharon winced and nodded. But as she hurried up the worn wooden stairs, she couldn't help feeling that the guys on second had somehow recognized her. They'd seen past the clean gray university sweats and zip-up fleece, seen past the clean skin and hair, and recognized one of their own.

"I'm *not*," she muttered.

But you're here.

She shook her head. "Shut up."

Reaching the third floor, she saw Micky clack down the hall in her high-heeled boots and in through a door at the end. Sharon followed. The four unmade beds inside, the wasted girl in one, the thick smell of unwashed clothes and unfinished food containers strewn around on the floor—they all triggered in Sharon a sudden, intense need to smoke. Worst cravings she'd had since she'd quit a year ago.

"Hey," Sharon said.

"Who're you?" the girl whined back. She was probably trying to sound tough, though she couldn't have been more than sixteen. The sunken eyes and pinched face made it hard to tell. She looked sick. Otherwise, she'd have been down on the street tonight.

"Shut up," said Micky, unknowingly mimicking Sharon's earlier command to herself. Micky scooped up a half-empty pizza box with disgust.

"Jamie'll kick your—"

"I said shut *up*! You talk and I'll cut you while you sleep."

The girl huddled back in her blankets and shivered. Sharon pursed her lips and nodded, remembering how you had to enforce discipline on the street.

Micky obviously saw it on her face because she turned with a kind of smug tolerance to acknowledge her. "Rose," Micky said, gesturing at the wasted girl in the bed. Something in the gesture said the older hooker probably considered herself Rose's surrogate mother. She'd just never show it, because that wasn't how you survived on the street.

God, Sharon *really* needed a cigarette.

A noise out in the hall signaled the arrival of Angel, the other prostitute Sharon had befriended over the last two months. She stumbled in through the door and grabbed the jamb, panting and looking around with her eyes wide. Unlike the hard little Micky, Angel was a good head taller than Sharon but fine boned and a natural dirty blond, like a swaying willow tree. Beautiful. Delicate. Clear signs she hadn't lived on the street long.

"Wow!" Angel gasped at last. "You showed up!"

Sharon half-smiled and nodded. "Yeah."

"Oh, but hey!" She straightened up. "Jamie! Someone said they saw him coming back from Commercial Drive. We got, like, two minutes!"

"Figures," said Micky. She crossed her arms over her chest and turned towards Sharon. "So? We're all here. What d'you got to say?"

"Nice place," Sharon said. "I'm sure you'd hate to leave it."

"Yeah, right."

Sharon's gaze flicked around the room and settled on the bed that, at first glance, looked like the others. Same sort of filthy mattress and box spring on a metal h-frame. Rumpled sheets and no mattress cover. But this one was more bowed in the middle—the abuse of regular male weight, plus.

"Jamie's bed," she said, pointing.

Micky and Angel looked at one another.

"We gotta *go*," Angel moaned suddenly. Probably not just from fear of Jamie, but from drug withdrawal too. Worse even than quitting smoking. Angel would be anxious not to miss her jailer/punisher/pimp/supplier. Just as Sharon was anxious *not* to meet him. Besides which, Sharon was going to be late for work if she didn't get going soon.

"In a minute!" Micky snapped. But her hard eyes actually betrayed a glimmer of hope as they looked at Sharon. They looked at Sharon's cropped, dyed-black hair, semi-goth. Tried to fit it with the clean clothes, the lack of makeup, the careful speech.

"You really did this?" Micky said.

"Nearly four years of it."

"Not here."

"No."

"Where?"

Sharon shook her head. She'd use her past this much, to get them to listen to her, but there was no way she was going to risk that past ever finding her again. "I was lucky enough to have someone help me get out."

"And we're payback," Micky said.

"You could say that."

The hard woman nodded.

Sharon pushed it. "You said something was changing on the street. New girls. New pimps. You've been thinking about my offer?"

"Shit," Angel burst out. She was dancing into the room now like she had to pee. "Come *on.*"

Micky ignored her. "This 'safe house' you been working on," she said to Sharon. "It's the hotel over the bar where you work, right?"

"Yes." Sharon forced her hands out of her pockets. Body language—nothing to hide.

"Why would we go there? What would we get?"

"It's a first step. A place to chill. You talk to people. You work out a plan. We get you on methadone...."

"Methadone!" Angel shrieked. Her long body shook, feet unable to stop their little dance. "I don't want metha-shit! They tie you down and pump you up!"

"You tell her," said an accented male voice from the door.

"Jamie!" Rose yelped from her bed.

The other three women whirled towards the door and Sharon felt her careful confidence shot through with ice. Whatever she'd told herself about who she was now, however much she'd made a new life, the situation and cues presented right here and now took over her like she was nothing but a puppet. She wanted to run so badly she thought she'd vomit.

It was all she could do to hold her ground. But she did, breaking out in a cold sweat over her forehead.

The girls' pimp lounged against the doorjamb—skinny, male, late twenties, dark-skinned with a black burn mark on his upper lip, Arab looking. He had none of the height Sharon's pimp had carried. None of Daryl's shoulder breadth, the rusty red moustache and crazy-ass glint in his eyes.

But this pimp was still just like him. In the threat. The attitude.

"Jamie" tugged a little white baggy from inside his jean jacket pocket and called softly to Angel. "Hey, baby. A little nanoo to cook."

He tossed it and she scrambled for it. Then he turned to Micky. "How about you? You are ready for some wings?"

"Don't," Sharon whispered. Not sure if it was to Micky, to Jamie, or to herself.

Micky swallowed and hesitated and Jamie's lips snarled up. He came towards Sharon with an odd sideways gait, snapped out a hand, and grabbed Sharon's upper arm. "Why are you here? You want a taste? Or you are just trying to fuck up my income?"

"No...," Sharon said.

It was all she could manage. Like the ice in her veins had wrapped around her vocal cords when he'd grabbed her. Like she was seventeen again and knowing that the way to avoid getting beaten was to simply stay as still as possible.

"We came up to check on Rose," Micky said from somewhere. "Sharon here's a nurse."

"Yeah?" said Jamie, the acrid smell of him washing over her, his bony hand still clenching her upper arm.

The hint of hesitation in his voice, Micky speaking her name, broke up just enough of the ice that Sharon managed to focus and clear her throat. "Rose...has pneumonia. It's serious and contagious. You could all get it. She needs antibiotics. I could take her. I—"

"No." Jamie threw her arm away from him and sidled over to where Rose huddled. "Micky will take her." He ripped the covers off the shivering girl. "Get up!"

Micky stepped close to Sharon and whispered, "Get out of here."

Sharon, trembling head to foot as the broken ice still flowed through her, nodded. She couldn't do this after all. She wasn't strong enough.

Then she glanced at Angel, who crouched in the corner, with a small jug of water, a hypodermic needle she'd found somewhere, and the baggy Jamie had thrown her. At Micky, whose hard eyes were scared silly underneath.

And she quickly reached to the zipper of her fanny pack, unzipped it, and slid out the little slip of paper she'd prepared. Her cell phone number.

"Take it," she whispered, and shoved it at Micky.

"Go," Micky whispered back.

"Call me. Or just come see me where I work."

Jamie suddenly gave an eerie, high-pitched roar and kicked at the bed Rose lay in, Micky stuffed the number into the top of her Spandex pants.

Sharon wavered, feet wanting to run. Needing to. "You remember where—"

"The Red Owl Bar," Micky whispered. "Yeah. Fuck. Go."

Sharon ran.

~~~~

Cross & Shiptite? Delivered. Done.

Griffin Walsh flipped the final file closed on his glass-topped desk. Then he loosened his tie, planted one Vigotti-shod foot on the lip of the desk, and pushed himself back on his chair with a bit of a spin, riding it like a cowboy until the wheels reached the edge of his carpet protector and bumped to a halt.

Griffin thumped down his feet, stood up and walked to the narrow, but very tall, window.

The whole of north downtown Vancouver spread out before him, from the Wall Building to the line of glass condos lining Coal Harbour, with Stanley Park beyond. It was hard not to feel a bit godlike up on the twenty-third floor. Hard not to feel, given the bonuses he'd be receiving this year, that he was already into the good life barely three years out of UBC Law.

Which was the danger, of course. Exactly the sort of things he'd begun warning some of his greener clients about, something passed on to him from his own parents: *Never let the people you're playing with seduce you away from your goals.*

The question was which people were trying to seduce Griffin here?

He tugged on his right ear. Was it his current bosses at Greene McNamara, with their fabulous performance bonuses and the incredible support staff and reputation that let him punch way above his expected class? Or was it—tug the left ear—Mr. Majo—hard "j"—Cruz, longtime friend and law school buddy who was dangling the classic temptation of starting up their own firm where *they* would be the managing partners and answer only to their clients and the law?

Greene McNamara—money, clout, solid career path.

Majo & Walsh—freedom and control. Though maybe no money, no career, business failure in two years.

Hmm, as his first year Commercial Law prof was wont to say, usually using one hand to hold his chin and tap his nose rather than tugging on his ears.

Hmm.

Without a knock, the door to Griffin's office opened and Griffin swung around to see the craggy form of Burt Lester swagger in. Lester, fourth partner on the letterhead. He rarely came down to the juniors' floor. In fact the grapevine said the appearances of this former football star were getting rarer and rarer in the office, even up on twenty-four where the other partners worked.

Not that anyone was surprised. The aging quarterback's main skill seemed to be looking great in an expensive suit.

"You broke their defense," Lester said, as if it was obvious what he was referring to. Which of course it was. The Cross-Shiptite merger. The same deal that had slipped through Lester's own fingers eight years earlier.

"Yes, sir," Griffin said and waited.

Lester stared at him, nodding his large head until Griffin decided to put him out of his misery.

"There was a sudden opening of the Chinese wheat barriers," Griffin said.

"Ah."

Since it was clear Lester still didn't understand, Griffin explained how Chinese shipping giant CSCL had found itself short and needed a fast deal but wouldn't go multiple because of government pressures. Which had led them to Cross, which had already been looking at

Shiptite again.

"Since you'd already laid the groundwork for their merger the first time around," Griffin offered, "I mostly acted as facilitator."

Lester, who'd been leaning forward intently as Griffin had talked, now huffed, as if about to take credit, then laughed with a snort and straightened.

"From anyone else, you know, I'd call that a major suck up."

"It's not, sir. It's just the truth."

"I know! That's what's so incredible. I couldn't believe it when I read your reports, but now, seeing you again, hearing you talk, damned if you're not just like they say."

"How's that, sir?"

"Goddamned humble. Goddamned honest. And goddamned self-confident. Supposedly smart too. That's why they all come to you, you know. They chose you because they know you play it absolutely straight with them."

"Thank you, sir. I like to think I provide good legal advice too."

"Oh, sure, sure." Lester shook his head and shoved his hands into his Hugo Boss trouser pockets like he was fishing for a football in there somewhere. "But this obsessive honesty thing... I've read the reports."

A hard tightness slipped around Griffin's shoulders. "Sir?"

"You really did use some of the templates I'd worked out for the deal. A little bit from there, a little bit from other deals."

"I...did say it wasn't that complicated."

Lester turned on him and his craggy shoulders hunched forward. It made him look like he was calling Griffin into a huddle. "You could have called in more help, stretched it out, covered more contingencies, billed for research time. My God, man. You just closed a merger between two of the biggest marine players out here and you billed them the same as some of the other juniors bill mom-and-pop stores to set up a franchise!"

The old man was shaking all over as he finished, like he expected Griffin to shout, "Yes, *sir!*" and run for position.

Griffin didn't. But the tension in his shoulders had spread right down his arms and chest now. And his office felt very narrow. "You want me to artificially inflate the cost of our services?"

"It's called *commercial* law, Mr. Walsh. The top lawyers cost top dollar. So if you want to be a top lawyer in our ranks..." He hovered over the thought, letting the hint of a sooner-than-expected partnership sink home. "You want to be a top lawyer, you have to learn not just to think like one, but to bill like one.

"Is that clear?"

Griffin's neck was too stiff to nod even if he'd wanted to. Keeping his voice neutral, he said, "Yes, sir. Very."

"Good," said Lester and hovered a moment longer, as if expecting Griffin to deke around him. "Good."

When Griffin didn't move from his stance behind his desk, Lester finally nodded his big head, swiveled about like a quarterback about to jog back down the field after a touchdown, and walked out the door.

For almost a full minute, Griffin stared after him. Then he walked to his desk, clicked up a number on his computer screen, and dialed the phone.

The other end picked up after two rings.

"Cruz here."

"Majo," Griffin said. "It's me. We gotta talk. Where?" A pause. "The Red Owl? Give me the address...Fine. Half and hour."

2

THE RED OWL BAR & HOTEL HAD BEEN BUILT IN 1903 and looked like it hadn't been washed since then. Four stories tall, it shared a wall for the first three floors on its east side with a meat shop that did decent business, but had heavy bars fixed over its windows.

On the Red Owl's west side, all four floors shared a wall with a poured-concrete garment factory that had been shut down for years, half the windows smashed, the bottom boarded up. Squatters and drug dealers usually accessed the factory's interior via an upended bedframe in the alleyway that let them reach the second floor windows.

The Red Owl itself, for all its dirt, was in decent repair. Above the tatty awning that advertised the first floor bar, its stucco facade rose up, patched and re-patched. A number of the windows looked newer. Most of the original simple cornice still ran across the top undamaged, and the tops of the three flat faux-pillars that bounded the two columns of windows—six windows, six rooms—still butted up under them.

It looked, all told, like a grumpy old man who'd squatted down a long time ago and refused to budge since.

This despite the deterioration of Vancouver's downtown east side into a skid row, the establishment of a major cop shop two blocks away, and the evolution of the nearby "pigeon park" into a place where mothers were afraid to walk their children for fear of stepping on a discarded heroin needle or crack pipe.

The Red Owl continued.

~~~~

Sharon got to the Red Owl's back alley door still running.

Her heart pounded so hard inside her that her chest hurt and her lungs forced her into a racking cough. It was as if all of her had been thrown into the past—her mind, her lungs. She hadn't been that scared since Julia Morrow had helped her get out of Kelowna. Hadn't coughed this hard since the first days going cold turkey on smokes.

Even her face, burning and running with sweat in the thick air, seemed clenched into the kind of mask she hadn't worn since Kelowna. She shook her head hard and blew out over and over again through her lips. She was *not* that girl any more. Hadn't been for almost five years, damn it.

She rubbed and slapped her cheeks then looked, embarrassed, up and down the alley. Two guys lolled at the rear of the garment factory just south of her, but they were too interested in their little tube with a Brillo pad—a homemade crack pipe—to see her. They probably wouldn't even be able to stand up soon.

Sharon coughed and spat on the pavement. Wiped her nose. At least...at least she'd never done that, thank God.

Desperately pulling herself back together, she grabbed the rough metal handle of the Red Owl door, squealed it open, and slipped inside. The greasy bustle of the kitchen cramped around her. Pushing past the six metal barrels of house draft and boxes of bottled beer, mostly Coors, she headed for the staff room.

Her friend Lisa caught her at the discharge rollers of the dishwasher, swinging the tray she was carrying around and up like a stop sign.

"Gotta *use* them tenny runners, hon! We was all beginning to wonder if you were coming in at all tonight."

"I'm not that late. It's only–"

"Fourth time this month. Henry's pissed."

"Shit."

Lisa tossed back her big, back-combed, blonde hair with a dramatic sigh and used her free hand to tug down her low-cut, tight tee-shirt. "Pete and Digger brought in prob'ly twenty-five Hard Riders for dinner. I barely got an ass left, all those boys pinched it so much."

Sharon smiled despite herself. If there was one thing Lisa Doigis, ex-pat Texan, never had to worry about losing, it was her substantial tits and ass. They were "her meal tickets" as she said. And they did indeed seem to have supported her since she'd fled her home state with her five-year-old son, Danny. Exactly what she'd run from she'd never volunteered and Sharon would never ask. Any more than Lisa would ask her where *she* had come from.

"I better run," Sharon said.

"Damn right." But Lisa grabbed her arm as she started to move. "Gotta talk to you sometime, okay? Just you'n me. Sunday?"

"Sure. Everything okay?"

Lisa couldn't answer because the latest young Chinese girl Henry had hired (going through them like firewood—he obviously didn't pay them enough) came jabbering back at them in Chinese, shooing them away from the girl's dishwashing station and towards the front. There Elrad, the cook, greeted Sharon and slid a basket of chicken wings along the counter towards Lisa.

"Clucks up!"

Lisa leapt over, caught them onto her tray, and rolled her eyes at Sharon. "Pete's, of course. Most of the others skedaddled but Pete and Digger just keep on–"

The door to the main room banged open and Henry's bulk stood there, white sleeves rolled up on impressive forearms, thick-lipped face bulging red. "Doigis! Finish your–" He saw Sharon. "Well fucking nice of you to show up."

"I–"

"Thirty seconds, on the floor, you want to keep your job!" He slammed back out to the bar proper.

"Mr. Wonderful," Lisa said, backing out after him. "But you better hurry, hon."

Sharon took a deep breath. Great. She wanted to press Henry about leasing rooms upstairs for which she didn't have financing yet, and he was ready to fire her. She was batting a million tonight.

She chewed her lip and went to the staff corner to strip off her fleece, track pants, and purse. Thing was, she thought as she got them off and balled them into her box, Angel and Micky, and now Rose, couldn't wait long. Even if things *weren't* sliding on their block, street life was always touch-and-go. Sharon had to get things moving. Maybe she could talk to Henry tonight after all. After she'd put in a good night of sucking up to customers, making the Red Owl's usual clientele feel happy and horny.

Something she was unfortunately good at.

She straightened her own white, stretchy top, adjusted her skimpy black shorts, switched her runners for the black shoes she kept at the pub, and did a quick spike gel on her hair.

Then she grabbed a serving tray and headed out.

~~~~

The dive reeked of sex, Griffin thought.

Why was that? And why had Majo chosen this particular place to meet?

Griffin let the grimy door of the Red Owl Bar & Hotel bang closed behind him with a jingle of the bells attached to it, and tried to figure it out. The room had eight old wooden tables, five of them occupied. Dark wooden walls. Door to the hotel stairs on the right wall. Dim light. Wood-shuttered windows. Seventies Elton John, "Goodbye Yellow Brick Road" playing somewhere.

Above it all wafted a greasy food smell cut with cigarette smoke, even though smoking wasn't allowed in Vancouver pubs.

The drinkers on the right side of the room looked like bikers with elaborate jean jackets, a stylized HR crest on the back. The left side of the room had just a few wasted-looking men at the tables and two female customers at the straight slab bar that looked like it had a Formica top and thick plastic front.

The sour-looking bartender behind the bar was eyed Griffin like he was some kind of foul roadkill.

Majo was nowhere to be seen.

And the sex?

Griffin grimaced. Obviously all in his mind. Even the two waitresses by the right end of the bar near the kitchen door had their backs turned to him as they whispered to one another. Both had truly fine rear ends displayed in shorts that might as well have been thongs, they rode up so high. But one was a big-haired blonde, and the other a spiky, black-haired model. Neither his type.

Nor did Griffin have *time* for sex. Especially not now. Majo may have initiated this meeting and chosen the place, but it was Griffin with the plan, Griffin who'd become unshakably gripped with a sense of destiny after Burt Lester's visit this afternoon.

It was a time for great beginnings. Here and now.

Just as soon as Majo showed up.

The waitresses still hadn't seen him, so Griffin made his own way to an empty table in the far left corner. The first item of business after putting this deal together would be finding a better place for social meetings.

He just got his trench coat and suit jacket off, tie loosened, when Majo Cruz came strutting into the pub. He spotted Griffin, waved, winked at the two women watching his entrance from their barstools, and sauntered over. "*Ola!* " he said.

Griffin rolled his eyes but still stuck out his hand to his darker-skinned law school buddy, whose conservative Mexican parents were probably rolling in their graves at the way he let everyone give his name a hard J. *Ma—joe.*

"Whaddya think?" Maj said as he gripped.

"About...?"

"The place! This pub! My all-time favorite downtown hangout!"

"Which caters currently to six bikers, three grizzled men who look like they work at the meat shop down the block, four underage Asian kids who followed you in, and two hookers at the bar trying for the Wednesday night after work crowd. Oh, and the thug-like bartender and two waitresses who are *still* ignoring us. Very nice."

"Isn't it."

"You troll for clients here?"

Maj slapped a hand over his heart. "I'm hurt. I'm mortally and morally wounded by that remark." He grinned and slipped off his own trench and sports coat. His tie had a dancing Hawaiian girl on it. "Actually," he said and sat, "I did pick up a client here. Bar fight. Clear case of self-defense. I slipped him my card while he was sprawled over by the bar, waiting for the cops. He was very grateful when I got him off quietly. He was a married stockbroker. The *cabrón* who attacked him was the boyfriend of the babe he'd brought here."

"Delightful." Griffin snorted.

"But mainly this place is close to the cop shop, so I come here to hang out and meet the other side."

"Business lunches."

"Exactly. And the prettiest barmaids in Vancouver." Majo swiveled around and tried to catch the eye of one of the two waitresses. "Yo! Customers here!"

Griffin sat back to watch his friend with amusement. Majo had always been the brashest of their law school group. Never the smartest, or most responsible, and rarely politically correct, you still had to admire him. He had guts, charm, and street smarts. No one had been surprised when he articled in a top criminal law firm and got hired back.

Most critical for Griffin, though, was that Majo's heart was in the right place. He cared about his clients. His ethics were solid. That had been the final kicker to–

"Hey, Sharon!" Maj stood up and cupped his hands around his mouth. "Come on! My friend's dying to meet you!"

Griffin frowned. The spiky-haired waitress had turned, seen them, then turned back like she wanted to hide. Something about the name... "I don't think—"

Majo cut him off with a grin. "Trust me on this one."

~~~

For the second time that night, Sharon felt like a young girl again, her heart pounding. It couldn't be him. Not here. Not like this. It had to be Majo's fault. She'd kill him for this. God, she wished she had a cigarette.

Henry leaned over the side of the bar to poke her and she almost shrieked.

"What?" Henry said. "Majo's calling for you."

"What is it, hon?" Lisa said.

Sharon turned even more towards the wall, trying to hide her face. "I can't."

"S'only Majo," Lisa said.

"It's not him."

"The other guy? What? Looks like a hunk to me. Ears stick out a little."

"I know him!" Sharon said.

"Yeah?" Lisa lifted one eyebrow. "Tell me on Sunday."

It was apparently all the interest she could muster. Her shift was done. She'd been just telling Sharon how Danny's after-school daycare was getting antsy about the times she showed up late. And, despite the usual Texas attitude, she was bagged. No help from that quarter.

Sharon was almost tempted to run into the back to grab one the young Chinese girls from the kitchen, but they all kept their heads down around men and spoke little English. No help from there either.

"Dekker." The big bartender's voice had an edge now, and some or the closer bar patrons were watching. You did not want to get this big man riled. "You with us? Or you like unemployment?"

"I'm going," Sharon said.

She straightened her bra under her the tight stretch of her top, tucked her tray under arm, and rubbed what felt like some sort of crap stuck to the corner of her mouth. Probably the fries she'd quickly scarfed in the kitchen for dinner in between Pete's food orders. Between that and her sweat from her run here earlier, she knew she looked like hell.

Of course, it wouldn't matter. Griffin Walsh—If it was really him. *Of course it's him.*—wouldn't even remember her. It had been what? Nine years? Ten? And she doubted she'd even had a real impact on him in high school. Despite her best efforts.

Sharon Dekker wasn't the sort of girl the Griffin Walshes of the world remembered.

She took a big breath, then strode out across the floor, circled the biker's table where Pete and Digger whistled at her, ignored the cackles of Brittany and Phyllis at the bar, and the crude stares of the kids near the back whom she was surprised Henry even let in the door. They looked underaged.

Then she was there, right beside Majo's elbow. She gave him and his buddy a quick, fixed smile. "Hi, guys."

And she'd been right. Griffin didn't remember her.

God, but she sure remembered him. Still square-jawed and serious, but firmed up now, with an adult set to his shoulders and a sky blue shirt that looked like Egyptian cotton or something. And when he looked up at her with those dark blue, serious eyes, it still made her knees weak and whole body respond. Like she was back in high school in Vernon, not virginal but innocent, and he was agreeing to be her debate partner in social studies. Grade twelve. Her final desperate play for brainy, unattainable Griffin Walsh. Virtually raping him behind the bleachers in the gymnasium. Ignoring her dying mother's advice that a girl who gives it up too easily loses everything.

She'd sure proved that right, hadn't she.

Now his vague smile nailed it home. He didn't even give her the usual male once-over of her body. She was nothing to him. Less than nothing.

"Sharon Dekker," said Majo. "Like you to meet a buddy of mine from UBC Law. Griffin W—"

"Walsh," Sharon completed. "Yes. I know."

She forced herself to lean onto one hip in exaggerated expectation and said nothing. She did drop her arms so he could fully look at her. She knew the tight top Henry encouraged her and Lisa to wear did good things for her figure. She wasn't huge up top, but was slim-waisted, and the low scoop and push-up bra gave her the cleavage of a pin-up girl.

Or a slut?

Her blood rushed from her toes up to her face. Her ears burned and she fumbled her hair back over them. But she still didn't back off. Majo, she noted, was goggling back and forth between Griffin and her. Somehow there were always spectators to her worst humiliations.

"I...um...," Griffin mumbled.

Majo plunged his face into his hands. "*Está fregado*," he moaned.

Sharon swallowed and made it even worse. "Vernon High. Ms. Robertson's social studies class. You and I worked together for a debate—'Whether Canada's military should assist in non-combat third world countries.'"

"Ri-i-i-ight," Griffin stalled, obviously wracking his brains. "Sharon Nells. No...Neal? Sharon Neal."

"You are pathetic, man," Majo said, raising his face. "I told you—"

"Griffin's right," Sharon said and Majo shut up.

"You dropped out before the end of the school year," Griffin said. "You didn't graduate."

"That's right," she said. A whole lost world behind that.

Yet for a moment even *that* was irrelevant. Beyond all reason, her mind and body were back in little girl mode around this man, back in high school when the world still had promise.

"You don't remember anything else?"

He met her eyes. Something there. She saw some...

He shook his head and everything crashed around her again— the rejection, the behind-the-hand whispers about her from his high school friends, her father finding out, and the whole snowballing, out-of-control mess that her life had become. It hadn't been Griffin's fault any more than it had been her own. But he didn't even re*member*?

Face burning now from anger as much as embarrassment, Sharon flipped her bar tray up in front of her and took a deep breath to steady herself. "So what'll you gentlemen have?"

Griffin started but Majo recovered immediately. "Beer. Whatever's on tap. Nice tall glass. Foaming head. Better music. You."

He grinned so pleadingly that Sharon gave him a laugh, glad to be looking anywhere other than at Griffin. "Coming up," she said, and hurried at a near run back to the bar.

But as she went, her insides steamed.

3

SHARON NEAL. Now with a new last name. By marriage?

Griffin stared after her, entranced by the movement of her hips, sway of her back, the bounce of her new spiky hairstyle as she turned her head to joke with other customers.

"Okay, Griff. Spill."

That profile. Those lips. He'd almost swallowed his tongue when she'd walked to their table. It had been as if his single, stubbornly recurring dream had stepped out onto the floor, flesh and blood, touchable, in front of him. And his first thought was that he had to be mistaken. Sharon Neal was almost like a movie in his mind, a once-upon-a-time from another time and life. This couldn't have been her.

Then she'd spoken and he'd known it was. The husky growl of a heavy smoker, though he never remembered her smoking in high school, even with her bad girl reputation. And that little scar across the bridge of her nose? Where had she gotten that?

"Yoo-hoo," Majo was calling, waving a flat hand in front of him.

"What?" Griffin tore his gaze from Sharon's back and looked at Maj.

"Yes, she's a stunner. Very hot. Dangerous. Every guy who comes in here, be they cop, crack-addict, or distinguished gentleman like myself, tries desperately to wrangle her phone number. Never get anywhere. And *you*, with your 'Uh...um...,' have her blushing and flirting and furious."

Griffin snorted and sat back. "What? No."

"High school," Majo said casually. "You know I seem to recall her mentioning her high school one time. It sounded familiar. I mentioned your name. She seemed to know it."

"You bastard. That's why you chose here for the meeting."

"And you debated together? That's like *oral* argument, right?"

Griffin narrowed his eyes at his friend. "Not like that." Except that inside he thought, *You don't know the half of it.* "We just shared a class. We were from two different worlds. You know the high school structure, right? All the little cliques? Let's just say our social groups didn't mix."

"And you never...?"

"Never." Griffin nailed down the lie by stabbing a finger into the table.

Then he bit his lips and almost took it back. He never lied, rarely even social lies. Yet here he'd lied vigorously at least twice in five minutes—the first time to Sharon in pretending he didn't remember everything about her; the second time now, denying Sharon had been anything to him physically or otherwise.

Not good.

He glanced back at her as she turned with their beer to came back their way and realized his mouth had gone dry. Good grief. He had no trouble believing what Majo said about guys coming onto Sharon. Even without the lithe body and punk black haircut, her face had a kind of big-lipped hurt that made you want to kiss all the bad stuff away.

Sharp eyes, though. She felt them slash him as she set down the drinks, then turned to Majo. "He paying?" she asked.

Majo spread his hands and looked at Griffin. "He's the business law guy. He's got the money."

"Business law, hunh."

"I'm paying," Griffin said. Was that mango he smelled?

"Good," she said, without looking at him, and flounced away, rear end twitching provocatively in her tight black shorts.

"Oh, yeah," Majo said as he picked up the beer to sip off the foam. "Definitely nothing went on between you two."

Griffin tore his gaze once more from Sharon's departing backside and said, "What?" Then, at Majo's smirk, shook his head as clear as he could. "Absolutely no—way—in—Hell. Okay? Even if she'd gone on to be a doctor, I wouldn't be interested."

"You sure? You know her last name is Dekker now. Doesn't that tweak your interest? Make you want to learn why?"

"I've sworn off women for awhile."

"If you say so."

"I say so." Come *on*, Walsh. "There are more important things to focus on."

"Than Sharon Dekker?"

"Maj!"

Majo sighed and sipped his beer. "Fine. Let's talk partnership. You and me go—"

"No." Griffin took a sip of his own beer to truly wash out the distraction of the woman now calling herself Sharon Dekker. "No. I'm thinking much bigger than that."

~~~~

"Hey, Honeybee," Pete called to Sharon as she worked her way back towards the bar. "Two m-more Heinies."

"Gotta watch those, big guy," she answered and looked pointedly at the hairy belly showing between the bottom of Pete's jean jacket/ tee-shirt combo and the top of his tent-like jeans. "Before you get too big for the ladies to hang on."

Pete shook his curly beard back and forth like a bulldog clearing its drool. "B-b-b-b-boobies!" he roared, making Digger, almost as big as Pete, laugh into his upended beer bottle and almost choke.

"May mine never hang as low as yours," Sharon shot back. She swung her tray up to the bar to get the two Heinekens.

The table of three Hard Rider guys by the door, heavy smokers, mean looking, and new to the Red Owl, stilled their conversations for a moment to watch Sharon come back with the bottles. She felt their creepy, dark eyes as she slung the bottles down. It was all she could do to not turn her back to them when she leaned over and popped the caps with that satisfying hiss. Besides, then they'd just be ogling her ass.

And as long as they just *watched*, they were no different than the old guys from the flea market or the underage boys near the door who were trying to catch her attention now. Lisa had served them earlier and hadn't said anything.

The watching, the leers—they were just part of the work, like the sticky woodwork and close air. As long as you knew when to back away, call Henry over, or call a cab to meet you after your shift, you were safe. You kept your nose out of their business and they kept theirs out of yours for the most part.

Anyway, Sharon could handle it. Always had.

Ironically, it was upstanding citizen Griffin Walsh who was the problem.

Now, as her anger cooled, she decided it was obvious that having someone appear out of her past like this would shake her up. And for that someone to be Griffin, of all people... Despite everything, it made a part of her she'd almost forgotten flare up inside her. He was a grown man now. And Sharon Dekker had learned what grown men liked.

She snuck a quick glance his way.

He wasn't watching her. He was leaning forward towards Majo, his fingers holding down the wooden table top, focused like a laser beam. Why? Was he in trouble? Hiring Maj to get him out of it?

The idea stuck a hot dart into her heart—sympathy or satisfaction, she wasn't sure. She only knew it twisted her up inside. Whatever this slick brainiac had done or was planning, Sharon wanted in. She wanted to see him operate again, share the classy intensity she remembered. Get some of that directed *her* way.

A shiver shot through her like the aftershock of an orgasm, and she almost gasped. Oh shit. From having no men for years to orgasming at the thought of having this one. If she needed any more proof her emotional time frames were screwed up, there it was.

And she still wanted him.

How?

And for god's sake, why?

Like she'd long ago learned to do with the unanswerable, Sharon simply closed down that part of her mind that wasn't coping well and went back to the bar to grab her receipt book and pen.

~~~~~

Griffin took another sip of beer—awful, sour—put down the glass, and came right down to it. "Look, I do my homework, I make things work, and I don't bullshit."

Majo's gaze flicked quickly across the room to where Sharon was serving another round to the bikers, but Griffin didn't look with him. It would totally shoot his concentration. "About business," Majo said, "I believe that."

"So?"

Maj turned back to him with an innocent smile. "So what?"

"I see five of us: me, you, Brent, Rotty, and Lillian. Best of the best. Walsh, Cruz, Major, Rothschild & Lee. We start as a total-service boutique law firm and grow it carefully. Break-even in two years. Steady fifteen percent growth every year after that. All our own."

The smile hadn't dropped from Majo's face, but Griffin could see the wheels turning behind the eyes. Maj tracked his finger around the side of his beer glass again, then picked up the glass and drank, clinked it down, burped dramatically, and wiped his mouth.

"How far have you gone with this?" Majo said.

"When you poked me about going out on our own, I started running projections. The odds go up with more of us. So I checked up on the others to see how they were doing. Little probes."

"And asked them if they were in?"

Griffin shook his head. "Not before discussing it with you. It's not going to happen without you on board first. You're going to be the social grease." Griffin smiled. "If you're in, the others will figure it's going to be a big party, right?"

"You've thought it all out, haven't you."

Griffin paused, looking Majo over. "Okayyy," he said. "What am I missing?"

Majo fixed him with the same stare Griffin suspected he used on a witness he was about to pull the guts out of. "Just this, Griff. You and me, I see us working together no problem. You say it doesn't work economically, I believe you and that's too bad. But if we have *five* lawyers, we have to have a managing partner. Which would mean you, since you know the business end. But you're stiff. I'm not sure anyone's going to want to sail on a ship your steering, even with me playing the hornpipes and dancing alongside."

"Ouch."

"Sorry." Majo raised his hands, palm up. "Remember that you're describing a small ship. Close quarters. Big risks. Not everyone can handle that."

Griffin sat back awkwardly, trying not to let the cuts deflate his sense of destiny. He knew this was the right thing, not just for him but for the others. He could see it all clearly in his head. He just hadn't expected his first big roadblock to be Majo. "Stiff?"

"Hey, it's better that than being a dick. We all love you. Just... small ship, you know?"

Someone other than Majo was watching him. Griffin raised his eyes to meet Sharon's gaze from across the room. She was getting drinks for someone again, filling her tray. She shot him a smile of encouragement now, like it was clear how badly this was going.

Embarrassment and determination heated his face and he swung his focus back to Majo. He wasn't going to let it end this easily. He knew Majo wanted out of his current firm, but the others? Majo was right that they might be no readier to jump than Griffin was even yesterday. They were all canny and brilliant and doing well where they were.

But they *would* jump if Majo came on board first. Griffin had a sixth sense about such things. Which brought it all back to this meeting. He hoped Sharon was watching.

"Okay, Maj," he said, sitting forward. "What would it take? I know we need to do this. What would it take to convince you? Anything."

"Whoo." It was Majo's turn to sit back. "Intensity time again."

"Well?"

"Chill, man. Finish your beer."

"You're thinking?"

"I'm thinking."

Griffin was spared having to climb over the table to wring Maj's neck by the return of Sharon. She planted her body unnecessarily close to him on his side of the table. Her bare thigh pressed against his leg. Her scent surrounded him. Definitely mango. It was like throwing a bottle of hairspray into his finally meshed gears of purpose. Everything got immediately jumbled again.

"You guys going to order food?"

Griffin couldn't look up to meet her eyes. He could barely wrench his focus off the warmth of her thigh to mumble, "Uh...no. I don't think so."

He almost felt Majo's shudder, which made his own face go red again. What? Majo did not know what it cost him to not throw himself recklessly at this woman. This woman was what had given him the tingles walking in here, he realized suddenly. He must have recognized her subconsciously, even in profile. But if there had been reasons to keep her away from him back in high school, there were double the reasons now. Just look at what she was doing to these negotiations.

Almost to spite his resolve, his gaze slid unconsciously up Sharon's body—bare thigh to crotch in tight black creases, to stomach in a stretchy white top so thin he could see the indentation of her belly button, to breasts, smooth-muscled arms, long neck, and...

She was looking down at him. Their eyes locked. And for that split second he was eighteen again, under the bleachers in the gymnasium, and Sharon had taken his hands and pulled them onto her breasts through her cotton blouse. A handful each. His mouth dry. His eyes wide. Worrying that his ears had turned red. His hands squeezing.

"You know what?" Sharon growled down. "That's just fine. That'll be six-fifty."

Griffin blinked then fumbled a ten out of his wallet and told her to keep the change.

"Thank you," she said, keeping her eyes on his. "And here's a receipt so you can write it off as business expense." Her long fingers slid something into his front shirt pocket.

Then she was gone and he could breathe again.

"Lemme see that," said Majo, leaning forward over the table and grabbing the paper Sharon had slid into Griffin's pocket. A second later, a slow smile spread across his swarthy features. "You want to know what would make me believe that maybe, just maybe, you have the *cojones* to make things work?"

"What?" Griffin reached out, grabbed the paper, and frowned. It was just a receipt. He turned it over. On the back was written in a big blue flourish,

I'm off at 2:15 a.m. Be here. Take me home.
Sharon

4

CLOSING PROCEDURE IN THE RED OWL:
  1) Elrad, in the back, closes the grill at 1:45 a.m., and, with the Chinese girl, cleans up for the next half hour;

  2) Sharon, the only waitress on a week night before Friday, collects last round orders;

  3) Denny, if he's been called in, hustles anyone who's drunk too much out the door and calls cabs for those stupid enough to have driven;

  4) Henry closes up the bar;

  5) Sharon wipes the tables, takes dirty glasses and ashtrays to the dishwasher in back, does a quick cash tally with Henry to count off her tips, dons her fanny pack, fleece and sweat pants from the back, and ducks out the back door and over to Gore then to Hastings to catch the 2:35 night bus home.

~~~~

Sharon couldn't bring herself to finish closing.

This night, technically morning, she wandered around the front room, giving all the tables a second wipe, wishing she had the chemicals to actually *clean* all the accumulated gunk there. Maybe then she could Windex the windows and framed "Naughty Dog" prints, clean the floor, fix the broken cuckoo clock on the wall, buy the place a TV...

Henry scowled at her, looking just bit like the pissing bulldog in the print over the back of his bar. "Dekker, are you—"

"Have you thought anymore," Sharon interrupted, "about loaning me just *one* of your rooms as a temporary shelter? We could work it into the final selling price when I get financing. There are these three girls..."

"What the fuck? I told you I'm not selling this place. You want to get some girls a room? Show me the cash and I'll rent them a room."

"I'm working on that. I just need–"

She cut it off with yelp as the front door opened with a tinkle of its bells behind her, and she spun around.

But it wasn't Griffin Walsh. It was one of the three new Hard Riders she'd seen earlier that night in the pub. This one had a short mustache, short hair, and a lurching gait to his walk that sent little cold fingers walking up and down Sharon's spine.

The man looked her up and down, then turned to Henry with a surly question on his face.

Henry said, "She was just going. Right?"

"Right," Sharon said. But even with the cold chill of the newcomer, she hesitated. Griffin hadn't come in to get her. Was he waiting for her outside? Because if he wasn't, it was high school all over again. She'd thrown herself at him, he'd seem interested, but then shrugged it off and walked away.

"You want to call a cab?" Henry said now, hunching over the bar.

"Hm?" Sharon jerked about to see both him and the biker staring at her. The noises in the back had stopped. Elrad and the girls were obviously done and gone. It was just Sharon and these two guys.

"Someone bothering you?" Henry said.

"Um. No?"

"Then go.

"Okay."

Smoothing back her hair and unconsciously rubbing the side of her mouth again, Sharon drew herself up and walked to the front door of the pub, opened it, and stepped out, closing the door behind her.

There was no one there.

As she heard the door lock behind her, she looked up into the misting night sky, lit garishly by the lights of downtown, and nodded.

Well, it was only what she'd always known. The streets had no sympathy. They were all about grit and slime and–

"Sharon?"

She almost screeched as she whipped around, but Griffin had stepped out now from against the wall where his dark olive trench coat had made him blend in like a shadow. His eyes were dark and pleading, almost like he'd been driven to come against his will. His need burned out of him in way that made her breath catch in her throat.

"Hello," she said.

"I...wasn't sure whether to come inside, whether you wanted others to know, or..."

Heart pounding, she gave a lopsided smile. "You were protecting my honor?"

"Um. Yes. I suppose."

Sharon stepped closer to him, a small step. Because despite the need she saw in him, he looked like he might bolt at any second. "Or were you protecting yours?"

"What?" His head jerked back a little and Sharon swore at herself. *Don't do that, you idiot. Don't. Not tonight. Not with him so close.*

"I'm kidding," she said and smiled.

He visibly relaxed. "So...I have my car just..." He pointed vaguely back down the block towards Hastings Street.

"Okay." She smiled again, packing her own fears away. This was like coaxing a skittish tiger. You yourself had to be totally in control.

"Okay," he agreed. He nodded his head, turned, and waited for her. And when she walked up beside him, they set off down the sidewalk together.

The click of his dress shoes, the scritch of her sneakers, seemed to echo around them like they were in a giant, empty fishbowl, dark, with intermittent rumbles of traffic, the middle-of-the-night mist drifting down around them, filling their mouths with the cold dankness of ocean. Her world.

Ahead on the corner, Sharon saw, Brittany and Phyllis both floated about in boredom, trying to entice the occasional fish cruising back from a more central downtown pub.

While Sharon already had her fish?

She looked sideways at Griffin in a sudden chill that almost made her vomit. "Are we going back to your place or mine?"

He stiffened. "Yours, I thought. Me driving you home?"

It cascaded a thrill of both comfort and wild regret through her. Yes, he'd take her to her little hole, plop her in, then recoil in horror. She'd watch him swim away.

From her safety. Her misery.

But she managed to put that all aside as they reached the sole car parked against the curb on this block, a BMW 3-series no less, and he opened the passenger door for her.

When he climbed in and the close rustle and smell of him—sweet and musky—and the car itself—rich leather—folded her inside it like a pilot in some high tech underwater craft. She held onto her seatbelt. Despite her determination to be in control, she was afraid to move.

"Where to?" he said, his own voice catching some of her fear.

"Burnaby. Duthie and Pandora. Just go east on Hastings. I'll direct you."

He gunned the engine to life and she nearly cried out. Then they were off.

~~~~

The insanity of it, thought Griffin as he roared them through the ugliest armpit Vancouver, BC had to offer, was that he would not even be here but for his need to start a law firm that was all about integrity.

Yet there was a gut-sinking inevitability to it. Almost from the moment he'd walked into the Red Owl, when some peripheral sense had picked up on Sharon's presence, a part of him had known he'd be cruising into this dark side again.

With Sharon N— Sharon Dekker.

The reality of her sitting beside him in sweat pants and blue fleece top, so casual-normal, was not fully there. He shifted gears to uncharacteristically tear through the changing yellow light. How exactly had he ended up back here?

Normally he'd have been long asleep by now, face and teeth scrubbed, reviewed work packed back into his briefcase for tomorrow, fresh workout gear in his gym bag beside it. That was his world. Instead he was tearing through the inky features of lower east side, sad-looking hookers and yellow street lights flashing by. He could smell the cigarette smoke from Sharon's clothes and hair. And he had a hard-on.

Forcing a smile, he shot her a glance and was surprised to see that, underneath that spiky black haircut, she looked as terrified as him.

"You okay?" he said. "My driving scaring you?"

"Hm?" She shot him a quick, scared look. "Oh. No."

Then they said nothing for blocks and blocks, until *Sharon* began directing him down one street, then another, finally to an apartment building that had obviously seen better days. On Pandora Street. Appropriate.

Less appropriate were the dark forests of Burnaby Mountain hunkered just a block to the east, daring everyone around to climb its trails and find the university, Simon Fraser U., spread out on its flat top some twelve hundred feet above sea level. Why had Sharon settled out here, so far from work, so close to that university? It had to hurt to live in the shadow of all the upper-middle-class kids studying up there, the life she'd obviously never had a shot at.

Most of the curbs here were filled with parked cars, but Griffin managed to find a spot just half-a-block from the building's front door.

He pulled in, shut off the engine, and got the inevitable, "Do you want to come up?"

For just a moment he considered saying no. Despite the throbbing in his pants, and a building need to touch this woman, it could end here. He could make some excuse about work. She'd get out, make some awkward comment about what a nice surprise it had been seeing him again. And...

"Yes," he said.

So they climbed out together, he beep-locked the car doors, and he walked with her to her building, to the elevator, up to the sixteenth floor.

Everything rattled and squeaked dust in this place—the elevator, the door of her apartment. But he almost didn't care.

And her place, when he looked around, wasn't that bad. It smelled like smoke, probably permanently stuck in the worn brown carpet from a previous tenant, but at least it was simple. Sparse actually. Second-hand furniture and a few framed prints on the walls, a simple computer table with computer and old laser printer. Interesting. For what? E-mail? The couch over by the balcony side of the room had well-worn claw marks along the right arm and leg. Which meant....

"Hey, Boobo," Sharon said (or was that "Bubo," like a swelling, diseased lymphatic node?), as a long-haired fat black cat with white splotches around its face and feet, rubbed up against her leg.

She kicked off her running shoes, then reached down and picked it up, cradling it in close against her neck and face. The sight of the cat's hair pressing against Sharon's cheek and long, smooth neck, shot envy through Griffin. *He* wanted to touch that skin, that cheek. *He* could purr.

"Can I...um...get your coat?" he tried.

She glanced up at him, then back to her cat. "In a minute." She wandered further into her apartment with Boobo. "Take your own off. Get comfortable. I need to change."

"No!" Griffin cried. He had a sudden vision of her vanishing into her bedroom and not reemerging until she'd had a shower, hunted

33

through every clothes item in her closet, redone her makeup. Despite his current excited state, he'd be asleep or gone by the time she reemerged.

"No?"

"I mean..." He shrugged off his trench coat and laid it over the back of the nearest chair. The cable-knit cotton sweater he'd worn underneath it suddenly felt foolish. "Can't we visit a bit...just as you are?"

"Visit?" She raised her eyebrows at him over the furry head of her cat and Griffin's blood rushed hotly through him.

"Tell me how you got that scar on your nose."

She stiffened. Then she slowly put down the cat—it padded off to the bathroom—smiled and turned towards him. She slowly unzipped her fleece.

"You don't really want to know about the scar on my nose, do you?"

Off came the fleece, dropping to the floor in a soft thump.

"Aren't there other parts of me you'd rather explore?"

She fluffed out her short black spikes, then slid her hands smoothly down the front of her waitress's top until her fingers found the front button of her black mini-shorts. She twisted it open. With a push and wiggle of her hips, the shorts dropped to the floor as well. She kicked them back by the jacket as Griffin's mouth went dry.

"Softer parts."

Now Griffin, speechless with his erection back to throbbing pressure in his pants, could see that the white stretch top was actually a unitard, snapped together below her crotch. The panties underneath were skimpy and pink.

Sharon planted her bare feet slightly apart, looked pointedly down at the snaps of the unitard, then straight into Griffin's eyes.

"Undo me," she said.

~~~

If he backed out now, Sharon thought, she would die. She would simply collapse on the spot and melt into a bubbling mess of... something.

Touch me, she urged him with her mind. It had to be him who came to her this time. They weren't in high school any more. She wasn't Sharon-the-slut. And she wasn't on the street, getting paid for it. And all the things that had happened to her since he'd known her... The awfulness she figured had killed her ever really wanting a man that way again...

It had to be him.

Touch me.

Then slowly, as if something deep inside him was taking over, she saw Griffin's face change. Whether a mask was going on or coming off, she wasn't sure. His jaw tightened, his chin lowered, his eyes narrowed. And he stepped towards her until his body was right up to hers and she was staring into his chest, smelling his cologne. Subtle now. Spicy. Hot. Like the subtle weave of his sweater—dark blue with a purply—

He cupped her pubes, pressed up with his fingers, and little electric tingles shot through her body.

"Right here?" he said.

His voice, lower than before, zinged a second electrical storm through her. She gasped and nodded.

The pressing fingers found the catch of the snaps and popped them one at a time. The bottom flaps of the leotard sprang up on either side letting a cool breeze wash over her damp panties. Not that it cooled her down much. She could feel herself swelling down there, aching for him.

For a terrifying moment, she thought he'd stopped, changed his mind, but when she drew back her head to look, the intensity in his eyes was everything she remembered and more. His gaze raked over her like a physical thing, raising goosebumps from her knees on up.

Then his hands had the bottom of the leotard and he was lifting it up and off her so quickly she had to jerk her arms up quickly to keep up.

"You too," she said.

He nodded wordlessly and tore his expensive sweater up and off, undid the buttons of his shirt, kicked off his wingtip shoes and kicked them to the side. Clunk clunk.

Stopped.

His nostrils were flared, his face flushed, and his brow was furrowed. Still *thinking*, damn it, even with his body ready to burst into flames. And that body! He'd put on nice slabs of muscle since they were teens together. Nice packs on his chest. A chiseled gut. She longed to explore its ridges with her tongue.

"Sharon," he said with difficulty. "Maybe we should–"

"Shut up!" she snapped. "I can't do it for you, but you're sure as hell going to do it."

"I..."

She shook her head, her eyes watering. "I said 'Undo me,' Walsh. So undo me."

And just like that it looked like his brain shut off again. He nodded, smiling almost ferociously. His fingers undid his belt and pants and he dropped them and his boxer shorts at the same time. When he straightened, it was clear his body, at least, had no trouble with this assignment. His cock stood up thick and proud. It bobbed eagerly as he stepped to her and jerked down her panties. He straightened, spun her around, and unclipped her bra.

When he spun her back, she forced her back up straight to stick her breasts out at him in offering.

He took it, diving in to wrap one arm around the small of her back and drop the other to her left breast, nuzzling around it with a motion like Boobo. Exploring. Possessing. His right arm ran up her body from her thigh, forcing her arm up in surrender.

He controlled her totally.

Then Sharon felt his lips open around her nipple and she quivered, arching it forward. "Suck it!" she said.

But he didn't. He just nibbled and played, and the shots of pleasure shook her in a crazy little dance until she had to bring her upraised hand down to claw at his shoulder, drag her nails over his back.

"Take me," she breathed. "Take me, take me, take me."

As if to shut her up, he grabbed both her arms and whipped them up above her head, held them together up there like she was in handcuffs. He glared down into her eyes, raking her naked body with his gaze. She could hardly breathe.

"Don't move," he ordered.

She gulped dryly. She couldn't have if she'd wanted to. His gaze, fear, something, pinned her totally to his will.

As she watched, wide-eyed, he released his hold on her hands, and stepped back to where he'd kicked his pants. Retrieving his wallet from the back pocket, he pulled out a condom, unwrapped it and slid it on. It made his erection look even bigger.

"Turn around," he said.

She did. Oh God, her heart was pounding so hard.

5

W ALK," he said.

She did, into her living room, until she was stopped by the side of the couch.

"Down."

Obediently she sank to her knees, her insides quivering in an over-the-top bubble of fear and excitement. He grabbed her under the arms, lifting her up and flipping her around so she lay back on the couch, her knees hooked over the arm of it.

Understanding, she shuffled her bum forward and up so it rested on the arm, her vaginal lips spreading wetly. Her heart pounded with sudden vulnerability, her mouth dry, as she watched Griffin through slitted eyes.

But rather than a rough, pounding entry, she felt his hands on her thighs and saw him drop down to his knees before her.

Then something hot and wet stabbed into folds of her vagina, just that far, and flickered about like a rooting animal. His tongue! He was tonguing her! No, tasting her, exploring. Her breath, already high in her chest, panted in and out like little sobs. Her knees drew up and bobbed jerkily on either side of his head. She didn't know if she was happy or humiliated.

Then the rooting became licking, sure and even, focused low and forward to catch her clit, and the sensations of pleasure overcame any doubts.

She started to moan. "Oh, oh, oh, oh..." She could hear herself, but couldn't stop it. Didn't care. As long as he didn't stop. As long as this didn't stop.

It built inside her then, the familiar tightening, running from her toes up her legs to her anus, down from her arms, her neck and chest on fire. She was going to come.

But she couldn't see his face! She wanted Griffin's face! Not this nameless, impersonal bobbing head down there.

Yet as she reached forward to raise him up, he forced her back with his hands and *kept licking!*

Then she couldn't stop it even if she'd wanted to. She was over the edge, shaking and yelping like a demented puppy. Her body jerked and spasmed and a small part of her mind wondered if she'd knocked Griffin backwards.

The sudden clamp of his hands on her hips told her otherwise.

Even as she shook, she felt him guide himself into her. The focus of the orgasm quaking her body became concentrated on the sudden jerking fullness between her legs. He bucked in and out and she bucked back at him, trying to match him thrust for thrust. Until his motion became too frantic for her to follow and she just rode it like a wave, her mind too gone in blood to care, surfing pleasure so close to violence that she was right on the edge, close to terror but laughing in ecstasy.

When he came, stiffening and holding, she still rode the wave, imagining Griffin's seed spilling inside her, willing the condom not there, wanting him to fill her with him, with his strength, his drive, his confidence, his life. She wanted it all inside her and through her.

To be anything but what she was.

~~~~

Holy....

It was as coherent a thought as Griffin could form as his body

39

clenched and released itself into her. Into Sharon. Though not really, since his condom would catch it all. But his passion and sweat, his muscled machismo. All those he'd put into her.

And where had those come from?

As he collapsed, breathing hard, across her chest, he felt a profound unease at how she'd poked at him, provoked him, made him release something inside he wasn't comfortable with.

It wasn't him. The real Griffin was—how had Majo put it?— "stiff."

So when Sharon shuffled beneath him, trying to push his face up so she could look at him, he withdrew quickly and stood, holding the condom on as he strode to the bathroom. There he was disconcerted to see Sharon's black-and-white cat sitting on the edge of the bathtub, watching him.

He removed and dumped the condom into the plastic bag she had as the liner for her bathroom wastebasket. Then he stared at it, feeling an anxiety he didn't want to name. Biting his lip, he reached down, scooped out the plastic bag with the filled condom, tied it up, and brought it out with him when he exited.

He tossed it by the chair holding his trench coat, then went for his pants.

Sharon sat naked on the edge of the couch, watching him, her face open, those lips still longing to have the hurt kissed away. His fingers fumbled on his zipper as he realized he had not even kissed her. It was like he'd done only what he absolutely had to do. What his body demanded. What Sharon, what Majo, had expected. What every man and woman probably who populated this city would have expected of him.

But it wasn't him.

"I liked that," she said. Her head was cocked to the side. Wistful? Hopeful?

"Me too," he said. Truth, just not the whole truth. Hey, he was a lawyer. He was supposed to be good at that.

"I guess you're not going to stay the night."

"Nuh-unh."

He looked at her. The way she just sat there, not covering up, not worrying about stains on the couch, or how she looked, or how this whole evening looked, both intrigued and repelled him.

He had a *law firm* to set up, damn it. He had a *career*. He had a life plan. He had a list of the milestones he had to reach, the places he would frequent, the sort of people he would have around him.

Sharon Dekker fit none of those lists and never had.

"No," he said more definitely. "I'm in the office by 8 a.m."

"Okay."

No, *Will you call me?* or *Please call.* She hadn't even pressed her phone number onto him. It was like she knew.

When he was fully dressed, she was still just sitting there naked, watching him. He picked up the tied garbage bag, went to the door, and paused, looking back at her. She was gorgeous. Everything around her, her whole life, was ugly, but she...

He sucked in the sight, feeling it clink and jingle through him like something his body was desperate to store up. Because this couldn't happen again.

"Goodbye," he said and let himself out.

~~~~

"Bye," Sharon said to his back.

Then she brought one hand up to her chest to massage the painful ache that suddenly shot through it.

"No," she said to the air, and shook her head hard, fighting off the depression that threatened. She'd faced worse things than this in twenty-six years. Not much worse, but worse. Goddammit, why had she chosen this year to finally quit smoking?

Perspective, she told herself. He doesn't know you. He knows nothing about you.

Like she, really, knew nothing about him.

She clenched her teeth and stood, walked to where she, with Griffin's help, had dropped her clothes. Scooping them up, she hurried to her bedroom, then separated out the white leotard to take with her to the bathroom. She quickly rinsed out the underarms and crotch and hung it up over the shower pole.

She opened her medicine cabinet to take out her toothbrush and her eyes fell on her bottle of no-name aspirin, extra strength. She'd seen what a full bottle of those could do to a person when that person became convinced all was lost. And she'd sworn to herself that she would never, ever go that route.

She, Sharon Dekker, was going to do the opposite. She was going to be a force for *good* in the world. Micky and Angel and Rose, others like them. They needed her.

She slammed the cabinet door and stared into its window to see her face still flushed with a mind-blowing orgasm. The contrast with her heavy thoughts made her smile lopsidedly.

"Get over yourself, girlfriend."

So Griffin Walsh had walked out on her again. At least this time he'd taken some responsibility for what he did. And what he did had been amazing. He'd shown her that she could actually enjoy that act again in some twisted way. That in itself was special enough that a tiny part of her insisted on taking Griffin's face and the need for her she'd seen there, and putting them in a special little shelf deep inside her—her "remote hope" shelf.

But rather than close the door on that inner cabinet, she kept it open, staring inward at it as she took off her makeup for bed.

What if he really knew her? What if he knew all that had happened to her and all she was now trying to be? What if?

The questions were still running around in her brain when her head hit the pillow and consciousness fled.

~~~~

"Awake!" Griffin blurted.

Then he turned to look at his beeping bedside clock. 6 a.m. He felt like he'd just closed his eyes.

Still, as he rolled out of bed he felt surprisingly good—alive, limber. Only there was something on his right shoulder blade that was stinging.

He jogged into the bathroom of his condo and flicked on the lights. Leaning onto the cool perfection of his marble sink top, he twisted his torso towards the mirror. Two long scratch marks, red and sore-looking, flamed down from his shoulder.

He had an instant flashback to the night before, only hours really. Sharon. *Sharon.* Her round face thrown back in passion. Her long arms wrapped around him as he sucked her nipples. Her need. Her command. Panting yelps. Him inside her.

Holy....

He looked down and saw he'd gone ragingly erect. So much so that he was going to have to calm down before he could even relieve his bladder.

"Unbelievable."

Shaking his head, he twisted the brass-plated taps, slapped some water on his face, and slicked back his short hair, his ears along with it. Then he jogged back into his bedroom for his running gear. It was Thursday and no rain. No-rain Thursdays meant a run around Stanley Park.

Five minutes later he'd dressed, relieved himself, and was out the door, running along Comox, left down Chilco, and right, onto the paved seawall that ran around the outside of the park's 1000 acres plus. Since daylight savings, it was no longer pitch dark for these runs, but the wind was up this morning, and the waves of English Bay crashed in so hard they sent cold gray mists up and across the path. He saw the dark shapes of other early morning runners and bladers ducking sprays up ahead.

A cyclist whirred up to his left and slowed to keep pace with him. It was Gill Alexander, the Westcoast Noram Media VP whom Griffin helped buy an office building last month.

"Thought you only did mountain biking," Griffin said without breaking stride.

"No time this morning," the young exec said. "I'm just on break from the hospital watch at St. Paul's. Nata delivered last night shortly after two a.m. Baby girl. Eight pounds, two ounces."

"Congratulations." It came out automatically, though Griffin nearly tripped forward at Alexander's words. Wife, baby. They'd never seemed as far away from Griffin as they did at that moment.

"Thanks," the man said. He ducked his head as he pedaled, then looked Griffin's way so that the happiness on the man's face shone like a lamp in the sludgy light. "Nothing like it."

Alexander powered ahead and the high energy Griffin had started his day with seemed to be sucked right away after him. But he made himself go on, forcing through the entire twelve-kilometer loop before staggering back to his condo for a shower and shave, breakfast cereal with fruit, brushed teeth and fresh clothes, and off to work almost twenty minutes earlier than usual.

By the time the other lawyers and Griffin's legal assistant came in, he was snapping mad.

"Where's the Dunbar file?" he barked. "And the Gilchrist? I've got three meetings today and no backup done on any of them."

His assistant rushed to find them and he threw himself back into his chair. Only to find some instant messenger text blinking at him from the bottom right corner of his computer screen.

Majo. Of course.

He considered not answering, but Maj would just follow up with phone calls, e-mails, faxes. He was persistent bugger, however charming.

Griffin clicked "Answer."

Did you go? Majo's little box asked.

Yes, Griffin typed back.

And did you do the deed?

Griffin considered, typed, *A gentleman never tells.*

Since you're no gentleman, answer the question.

Griffin grimaced. His fingers hovered over the keyboard. Then he typed, *No. I drove her home. We chatted a bit. We were both tired. I said goodnight. End of story.*

There was a long pause where Griffin wondered if Majo had been called away from his computer or had to blank it out when one of the partners walked in. *I don't get it, man.*

What?

You never used to lie.

Griffin had no answer to that. His insides knotted up.

Meet me for a 1 p.m. lunch, Majo's words came up.

Why?

I spoke with the others. We've got a business proposition. It may involve Sharon.

Griffin's mouth dropped. Majo had gone to the other three without Griffin? And what had he told them about Griffin and Sharon? What did she have to do with this? (Besides turning around and around in his head, naked, thrusting her nipples forward at him.)

Griffin rubbed his temples hard, then typed, *Okay. Where?*

Majo's response: *You know where.*

6

Y ES, MS. DEKKER?"

For a second Sharon's hand wavered in the air, not believing Professor Tighe had actually called on her. The amphitheater-style room of her Social Psych 260 class at Simon Fraser University was so jammed, standing room only, that in the six weeks since the term started, he hadn't picked her once. And now he knew her name? She rubbed the side of her mouth and wondered if something of her night with Griffin was somehow still on her face.

"Ms. Dekker?"

"I...um...don't think you've got the power balance right, Professor."

He smiled faintly and tugged down his tailored suit. His vaguely-East-Asian features made it hard to tell if he was amused or annoyed. It was part of his whole power persona, that came from his having been in government, then a professor who claimed he was still consulted by government when they designed their social programs.

"The power balance between...?" Tighe prodded.

"You're making it sound like a class warfare, the haves versus the have-nots. That's not the way it is on the street."

"No?" He cocked up one dark eyebrow.

"No. It's a struggle between the strong and the weak. It's not just money."

"Ah," said the professor, prowling forward to the front rows to see her in the back more clearly. The rest of the students were craning their necks around to see who was taking him on. "But isn't it money that makes some strong, others weak?"

Sharon licked her dry lips, thinking about the night before, the ride in the BMW, Griffin's clothes that were so rich they made Tighe's look cheap.

"Of course it does," she said. "But it's more about your family support. Whether your friends are trying to make it or are just addicts. Whether guys with guns are after you. Whether you've got your head on straight or you're a schizo."

"You mean schizophrenic," Tighe said, jumping on the last one. "A clinical term from the DSM-IV, indicating a profound disruption in cognition and emotion, affecting a person's language, thought, perception of reality, emotions, and sense of self."

"You mean the DSM-IV-TR. And a narrower definition still in the upcoming DSM-V. Yeah, that's what I meant."

She folded her arms across her chest as the students around her gasped.

Tighe's dark eyes glittered like his short, oiled-back hair. "I'm gathering from your advanced age and your clothing that you've had some experience in this area."

"Not with being schizo, Sherlock." Her mouth had gone dry on her.

Tighe's eyes were dangerous slits, but he didn't seem to know what to say.

"And one more thing affecting a person's power?" Sharon blurted. "How well they deal with people outside their normal comfort zone."

The laughs of her fellow students felt good. She only wished, as she crossed her legs and remembered Griffin between them last night, that Griffin understood the truth of it.

"You know what, Ms. Dekker?" said Tighe from the front of the room, jerking back her attention. "You're right. And I think the appropriate response to this behavior of yours—that is 'outside my comfort zone'—is to assign you a special essay where you can put forward your views. You'll meet me at five o'clock in my office. That's the third floor, northeast corner, 3112. Write it down."

"But—"

"You have other things to do? So do I. Be there and we'll make it brief."

He turned to the rest of the class to continue. Sharon wrote down his office number, checked through her already overloaded schedule, and tried to figure out how she was going to meet him, follow up with the guy from Avirona Engineering who thought they might be able to kick in some money for the Red Owl safe house, and still get to work on time.

She rubbed her eyes. The day just kept getting better and better.

~~~

The Red Owl at lunch was even more of a dump from the outside, Griffin observed as he walked up to it in the full daylight.

An edge-of-Chinatown, gray stucco monstrosity from another era. Signs up and down the street were in Chinese. Half the people on the street looked Asian too. But there was spillover. Wandering crackheads and drunks from Hastings on up to Powell sat in the doorways or shuffled along aimlessly.

He could almost understand how Majo was attracted to the place. He'd always had a fascination for the seedy side of life. It was why he practiced criminal law.

But why Sharon had chosen work in this part of town puzzled Griffin. In fact the more he thought about her, the more everything about her puzzled him. The name change thing, for instance. Something about her said she hadn't been married. But she still had this mix of hurt and incredible strength, neediness and commanding sexuality. It tickled his brain and groin at the slightest memory jog.

Like this place. Her workplace.

He stopped at the front door and glanced at his watch. Since she obviously did night shifts, she probably wouldn't be in this early. He felt a pang of regret at that, though he knew it should be relief. Meeting whatever Majo was about to hit him with would probably take all his concentration.

He took a deep breath and entered.

The gloom closed around him again, even with the noon sunlight fighting to get in through the wood-slat window blinds. The cigarette smoke didn't hang in the air like last night, but the place still reeked of it. Depressing. He coughed. Why couldn't those two cops eating lunch on the front right tables slap down a fine or something?

"Griff! Over here!"

Maj was at the same left-rear table Griffin had chosen for the two of them last time. He'd brought Lillian with him.

Lillian Lee, immigration lawyer. She'd easily been one of the smartest students in their year, with a Chinese-Canadian family behind her driving her harder than most Caucasians would ever understand. Yet she'd chosen the relatively poorly-paid area of immigration law when she graduated. Because, even more than Majo, Griffin, Brent, and Rotty, Lillian had a social conscience.

And great legs, Griffin thought as she pulled them in so he could sit down. Then he mentally checked himself. Since when had he noticed Lillian's legs? It was like his quick one-night with Sharon had awakened this whole repressed sexual side of him. This wasn't really a good thing.

Shaking himself, he took one side of the table, with Maj on his left, Lillian on his right.

"Hi, Lillian," he said. Nice lips too, all long and sculptured. Not as puffy or hurt-looking as Sharon's. Not calling to him the way hers did. He blinked as he caught himself looking around the room.

"She's not here, Griff." It was Majo.

"What?"

"Daytime shift. Nighttime shift."

"Right."

Lillian cut in. "What are you two talking about?"

Majo leaned back and smiled at her, rubbing the bristle on his chin as he'd apparently forgotten to shave today. "A bet. A little romantic adventure Griffin's engaged in."

"Really?" Lillian looked at Griffin with such surprise that Griffin's annoyance at Majo turned towards her, and to the world in general.

"The only 'adventure' I'm engaged in right now is getting Vancouver's newest law firm off the ground. That's what we're here to talk about, right? And some sort of 'business proposition'?"

"Indeedy," said Majo. "I'm glad you're making the conviviality of it all so appealing."

Before Griffin could respond, the big-haired, big-chested blonde he remembered being there briefly the night before showed up at their tables and took their orders. Majo ordered an extra beer and plate of chicken strips that made Griffin frown.

"Brent'll be here soon," Majo explained. "Rotty couldn't make it today."

"Ah."

Majo let him hang in suspense for a minute while the waitress returned with their drinks—beer for Majo, Lillian, and soon-to-arrive Brent; Water for Griffin. She leaned in close to Griffin as she put his down and drawled in her Texan accent, "Sharon says hi."

Griffin flushed and gripped his glass hard while Lillian gave Majo another raised-eyebrow look. "This *place*," Griffin said.

"Is one of the reasons we're here," Majo said. He leaned forward on the table and lowered his voice, though the only customers in the place besides them and the two cops were two guys slouched forward on the bar. The could have been the same two men that were here last night. Regulars.

"You're going to tell me?" said Griffin.

Majo nodded to Lillian, who took over in her carefully clipped voice. "It's like this, Griffin. You've heard about snakeheads, Chinese who extort life savings from poor Chinese to ship them to Canada packed in dirty boats and shipping containers?"

"Ye-e-es."

She flashed him a quick, tight grin. "It's not about Cross or Shiptite, don't worry. Congratulations on that deal, by the way."

He nodded, relieved.

"I end up working with a bunch of illegal immigrants who come into the country that way, on boats. Usually it's a matter of helping them through the red tape, sometimes claiming refugee status, sometimes finding them a sponsor after the fact. Sometimes it's just rescuing them from the indentured servitude they've been tricked into to pay their ways here."

"And...?"

"I've been twigged to two Chinese girls already who were brought over and assigned work here before they were shipped off to who-knows-where."

"'Twigged'?"

Majo raised his hand as he took a long pull on his beer.

Griffin frowned. "I still don't see what–"

"The cops won't move in without proof, particularly because it looks like the Hard Riders are involved."

"Local motorcycle gang," Majo supplied. "They were the guys in here last night. They run drugs and girls, mostly. Led by a scary, bald, shriveled dude named Jean Calibeau." He said the French form of John with a nasal Montreal accent.

Griffin felt that bad tension creeping in across his shoulders. "You said this might involve Sharon. Are you–"

"Not that way," Majo said. "It's just that this is her place of employment."

Lillian leaned forward. "That wouldn't necessarily change. There's a group of businessmen who want to buy up this whole block, renovate it, and use government incentives to turn some of it into low-income housing. They need help working out a deal."

51

"Ah," Griffin said, finally seeing why they were pulling him into it. "But that sounds more like real estate law."

"The group wants it to be an independent commercial entity, separately incorporated, separate charter, and mostly run by a second group via a loose partnership agreement. It's complicated."

"Uh-hunh."

"However it's done," Lillian said, "new ownership would effectively end this bar as a transit point for abusing these girls."

"Hello, ev-er-y-body!"

The rich baritone boomed into the smoky gloom along with the light from the door. Griffin turned to look and saw a tall man backlit in the doorway like an armor-clad knight. The door swung shut and Griffin's eyes readjusted.

It was Brent Major, handsome firefighter-turned-litigation lawyer, the oldest of Griffin's chosen, but probably the fittest. Certainly the most physically and emotionally imposing. Bully knight wasn't too far off as a description. Or maybe just bulldozer. Certainly a guy you wanted working *for* you, not against.

Ignoring the annoyed looks from the bartender and the other few patrons of the Red Owl, Brent strode over to Griffin, Majo, and Lillian, and took the fourth chair.

"Where's Rotty?" he said as he sat.

"Couldn't make it," Majo said. "Clients."

Brent rolled his eyes. "And you've started without me? Beer here! I need—"

He cut it off as Majo shoved him the extra glass he'd ordered earlier. Majo outlined more details of the housing project as Brent drank. When he'd mostly finished, he sat back, fingering his mostly-empty beer glass, and looked questioningly at Griffin.

"Well?"

Griffin frowned. "It sounds doable. Not much money involved, which might be a problem..."

"You see?" Lillian said to Majo and turned half away from Griffin at the table.

"...for my current firm," Griffin finished.

"Lill?" said Majo.

She turned back with her eyes hard. "This is what I told Majo, and I'll tell you, Griff: I'm not going to belong to a firm, even of friends, if it's all about the bottom line. I got enough of that from my parents growing up."

"I see," said Griffin. "So this housing deal is what? Some kind of test, then? A precondition to your considering joining us?"

She didn't even blink. "You could call it that."

"You, Brent?"

The big man smiled broadly. "Hell, no. Majo's in, then I'm in. Long as you can guarantee me a big enough line of credit to properly build my cases. The big ones take money. No penny-pinching."

"Understood," said Griffin. "What about Rotty?"

He directed it at Majo, since his friend had obviously gone straight from their meeting yesterday to call the others and actively canvas the issue of the proposed partnership.

"Rotty's...complicated," said Majo. "But I think he'll kick in if the rest of us are a go."

"So he's in if all of us are, Brent is if you are, Lillian is if I do this housing deal. Am I missing anything?"

"Our little wager," said Majo.

"About?"

"Showing me you have what it takes. Lillian needs your morality. I need your—How do I put this gently?—flexibility."

"On what?" Brent broke in. Lillian too raised her eyebrows. Majo held Griffin's gaze until the criminal lawyer's little smirk made it absolutely clear what he was talking about. Sharon. Griffin's penis twitched. *Down, boy.*

"I already did that," said Griffin.

"Not according to you. I want a serious effort."

"As judged by...?"

"Me, of course."

"You're not serious." Griffin felt tension creep around his shoulders.

"One hundred percent serious, man," said Majo, sitting up. "You answer Lillian's challenge, you answer my challenge, and you end up with a new law firm. We all do."

"How do I measure whether I've met your challenge?"

"Hey!" said Brent, impatient now. "I want in on this. What's Majo's challenge?"

Majo smiled slowly, drained the last of his beer, and clinked it down. "One just for our boy Griffin. Let's say...four more dates, at least one where she meets either all of us or your parents. You up for it, Griff?"

"A woman!" said Brent, and even Lillian looked at Griffin curiously.

It felt like the bartender was watching him, the Texan waitress too, maybe somehow even the partners of Greene McNamara or his parents living back in Vernon.

And then, incongruously, he saw a vision of Sharon sitting naked on the edge of her couch. Her open face. Her hurt-looking lips.

You up for it, Griff?

His rational, career-driven self wanted to scream no. No way. The thing with Sharon was a one time (okay, two, counting high school) mistake.

His mouth said, "I'm up for it."

"Good." Majo grinned. "Lillian's already given the investors your office number. They'll call you this afternoon."

7

A T 4:55 PM, Sharon was panting up the outside stairs to the academic quadrangle, hissing curses under her breath.

She'd had to cut her four p.m. study group, jog home down Burnaby Mountain, ditch her backpack, change into her work clothes, then grab the bus up the mountain again to the university, all so she could meet Professor Tighe and still have a shot at getting to work by six.

Of course with all the rushing, she was sweating up her work clothes as bad as she had yesterday. Before she even got to work.

Not that she had a choice about seeing Tighe. She needed to keep a minimum grade point average for her scholarships. And for grad school? One thing at a time. She just wished she'd held her tongue this morn—

Her cell phone dingled Beyonce's *Sweet Dreams* and she almost stumbled.

She stopped, two steps from the top, and checked her watch as she pulled out her cell phone. 4:56. Yikes.

The phone kept playing. She didn't recognize the number on the caller ID.

Gasping for breath, she flipped it open. "Hello?"

"Is that Sharon?"

Even across the thinning channel of the cell, Griffin Walsh's voice made her legs wobble. Or was that just the run from the bus?

The climb up the stairs?

She sat down in any case. "It's me."

"You're out of breath. And I hear birds. Are you outside?"

"Yes. Cell phone."

"But I got your number from Directory Assistance."

"It's my only phone. City plan. I'm not home much."

"Ah."

There was a bit of a silence when all she could hear was her own breathing. And her heart. It was thumping ridiculously hard for just that little run, even for a former smoker. Her hand clutching the phone was slick with sweat and cramping from holding on so hard.

Finally she heard Griffin take a big breath. "I...wanted to call you to...apologize," he said, "for leaving so abruptly."

"Mm-hm."

"I'd...um...like to see you again."

"At the pub?"

"No! I mean, not just there. I'd...like to take you out somewhere. Lunch, dinner, just a walk. Talk. To catch up. I don't know."

An incredible pressure Sharon hadn't even been conscious of lifted from her chest so she virtually floated up to her feet. The wind seemed suddenly fresher, the view from top of the steps over the grounds of the campus suddenly magnificent, green and alive.

"That would be nice. A walk. You know the trails around Burnaby Mountain?"

"No."

"Doesn't matter. I do. You could just pick me up and.... When?"

She heard him clear his throat. "This afternoon?"

"Can't. I've got work."

"Right. Of course."

There was a beat.

"I could pick you up after work tonight," Griffin said.

Sharon laughed, surprising herself with the sound. "A little late to go hiking."

More throat clearing. "Right. Right. Okay. Tomorrow? Thursday. The afternoon sometime?"

"Don't *you* have work?"

"I can get out of it."

Sharon laughed again. She felt so light that she might just fly away on this autumn breeze. She had no classes tomorrow afternoon. "One o'clock. My place. Dressed for a serious, two-hour hike. Shorts. Water bottle. Power Bars."

"I'm up for it."

"Even if it rains?" Not that it looked like it would, but something told her to tie this date down. Make *sure*.

"Even if."

"Okay, then."

"Okay."

There was an awkward pause. "Tomorrow." He hung up.

Sharon caught herself smiling foolishly as she hit END and flipped her phone closed. Then her eyes went wide.

Her appointment with Tighe!

~~~~

Jocasta, Griffin's legal assistant, stuck her head into his office and held up the Gilchrist file. He nodded it to his desk without a word. She dropped it and left quickly like she was scared of him.

Griffin looked at his hands, clenched tightly on his knees. He was sweating. His collar and tie felt too tight.

Hiking! With Sharon!

Damn Majo.

Griffin was a swimmer. He'd even captained the swim team in high school his senior year. And played racquet ball, lifted weights, ran Stanley Park. All mostly solitary pursuits, highly focused. Hiking had always struck him as the equivalent of a rambling daydream, something people did who had more time on their hands than they knew what to do with.

Of course *mountain* hiking was probably a good cardio workout, but...

He stopped himself. It wasn't the hiking aspect that had him sweating, was it. It was this whole "romance Sharon" thing. It made no rational sense. Sure, princes married peasant girls, but that was only in fairy tales. In real life their worlds didn't mesh and they had nothing to talk about. Nothing at all.

He leapt up from his chair and began to pace around his office.

That was the real nub of Griffin's immediate discomfort—talk. With Sharon. For two hours. Because Majo was painfully right about one thing—Griffin *was* stiff. He'd never learned how to talk about stupid nothings.

Learning, yes. Achievement, yes. Destiny, yes. But trivia?

His friends in university and law school, they accepted that about him. He knew his stuff. He did what he said he would.

Somehow he didn't think that would interest Sharon for long.

Two hours!

Jocasta stuck her head in the door again. "Griffin? The men you're going to help buy some properties down on Pender? They're on Line 2."

Griffin pulled his focus back to law. This had to be Lillian's investors. "Names?"

"I asked. They wouldn't give them." She was keeping her face blank, but Griffin knew her curiosity was twitching.

"Thank you," he said, waited for her to leave, then lifted the phone. These people, at least, he knew how to talk to.

~~~~

Tighe was closing up his briefcase and taking his trenchcoat from its hook when Sharon rushed in through the door.

"Professor!"

The middle-aged man casually looked at his watch and continued to pick up his trench, sliding it casually onto his arms. "You're late, Ms. Dekker."

"I know. I had to run home and grab my work clothes. I had a follow-up phone call for this project I'm working on. Then I got this other phone call on my way here..."

He looked her slowly up and down as Sharon wished she hadn't been so hot that she'd unzipped her fleece. The man's dark gaze made her feel naked. She was used to it at the Red Owl. Not at school.

"You don't even have anything to write on," said Tighe. "Did you think I'd simply type it all out for you? Or were you planning to 'convince' me to simply drop the whole matter?"

Sharon flushed hotly and fumbled into her fanny pack for the pen and folded sheets of paper she'd brought. "No! I just—I don't bring my backpack to work because where I work... I mean. It's not a good idea."

"I see."

He simply stared at her a moment longer and Sharon's long-honed self-defense mechanism clicked in, making her stare right back, assessing him now as a man, not just a professor. He looked mid-forties, with short, oiled-back black hair and vaguely darker skin that might have signaled Middle-Eastern blood but for the oriental cast of his eyes. A sweet, exotic scent filled the tiny office, and Sharon worried it might be coming from him. He stood trim and straight. Well-kept to the point of vanity.

In Griffin, Sharon realized, the well-kept look was part of his class and job, part of his appeal. But in a psychology professor, particularly one who now had her alone in his office after hours, it was kind of creepy.

He seemed to sense it and retreated behind his ornate teak desk. That and the matching tall bookshelf were the only furniture with personality in the room. As if he'd brought them with him like suitcases, plunked them down to claim this space, and done nothing more to settle in. The rest—the degrees on the walls, the gray melamine credenza, the metal-and-fabric chairs—all looked rented. Like Tighe thought of himself as just passing through.

He pulled a file out of his top drawer. He'd obviously been looking at it just before she arrived because he fingered it open to just the page he wanted.

"You're here on four different scholarships," he said, reading. "One you got after presenting a collection of photographs you took of prostitutes on East Hastings and Cordova last year. The comments— 'heartfelt', 'searing', 'genuine talent', are attached." He looked up. "Are you sure you shouldn't be in the fine arts program, or perhaps journalism?"

Sharon's face burned and she felt comments rising up again that would only get her into more trouble. She bit her tongue. "No, Sir."

"You have no financial help from your parents, I presume."

"No, Sir."

"Let me guess. They kicked you out of the house when you were still a teen. You became a street kid, did drugs, almost died. You somehow managed to claw your way out, and now want to help others do the same."

Other than the part about the drugs, it was close enough that Sharon's jaw dropped. She shut it again at the cold glint of satisfaction she saw in Tighe's eyes.

He closed her file and set it down again in the middle of his desk like a clear signal that he was far from done with it. And it finally struck Sharon that he shouldn't even have been able to get it, should he? Just how public was all of her history? The reference letters from Julia—were they in there too? Sharon's stomach suddenly went so cold she thought she might be sick.

"You think that living on the street gave you a clear perception of our society's class problems?"

"No, s– Yes, Professor. I think it did."

"Well which is it? No or yes?"

"Yes."

"Better than the social scientists who've been conducting studies and research in the area for the last twenty years."

Sharon licked her lips. Did he want her to just shrug and agree she was being foolish? But this was a university. She was *supposed* to think here. "I think...that sometimes theories and studies get lost in trying to find commonalities of experience. They want all the problems to make sense. Otherwise how do you deal with them?"

The small sarcastic smile that had been dancing on the edge of Tighe's mouth dropped away and his eyes sharpened. "Ah. And how would you deal with them?"

"One person at a time."

"One at a time."

"Yes."

"A door-to-door personal salvation mission."

"More like corner-to-corner," Sharon said. "Most of the street kids, and especially the girls on the street, don't have particular doors you can go to."

"Speaking from personal experience again."

"Yes, sir."

"Did you know that I've spent time down 'on the street', talking with the kids there—the prostitutes, the drug users?"

Sharon regarded him doubtfully, trying to imagine someone like Micky telling this cold customer anything real about her life. "I didn't know that," she said at last.

"Do you think that might inform my lectures on the subject?"

"I still don't think you get the real picture unless you actually live there. Sir."

Tighe stared at her long time, his long fingers tapping lightly on his desktop. Finally he said, "Alright, Ms. Dekker, here's your assignment. I want you to actually go out onto our mean streets again, find at least two destitute persons you believe you can save, and write up a report outlining their histories, living conditions, current challenges, and your proposed solutions. I want it typed up in grammatically correct sentences and submitted here on my desk by this time a week from today. Thursday."

The ice in Sharon's belly had vanished and a smile spread across her face. "Yes, Sir. One thing, Professor?"

"Yes?"

"If I can get that report in to you by next week, and my proposed solutions are viable with a little government support, could you see your way clear to putting me in touch with some of your former colleagues? Getting anyone to talk with me about the methadone programs has been a real bear."

Tighe frowned. "Pardon me?"

"Daniel McGlough, Jarmin Sandeep, Betty Klintock. The first two are now in the Ministry of Family & Child Services. Ms. Klintock, I believe, is the MP for the riding of East Hastings. I think they'd speak to me if a former colleague and current consultant were to ask them nicely. That is, if *you* were to ask them, sir."

Tighe stared and Sharon smiled back.

"Before I signed up for your course, I did my research on you too."

Tighe cleared his throat. "This meeting's over, Ms. Dekker."

"The support, sir?"

"First do the work, Ms. Dekker. Then...we'll see."

"But if–"

Tighe strode out and scooped up his briefcase. "Go!"

And Sharon did, running out the door, down the hallway, and not slowing to check her watch until she was outside and halfway down the quadrangle's broad white steps.

She was going to be late for work again but didn't care. From rejection by Griffin and threatened expulsion from university, to a sign of hope with Griffin and a promise of help for Angel, Micky, and Rose. This had to be a record turnaround for her. And it was maybe, just maybe, a sign that this hard-luck kid might have a chance for happiness in this world after all.

She looked back at the quadrangle building and almost stumbled when she saw Professor Tighe's face staring down at her from one of the upper hallway windows. Watching.

She shook it off.

He was going to help her. She already had *three* women picked out who needed help. She had her solution. Avirona Engineering had come through with a promise of cash to help buy or lease the building, which meant two corporate sponsors so far—just enough to show that a business-government partnership on this was possible.

Yes, Tighe was going to help her whether he wanted to or not.

Like Griffin was going to love her, whether he wanted to or not.

Sharon would simply *make* these things happen.

8

I N FRONT OF THE RED OWL. 2:20 am.

What was he doing? What the hell was he doing?

Maybe it was the unsettling meeting Griffin had had about this place this afternoon. The two goons he'd talked to had been wearing nice suits and been groomed like businessmen, but something about them felt wrong. If Lillian hadn't vouched for them ahead of time, Griffin's scuzz detector would have gone off big time.

Okay, it *had* gone off, but he'd silenced it. And they'd talked the right talk, described their plans for affordable housing, laid out the problems they were having with the co-developer they wanted to bring into this project.

Maybe it was just the tiny size of the deal. Maybe Griffin had gotten so used to going after the big ones that it was just like Lillian had accused—he was all about money, not about caring.

Hm. So an identity crisis that had brought him here tonight? And what? He hoped Sharon Dekker was going to solve it for him?

Absurd. As stupid as Majo's insistence on him dating her four times.

Ridiculous.

He turned up the collar of his trench coat against a cold wind that whistled around the brick wall where he stood. The night sky was overcast. The chill air was thick with impending rain. The street was deserted.

Jeez, it was so quiet Griffin could hear the buzz of the street lamps. The only people who came through here at this time of night were drunk, stoned, or driving like hell to get home after doing something they shouldn't have.

Or they were mixed-up lawyers who were slumming to find themselves in the arms of—

He cut off the thought as a dark-paneled van pulled past him and stopped against the curb, directly in front of the Red Owl.

Griffin shrank back into the shadows.

Two rough-looking men in jean jackets piled out of the front of the van, walked to the back, opened the doors, and dragged out what looked to be two girls who seemed to be staggering—either drugged or beaten.

A third man stuck his head out of the van and looked up and down the street, his gaze traveling right over the place where Griffin held his breath. His face was shadowed but it looked like he wore a short moustache. He had a compact, prowling sort of look to him.

After a moment, he motioned to the men with the girls and they dragged the girls to the Red Owl's front door. Before they could knock, however, the sour-looking barkeep—whom Griffin had learned was named Henry—flung open that door and stormed out.

"Not too fucking brilliant bringing them to the front door," he said.

Henry walked over to the van and talked in a low voice with the mustached man. He became whiny and weaker. The words "back door" were the only ones Griffin heard clearly.

A moment later, the two men with the girls jumped back into the van and it roared forwards, turning right on Hastings, no doubt coming back down the alley behind the bar.

Which was also the door through which Sharon must have left for the night earlier. D'oh. She wasn't even around anymore.

To compound the stupidity of it all, it wasn't until Griffin had his cell phone out of his pocket, 9-1-1 already dialed, that he realized he couldn't explain his own presence here at 2:30 am. Or even why, exactly, he was convinced there was anything wrong going on.

"Shit." He tugged on his free ear.

The 9-1-1 operator answered. Griffin muffled his voice to give a brief, anonymous tip, and hung up.

Then he paused, staring at the phone.

Truly gallant behavior might be to go to the front door of the Red Owl now and knock. But then what? Most likely he'd face a pissed-off owner/barkeep who'd recognize him from last night and mess with Sharon or the upcoming building negotiations. And if this really was the sort of thing Lillian had described—girl smuggling—then he'd face some really badass criminals who'd decide Griffin had seen too much and promptly vanish him.

Swallowing a bitter taste, he shoved his phone back into his pocket and jogged to where he'd parked his car further up the block. When he started imagining either ramming his car through the front doors of the Red Owl in a crazed rescue attempt, or chasing the night bus along its route to see if he could spot Sharon, he knew he needed to head home. Selfless honesty was one thing; stupidity was another. Let the cops handle it.

As for his lingering sense of creepiness, he'd get over that by seeing Sharon tomorrow. Today, actually. Their hike. In 10.5 hours.

Maybe if the conversation lagged, he could suggest she look for signs of smuggled sex-trade workers in the back of bar where she worked.

Not that it mattered. He was going to help these questionable businessmen of Lillian's do their deal quick and slick. Then the Red Owl would simply no longer be in the game.

Would that ease his conscience?

Bet on it.

Now he needed sleep.

~~~~~

East Hastings and Woodland. 2:31 a.m.

Sharon, who'd slipped out the back of the Red Owl and run to the bus stop now let the 2:30 night bus roar past her. There was something about the way Lisa had shrugged her off when Sharon had come in today. The older waitress had looked more than just tired. She'd looked troubled, obsessing over something. Sharon could tell she needed help, but couldn't tell what for.

"Sunday," was all she'd say. "The Glad Rose at eleven. 'Kay?"

And Sharon had nodded, a little overwhelmed suddenly by all the women she was committing to help.

It got her walking further north and east until she reached Micky and Angel's turf.

She saw Micky's compact shape from a half a block away. Hanging back until she was sure that their pimp, Jamie, wasn't hanging around, Sharon jogged quickly forward.

"Hey, girlfriend," she said when she got there.

"Shit. What are you doing here?"

"Finished work. Jogged over. How's Rose?"

Micky, who was dressed far too lightly for the weather, in a mini-skirt and a green jacket that clashed horribly with her hair, sniffed and looked at her with bright eyes, like she'd already done a line or two tonight.

"She's fine. Clinic doc gave her some pills. Rose loves any kind of drugs." She snickered a bit at her own wit. "How bout you? How bout that 'safe house' of yours?"

"I'm working on it."

Micky giggled at that, then sneezed. The red streaks of her hair popped up and she began to look like a Pomeranian—giggle and sneeze, giggle and sneeze, the green jacket jerking up around her ears, her naked legs twitching about underneath her.

"What?" Sharon said, annoyed.

"I asked around...hunh...about your place, the Red Owl." Another giggle. "You know what the word is?"

"Tell me."

"The Hard Riders are buying it. All that buzz about changes round here? It's like they found out what you were trying to do with the Red Owl and figured, 'Hey! This is *our* place.' Yeah. So now they can use it like a headquarters. Keep tabs on the cops from there, move the drugs, move the girls."

Sharon felt a chill in her gut as she thought about the new Hard Riders she'd been seeing in the Red Owl. And Henry's late night meeting with the mean-looking one. Had Henry told them she was trying to buy the building? Used it as leverage?

Henry said he won't sell," she said.

"Might not have a choice," Micky said. "This is the Hard Riders, right? And they've hired some slick lawyer. He's supposed to be so good he's gonna push it through in like a week."

A week! There was no way she pull together a counter-offer in a week. "I'll talk to Henry."

"You do that."

Micky turned as a low-riding Acura Legend slowed to at stop at the curb. Silver. An old-fashioned car-phone antenna sticking up from the rear window like a skinny penis. Micky's smile went wide and she strutted over to the lowering window. "Hey, handsome. Haven't seen you in almost three days."

Sharon stepped over behind her and dropped her face to scowl over Micky's shoulder, saying, "You there!"

Inside the shadows of the vehicle, Sharon got the flash of a vaguely-familiar face before the man covered his face with his one hand and slammed his foot to the gas. The car squealed away from the curb so fast it dragged Micky onto the street with it. The hooker yelled and ran and ripped her arms away, stumbled, almost fell.

Then Micky spun around, smack in the middle of the Hastings east-bound land, and stabbed her index finger back at Sharon. "You! You get the fuck out of here! Go build your fucking 'safe house' and leave me'n Angel alone!"

Shaken, Sharon stepped backwards. "And Rose too? How old is she, Micky?"

"Get OUT!"

Micky was screeching now and Sharon thought she heard running footsteps. The pimp, Jamie?

A visceral memory of him grabbing her burned through her like ice, freezing her in place. But only for a second. Then she turned back towards Dunlevy and ran.

She heard the footsteps turn to run after her. She put her head down and sprinted down an alley, sharp-turned into another, and another.

The night air whipped smells at her face. Garbage. Charred brick. Memories of other nights running—*Daryl catches her, drags her back to their stinking room in Kelowna, slaps her, punches her in the arms and gut with those gym-pumped muscles of his, then rips off her clothes. "You know you deserve it, Baby! You know you do!" Rapes her...*

Her feet caught on something and she stumbled. Staggered. Regained her balance and kept running even though her lungs were burning now.

Because she *wouldn't* go back to that life.

Never.

Never!

Never!

When she reached the night bus stop on Hastings, it was deserted. She slowed to a halt and danced around it warily, breathing hard, looking back the way she'd come, listening for the footsteps.

She heard nothing. Saw nothing. They must have given up.

She stopped and looked at her hands. They trembled like little buzz saws. Her heart still pounded. Her face was wet with tears. She could feel hot trickles of sweat running down her underarms and temples and back.

And, incongruously, her first thought was she was glad that Griffin couldn't see her like this—helpless, dirty, shaking, afraid. God, this was not who she wanted to be. This was *not* who she was anymore.

Go build your 'safe house!'

The sneer in Micky's voice came back to her, announcing how naive Sharon was. For all Sharon's years on the street, she'd still believed she could just find some angel investors, tap some government programs, and do exactly what she'd told Professor Tighe had to be done—start rescuing streetwalkers one at a time.

Sharon forced herself to stop dancing about by planting her feet by the night stop. She gritted her teeth and breathed hard, still scanning the street.

She *wasn't* naive. She'd managed to find two corporate donors so far and she'd find more. And she knew the government programs were there if you knew who and how to ask. With Tighe's help she'd access them.

All she had to do was make sure the Red Owl building didn't get bought up by biker scum before she could get things in place.

...they've hired some slick lawyer...

Yeah? Well that was a problem she'd have to address. She certainly didn't have the money to hire a legal gun of her own, but...but....

No. She couldn't do what she was thinking. Not when she'd just managed to separate out the parts of her life so nicely. No classes tomorrow and a nice hike with Griffin. He'd get to see her as a real person, not just some slut.

But if she asked him for help with this Red Owl thing, he'd ask, and have every right to ask, why she'd gotten involved in this in the first place. And their relationship wasn't ready for that yet.

Never will be, whispered a voice inside her

"Shut up," she whispered at it.

A rumble from her left told her the night bus was coming. With a grimace, she turned to face it. Right then it looked just like the ones back in Kelowna, and she felt her mouth fill with bitterness.

Was she going to spend her whole life running and hiding? Or was she going to ask Griffin for help?

The bus stopped. She climbed aboard and grabbed the front rail as it pulled out.

As it did, two things happened. One, she decided she *would* ask Griffin and damn the consequences. Two, she thought she caught a momentary glimpse of a face watching her from an alley to the north after all.

But it had to have been some kind of trick of the light.

It had looked like Professor Colm Tighe.

9

B Y FRIDAY NOON, it had started to drizzle. By one p.m., the drizzle had turned to steady, concrete-splattering rain. It grayed out the north shore mountains and drummed loudly on the roof of Griffin's car.

Inside that car, Griffin steered carefully up to the front of Sharon's building. He squinted up at Burnaby Mountain just beyond as he stopped. Could he picture himself happily slogging up a bunch of steep muddy trails? Nope. All he got was something out of a bad war movie.

There was a thumping on his passenger side door.

Griffin turned and saw Sharon's soaked face grinning happily from underneath a yellow rain slicker's hood. He reached over to open it for her.

She burst into the Beamer's front seat like her own little typhoon, swinging her knapsack down beside her boots then reaching back to thunk the door closed behind her. She smelled like wet grass and peaches. No, something else. Fruity. Sweet. He remembered—*mango.*

"Hi!"

Her rain-dripping smile was so broad and eager that Griffin found his own lips pulling up to match it. And while the glimpse of her wet, bare red legs called to him, it was her smile that held his attention. She was actually heart-stopping beautiful. With the distractions of her spiky hair and wild body hidden by her rain coat, her face shone like something untouched. Her smile showed small, perfect teeth inside an expressive mouth. Her cheekbones were round and full. Her nose—tiny and pure, even with the scar across its bridge. And the eyes—smoky green. Yes, they held some sort of sadness in them, but the long lashes framing them made it such a pretty sadness.

"Hello?" she repeated.

Griffin cleared his throat to speak over the drumming rain. "You don't seriously still want to go hiking."

"Any kind of weather. I told you. You did bring your rain gear?"

He looked at her rain coat. It was on the cheap side, but looked waterproof, with a nice little bill sticking out from the top of the hood. Whereas his...

He lifted an arm. "Gore-tex. Water-repellent."

"Last sprayed...?"

"Pardon?"

"You do know you have to spray those occasionally to keep up their water repellency."

He raised his eyebrows at her. "Actually, no. I try to avoid going out in the rain much. I'm more a weight room, indoor swimming pool kind of guy."

"And you live in Vancouver?" She clucked. "Don't worry. The rain'll let up. And most of the trail's under tree cover."

"You're still going to make me hike?"

"Oh, yeah." She pointed straight ahead. "End of the street. Find a parking space up there and we're set."

With a dramatic moan, Griffin put the car in gear and drove slowly towards the mountain. It felt like the dark mass of evergreens was a great slumbering giant ready to pounce through the splattering rain at them.

Truthfully, though, he wouldn't have noticed if it had. Griffin was only half-looking that way. Mostly he was studying Sharon out of the corner of his eye. Despite all that perkiness, the casual act, there really was something sad in her face. As if she was struggling with some image of how bad life could be. It showed even in the way she kept pulling her raincoat sleeves back into her lap when they started dripping onto the leather. Like she could get slapped or rejected for something so minor.

Why?

And how, through all that, did she keep up such an outward appearance of cheer? That had to take amazing act of courage. Like the way she'd opened to him up in her apartment, then watched him without covering up or asking him to stay.

Where did strength like that come from?

"Anywhere here," she said suddenly.

Griffin slammed on the brakes and slid through a puddle. They'd reached the end of the road. Lots of curb parking since no one else was crazy enough to hike in this weather.

The mountain loomed directly in front of them.

Oh boy. Was he starting to find himself yet?

~~~~

Sharon stifled a laugh as she saw Griffin crane his neck forward to look up the slope. Mostly because the laugh would have come out wrong. A nervous laugh.

She'd felt him studying her. Judging.

Oh, God. Didn't she get even a half hour's grace? Just a little time when she could pretend they were starting fresh? That the night with him in her apartment hadn't happened and they were two old friends with normal lives who were catching up on old times? Sharon had skipped classes and spent three hours on the phone this morning to push her case for the Red Owl to corporate P.R. people, CEOs, charity groups. She'd bagged another thirty-thousand dollar commitment. That had to earn her *some* kind of reprieve.

She swallowed.

Come on, she thought. Like me. Respect me. Both for me and so I can ask you to help me fight the Hard Riders' preemptive strike.

She looked away quickly as Griffin turned towards her.

"Okay," Griffin said, leaning over to touch her arm. "We going?"

Even inside her wet raincoat, she could feel the sudden electricity of his touch. He seemed to as well. His eyes smoldered when she looked at him, and he didn't pull back right away. Almost as if he was urging her to change her mind and drag him back to her apartment after all.

But that was wrong. Wrong! It complicated everything too much.

Pulling back from Griffin, she grabbed her backpack and scrambled out into the rain. She fought an urge to run as she shouldered her pack and jogged forward to the head of the trail. There she swallowed and looked up, sheltering her eyes from the rain. The two tall cedars trees on either side of the path calmed her again as they always did.

"What are you looking at?" said Griffin, close at her elbow.

She glanced sideways at him and saw he'd raised his hood, pulling it around his face with a silly drawstring. His face was dripping as the rain splattered down on them.

"They're my two big brothers," she said loudly. "The ones I never had and always wanted. They look out for me. Take care of me."

Now why had she told him that? She'd never admitted that to anyone.

Griffin didn't laugh but spoke back as strongly. "They're overrated, brothers."

"You don't know that. You don't have any."

"I do. One older one."

"But–"

He held his hands up over his eyes so he could see her better, not pushing her to move. "Keith. He's sixteen years older than me. He wasn't living at home when you knew me in school. He was in L.A. becoming an actor. I was an accident."

She stared at him, trying to tell if he was joking or bitter. "Where's your brother now?" she asked.

"Pardon?"

She repeated it louder, because he'd drawn back from her and the rain had drowned her out.

"Can we start the walk?" he said, pointing to the path.

She laughed. "Sure." And they ran together under the canopy of cedars and spruce. All of a sudden they could hear themselves think again. No more rain, only light drips. And all around them, curling through the trees, was a kind of floating mist.

"It's part of the TransCanada Trail," Sharon said. "Eventually supposed to stretch through every province."

He turned back to her. "That would be one helluva hike!"

She grinned. "Starting now." She tugged him by the arm and they started the climb.

"Not muddy," he said after a while of climbing. The trail had started uphill and only gotten steeper, but underfoot was only needles, twigs, and rock.

"No mud."

"Warmer than I thought."

She shot him a lewd smile, threw off her rain hood, and unzipped the top of her slicker.

He followed suit, exposing the white of his throat and top swell of his chest. Through his rain pants she could see his powerful thighs bulged as he crunched up the trail beside her.

"Damn, I knew I should have told you to wear shorts," she said.

"Hunh?"

"Pretty up the place."

She was delighted to see him blush, but then scolded herself and turned away, focusing on the climb. This was *supposed* to be her earning his respect. Why did she slip so easily into her old, crass flirting? Too many years of practice.

They climbed in silence.

"It would be an adventure," she said finally. "Hiking across Canada. You know I've never been anywhere but Vernon, Kelowna, and here. With this, you'd get maps, a GPS, trail breaks for re-supplying, and take, what? Six months? A year?"

"Too long. I couldn't get away."

"Work?"

"Building a new law firm."

He looked at her with a flash of anger as he said it, like she was contradicting him. Then the look was gone. Imagined?

"What about you?" he asked.

"Hunh?"

She wanted to clap a hand over her mouth. It had come out like a hooker's grunt.

Thankfully she could blame it on the trail. It was getting ever steeper, and it was harder to talk and climb at the same time. Griffin had to pause and catch his own breath before he said, "Do *you* have anything going on that you wouldn't want to leave right now?"

Sharon flushed. So much for light and breezy. He was judging her again. This was his way of asking if she was doing anything with her life.

"I've got some things going," she said.

"Like...?"

Before she could stop herself, she said, "You'll see when we reach the top of this trail."

"What? A lookout?"

"Something."

"A mystery."

"Yep."

Before they started climbing again, she took off her raincoat and stuffed it into her sack. No skimpy top on underneath, though. She'd purposely worn a thick blue tee-shirt with a sports bra underneath that squashed her almost flat.

She grinned at the look of disappointment on Griffin's face, handed him the water bottle.

He took a long drink, capped it, and took off his own jacket.

Unlike her, he'd worn a top as tight and stretchy as her waitress shirt. All purple and black, it molded tightly to the gorgeous vee-shape he'd developed in those weight rooms and indoor swimming pools. My, the taut slabs of muscle on this man!

No, no, no. Wrong agenda. Focus somewhere else.

"Running shirt," he said with what sounded like laughter in his voice. "Wicks the sweat away from the body so I keep smelling clean and sweet as a baby's bottom."

"Okay," Sharon snapped. "Let's see how good you really are."

With a spurt of nervous adrenaline, she started tearing up the steep slope at a near run. Which was saying something, since they'd now reached the part in the trail that was so steep the trail keepers had done like the Grouse Grind, with sideways-piled four-by-fours reinforcing sharp switchbacks. The ground underfoot was almost all rock or roots and stone.

When Sharon glanced back, though, Griffin was right behind her, breathing a bit, but easily matching her pace with his longer legs. Not fair! She did this climb two or three times a week, and he was just some kind of weekend warrior.

But through the wound of injustice, she felt a tingle of excitement too. She remembered the ripple of his muscles when he'd stripped in her apartment. She remembered the ease with which he'd taken her. None of the pumped brutality of Daryl; just clean strength.

That and a strong mind, one that could touch her in ways she—

Stop it!

Why was she torturing herself like there was any kind of future here? She didn't want to end up dying with a life of wasted passions like her mother had. Sharon was going to pursue things she could get. Here that meant Griffin's friendship, hopefully. Respect. Help.

Gasping, she stopped just shy of a switchback and put her back to one of the wooden crossbars someone had nailed between the upright four-by-fours that served as guard rails over the steeper drops.

"Tell me about your brother," she managed as he stopped beside her and—*Yes!*—leaned over his knees to take deep breaths. "The one down in L.A."

Griffin straightened, asked for the water bottle again, drank, shrugged. "His life determined mine."

"How?"

"Tell me about Kelowna."

"You first."

"How much further to the top?"

"Ten minutes. Maybe fifteen."

"Okay. Let's go, and I'll tell you on the way."

So they did, slower now. Which was good because Sharon's thighs were quivering with fatigue from that last sprint. She had to use her hands on the railings and rocks to pull herself up now.

As did Griffin, but he talked as they climbed.

Brother Keith had been raised as a spoiled, only child. He was talented, smart, athletic. Then, right around the time Keith was going into grade eleven and already thinking about applying for scholarships for university, something happened with Father Walsh's vasectomy and Griffin was conceived.

"A vasectomy problem?" laughed Sharon as her foot struggled to find purchase some roots that snaked over a rock like gnarled fingers. "You sure it wasn't..."

She let it die and bit her tongue.

"Doctor checked it," Griffin said, up ahead of her. "It happens. Anyway, Keith suddenly wasn't Mommy and Daddy's one-and-only any more. He started acting out, literally. Got involved in drama. He was good at it. So he ditched going to university and came here to Vancouver. He got commercials, bit parts in series. It beat working."

This time there was no mistaking the disapproval in Griffin's voice. And envy? It was unsettling. Envy was a weak emotion. It was petty. It made Griffin almost...attainable?

Sharon cut off that thought brushed her hands off on her hiking shorts. It was just her subconscious compensating for her feelings of inadequacy. She had to keep that under control. She had to be normal for Griffin, worthy of his friendship.

So why had she ever mentioned Kelowna? What was she going to say if he brought it up again.

Thankfully, though, the trail was leveling off. They were reaching the top of the loop.

"He went down to L.A.?" she asked. "Your brother?"

"He tried to make it for about ten years. Did bit parts, a few commercials, lots of extra work. Got involved in the health food industry somewhere along the line. Now he designs power drinks and workout diets for the stars." He stopped and let her pass him.

"He's successful."

"He's turning a profit."

"Your parents aren't impressed."

"It's not a profession."

"A profession." Like streetwalking?

"Something funny?"

"Only if you're very strange like me." Before he could pursue that, she turned and strode out over a flat portion of trail to a break in the trees. There she mopped the sweat from her forehead, retrieved the water bottle from her backpack again, and pointed.

"That's the Burrard Inlet. On a clear day you can see Belcara, Deep Cove, even most of North Van."

"Rain's almost stopped," he said, coming up close beside her.

She moved off, handing him the bottle and shouldering her pack. She nodded to a steep trail cutting up off the main path. "Short hike straight up here and we're at the campus."

He took a glug from her water bottle and handed it back. "The campus? SFU?"

"I told you I had something to show you."

"Probably not what I'd *really* like to see right now, but lead on."

10

THEY BROKE OUT OF THE TREES to a road, across which was a short strip of grass and a row of what looked to Griffin like residence buildings.

The rain had almost stopped and a steady stream of students were walking along the road or on the grass, arms full of books or carrying backpacks or briefcases—presumably heading to class.

It all gave Griffin a wistful tightening inside. He'd enjoyed UBC, the University of British Columbia. Both his undergrad and his law school time. Everything was so simple in school. Your goals straightforward. Your path given to you.

Of course, he'd done the whole thing in a bit of a vacuum. He'd cultivated few friends other than Majo (who'd brought in the others). Mostly Griffin had just worked like mad. Proven that at least one Walsh brother had the grit it took to really make it.

As he stood remembering, Sharon pushed past him and headed in the same direction as the general flow of students.

"Come on," she said.

He grinned and followed without hesitation. At least in part, it was to keep watching the delightful twitch of her bum as she walked. She'd denied him her upper body with that bag of a shirt, but that very fine rear end had been mesmerizing for the last twenty minutes or so of the hike, ever since she'd doffed her raincoat. He wasn't about to let it out of his sight now.

Suddenly, as she walked, she threw her head back to laugh at the spitting gray skies, and Griffin felt something almost akin to pain shoot through his chest.

My God, how different his university years would have been if someone like Sharon had been around. He probably wouldn't have made the honor roll four years running. Nor won all the graduating awards he had. Nor landed his Greene McNamara job before he was even finished his second year in law school.

Maybe that would have been better.

He blinked and stumbled to a halt.

Better?

He studied the faces of the students around him, especially the ones walking with a boyfriend or girlfriend. Most of them looked half-asleep. They didn't know, didn't *care*, that they were preparing themselves for the rest of their lives.

If you didn't *work*, you didn't achieve.

If you let yourself get distracted, you didn't *work*.

That was all going to be doubly important when he got Walsh, Cruz, et al., off the ground and generating income.

So he could work even harder? Become even more cut off from everyone? More work-obsessed? More impossibly separate from people like Sharon Dekker, for instance?

Oh, yeah, he thought, remembering his angst over Sharon yesterday and last night. She was really helping him sort himself out.

"Hey!" Sharon called to him. "You coming?"

He hurried to catch up. She stood in a large triangle of grass beside a six-story box to her right and concrete paths and walkways ahead. When he reached her, he found himself sliding his arm around her waist. Just to confirm that incredible body still existed under that shirt.

She jerked in surprise and he smoothly withdrew his hand, swearing inside.

Idiot! It wasn't like she wasn't making it plain to him. This hike was all about resetting their relationship. To friends, not lovers. The other night had been...the other night. He had to forget the body. Even if she was still interested in him physically—and he was pretty sure she was—she wasn't going to that place with him again for quite some time. If ever.

Which was fine. Really. It would keep this whole exercise controllable, something he could present neatly to Majo for the simple thing it was. Better for everyone. Really and truly.

Damn, he wished he didn't want to touch her so much.

She was pointing. "That's the academic quadrangle."

Ripping his gaze off her, he saw that past the concrete walkways and paths ahead was an enormously broad white building. It had two upper floors held up by evenly spaced rows of square concrete pillars. Wide concrete steps led up to it on this side. There might have been a fountain and grass beyond.

"It's a big square, open in the middle" Sharon said. "Most of my classes are held in there."

He didn't hear it at first. Then it sank in. "Your classes. You...teach?"

She blushed and pressed her lips tightly together.

"I mean, you're attending university here?" he corrected quickly.

Neither one made sense, actually. She'd never been that brilliant in high school, more a rebel than scholar, with pink and red hair. And she hadn't finished grade twelve. Now what...?

"I'm studying psychology," she said with her arms folded in front of her chest. "And sociology. My second year."

"How? Your father? Or stepfather?"

"No."

She said the word so coldly that Griffin almost took a step backwards to avoid frostbite. There was obviously no love lost in either case there. And Griffin remembered grade twelve when he heard Mrs. Neal, Sharon's mother, had died. He'd always assumed that was why Sharon had dropped out.

"But you obviously finished high school," Griffin said. "Back in Vernon?"

She shook her head.

"Kelowna?"

Another shake.

"Here?"

She nodded and for a moment he didn't think she'd speak, but then she said with careful clarity, "It took me two years. I was working at the same time. Two jobs. Then I applied here and got in."

He noticed she was pointedly not talking about Kelowna or filling in the time gap of six years between Vernon High and going back to school here in Vancouver. Griffin decided not to press it.

"You like it?" he asked. "Your courses? Coming up to the top of a mountain to study?"

She looked close to tears and he yearned to lunge forward and wrap his arms around her, squeeze away the hurt. But that wasn't his place. He didn't know her that well. He was starting to realize he wanted to, crazy as that seemed to him—their life plans were so obviously not in synch—but she didn't seem to want him to. And it wasn't the Walsh way to just randomly ride to the rescue of every hurting soul one encountered, sex goddess or not.

So he just wavered there uncomfortably as her eyes welled up.

"Sorry," he said. "Wrong question."

She laughed, and the sound was so painful it almost broke his reserve. He felt that squeeze in his chest again.

"No," she said, dropping her arms and grabbing the straps of her backpack. "It's an innocent question. It's just...you have no idea how much it cost to get here."

"The money?"

She laughed again, this time mocking him. "That was simplest cost."

"What, the application? Finding–"

"Don't." She held up her hand. "Just don't. The costs were really personal, and I'm not sure I know you well enough yet to trust you with them."

The turnabout of his own thoughts rocked Griffin backwards like he'd been hit. "Oh, sorry. Excuse me. Fine. Don't tell me."

"Don't be a little boy. What? You're used to women confiding their deepest secrets to you on the first date?"

"Usually."

"Oh, Mr. Wonderful."

"And this isn't our first date."

That shut her up. She pursed her lips together again and turned away from him. "Maybe this wasn't such a good idea after all, bringing you up here."

"Maybe not."

"Would have been better just to take you back to my apartment and screw your brains out."

He said nothing but was angry that her words made his internal temperature jump wildly. Especially because she was saying the words with such obvious sarcasm.

She saw the effect and stepped right up to him. Even through her blue bag of a tee-shirt, he could feel her breasts press against his arm.

"And if I did take you back and fuck you," she whispered, running a hand lightly up his chest, "and afterwards asked a favor of you, would you be willing to help me, or would you have already mentally run out on me like you did last time."

Griffin felt a heady mix of anger and lust rush up to his already flushed face. "It would probably depend on the favor."

"Okay," she said, voice breaking.

The meanness she'd put into her move seemed to drop away at once and she pulled back just a little, like a scared girl. It was all Griffin could do again to stop putting his arms around her and crushing her to his chest. He felt awkward and helpless. Not a feeling he was used to or liked.

"You're...a lawyer," she said.

"Yes."

"Real estate?"

"Not really."

"Right. Business law, Majo said. But...buying commercial buildings. Do you ever, like, deal with business people who are buying whole blocks of them?"

Even unsettled as he was, he couldn't miss the irony of her question. "Not my usual field, but I was handling one of those yesterday afternoon."

There was a beat where he swore her breath choked to a stop in her lungs. "Yes?" she said.

"A group of three businessmen who are trying to hook up with another group to buy a group of buildings downtown Vancouver."

He suddenly remembered the deal had the potential to put her out of a job, despite what Lillian had said. In fact he himself had been so bothered by the scuzz vibes he'd had at the meeting with Lillian's developers yesterday that he'd completely forgotten that point. That was unforgivable.

"I...should tell you," he said. "The deal could affect your job at the Red Owl."

"*My* job." Her eyes went wide and he could visibly see her mind racing as her pupils twitched back and forth. She pulled back fully from him now and said, "How?"

He cleared his throat. "The buildings these guys are trying to buy—one of them is the Red Owl Bar & Hotel."

11

S HARON COULDN'T BREATHE.

It was him. The slick lawyer the Hard Riders had hired. It was Griffin Walsh.

But–

It made no–

"These 'guys'," she said at last. "Who are they?"

He shrugged. "They call themselves the Coogan Group."

"The Coogan Group," she repeated numbly. "Which means what? What do they do? Who are their members?"

Griffin looked suddenly uncomfortable and shoved his hands into the pockets of his sweaty rain pants. "They're property developers," he said. "They're committed to developing profitable low-cost housing."

"Ha!" It burst out like a smoker's hack, driving him a step back. Sharon didn't care. "You believe that?"

"Why shouldn't I?"

"'Profitable low-cost housing.' They have a word for that, don't they? Oxymoron."

Griffin's brow lowered. "Full of big words today."

"Oh...." Sharon shook her head slowly at him, feeling her heart pressing so hard into her mouth she thought she might choke. "You want some simpler ones? How about stupid? Or liar. Or consciously self-deluded. You, not me. I thought you were Mr. Integrity."

Now Griffin's brow not only puckered but grew dark, his mouth tight. "You want to tell me what you're getting at?"

Sharon couldn't stand still. She found herself stalking, half-dancing, around him as he stood his ground. She probably looked like some crazed she-wolf, even with her backpack and shorts. Awful. Sordid. She just didn't care. This was too much like Daryl. The man looks perfect. He looks like your savior, your way out, someone you can trust.

Then *this* shit.

"You're in bed with the bikers, Griffin! With criminals! You're helping them abuse kidnaped girls and sell drugs to abusive psychopaths!"

She poked a finger at him, fully expecting him to hit her back, make it all fit the pattern.

But he didn't. His brow just pulled in even tighter, and he glared at her like he could slice-and-dice her up with his eyes. "I don't know what you're talking about."

"The Hard Riders!" she said. "The guys who were in the Red Owl the first night you came in there! That's who you're dealing with! The Coogan Group. Pagh!"

"No."

"No? That's it? *No?*"

The arrogance of the denial was as bad as Tighe's dismissal of her yesterday, as bad as every guy who'd ever bought her body and laughed at her. And suddenly she wasn't going to take it anymore.

"You don't know what the *fuck* you're talking about! You conceited asshole! I used to *worship* you and now you're doing deals with scumbags! Goddamn you, Walsh! God*damn* you!"

Then she was turning from him, unable to help herself, conscious of the stares from all the students who'd stopped to watch. How many of them had classes with her? How many would remember this and pass it on in whispers behind their hands? Just like every other normal crowd Sharon had ever tried to fit into. It was like they were programmed to smell weakness, then attack.

Like her stepdad had done with her mom.

Like... No, she wouldn't even go there. Any more than she'd moan and gnash her teeth over the fact that the last great hero of her imagination, Griffin Walsh, had just shown he had feet of clay.

"Sharon....," Griffin said from behind her. His hand grabbed her bare arm just like Jamie had in Micky's place.

Sharon screamed. Two birds burst into flight from the nearby rhododendron. People all around her drew back. Griffin jerked off his hand and stepped back.

When Sharon whirled around, she could read what was in all their faces, even Griffin's. *Crazy bitch.* Meaning her. *Crazy dropout whore. Who does she think she is coming up here anyway?*

And they were right, weren't they? They were right.

Fuck them. Her eyes were so wet she could hardly see. Fuck Griffin especially.

"Stay back," she said. "Don't touch me. Don't come near me. Don't follow me."

Then she turned and ran back towards the top of the path she'd come up with Griffin. She felt the clouds parting somewhere far overhead as she reached it. The bushes and ground went all eerily silver on her.

She dove in among the trees and stumbled down the mountain.

~~~~

What—the—hell—just—happened?

Griffin stood, literally open-mouthed, as he watched Sharon Dekker, née Sharon Neal of Vernon, jerk away from him and run to the line of forest where he'd hiked up with her. She disappeared.

He was vaguely conscious of the students who had stopped their march to class to watch the show. Vaguely conscious that the clouds were breaking up overhead as well, that the air up here on the mountain smelled fresher than downtown; pure and clean. More irony.

Or was it just fitting? Was this place a special haven from the grit of downtown that Griffin had somehow driven her from?

By his work with the Coogan Group?

If Sharon had given him just another minute or two, he might have explained that he certainly had misgivings about working with them. That "scuzz" alert that had gone off in their first meeting.

But...bikers?

He looked around at the gawking students and shook his head at them, dismissing them. Then, because he had booked himself out of the office until five, he began walking to what Sharon had called the "academic quadrangle." He might as well see if he could learn anything about what Sharon was doing up here. Make sure she really was a student, for instance, and not pulling some elaborate con on him.

Bikers?

Inside, a few inquiries sent him to administration, but the workers there weren't willing to give out any information about their students.

As he turned to go, however, a big-bosomed bespectacled woman in her sixties came quickly out from behind the administration desk and hurried out the door with an almost imperceptible nod to Griffin as she passed him.

He followed her out to the hallway. She was waiting for him two offices down, straightening her silk blouse.

"You do understand the need to protect the privacy of our students?" she said curtly when he caught up.

"Of course."

"Is Sharon in some sort of trouble?"

A knot Griffin hadn't been aware of loosened up in his gut. Sharon *was* a student here. No lies. No con game.

"I...don't know," he said. Sharon's extreme reaction to him telling her about the Red Owl haunted him. And her reaction to being touched.

The woman nodded and adjusted her glasses just the way his twelfth-grade biology teacher used to do when considering whether to give him time off to prepare for his debating competitions.

"What's your interest?" she said at last.

Griffin sighed. "It's like I said in there. I knew her in high school, ran into her here in town, asked her out. Found out she was a student here. I'm just curious."

"Curious?" She looked at him over the top of her glasses.

"I— Okay. She brought me up here on hike and we had a fight and— I don't know what I did wrong. I'm trying to understand her."

"Hmph. That might be a challenge."

"What do you mean?"

The woman took a considering breath and tugged a little at the bun she'd pulled her hair back into. "Sharon Dekker is a special student. I mean, of course every student is special, but it's hard not to care deeply about Sharon."

Griffin said nothing, but the woman seemed to see agreement in his eyes.

"She's sharp, hard-working. You know she's paid for her entire tuition with scholarships? And such heart. You said you know she's studying psychology and sociology, but do you know why? What she wants to do? I find her personally inspiring. For her to have gone through so much and still care like she does."

Good grief, the woman was actually choking up. If he'd been wearing his suit, Griffin would have offered her a handkerchief. As it was, he could only nod sympathetically.

But once the woman regained her self-control, his patience vanished. "What, exactly is it that she's gone through? And what is she aspiring to be?"

His informant gave him her over-the-glasses look again, but then jerked up her head to peer past his shoulders. Griffin turned to see a man standing at the administration office door. He wore a suit-jacket and tie, and looked ready to call security on both Griffin and the woman he was questioning.

"Time's up," she said.

"But—"

She touched her nose and said, "I think both your problems might be answered by a quick trip to our fine arts wing in the quadrangle. Look for Sharon's photograph collection there. I think you'll find it illuminating."

~~~

Illuminating wasn't the word.

Terrifying, maybe. Or heart-rending.

Griffin walked back along the polished granite to start again at the beginning. Sharon's work was all at the west end of the hall, on one wall, spread out, one after another, in simple silver frames with black mattes. The photos themselves weren't black and white, but the subjects were mostly taken at night and so bleak that they seemed that way.

Photograph: Woman sitting on the pavement, back to a forest green Dumpster, naked from the waist up, no shoes or socks. She's sticking a hypodermic needle into her forearm.

Photograph: Different woman standing just back from the curb, smoking. Her hand's on her hip, shirt unbuttoned to her navel. Lace pink bra underneath. She stares at the camera like she's figuring how much she could get for it.

Photograph: Dark-skinned woman on her knees in an alleyway. Her head's in the groin of some man who's face is lost in the shadows.

Photograph: Three skimpily-clad women standing together near a street lamp, watching traffic. The building behind them is dark. One of the women is obviously pregnant. Barely visible in the background, in the alley beside the dark building, is a child, no more than three, playing with a truck.

And on. And on.

Griffin counted twenty-seven photographs, in sizes ranging from eight-by-ten inches to one horrific one of a street girl, maybe seventeen, screaming at the camera while her fingernails tore at her scabby face. That picture must have been four feet high, three wide.

None of the photos had backlighting. Even the composition was crude, the subjects sometimes in fuzzy focus or half out of frame.

But the power of them was they were real. You had no doubt, viewing them, that nothing was staged. This was just things as they were.

Which begged the question how Sharon had managed to photograph them. And why?

Rather than get Griffin more into Sharon's mind to understand her, the display just tumbled him more into confusion. Yes, it accounted for the sadness he saw in her eyes. Maybe even for her sudden explosion at him over what she thought was a deal with a biker gang. A bottled-up rage against people she saw as responsible for the misery in her photographs.

But what set her into that world to start with? Had some friend of hers gotten caught up in that life? Had *she*, God forbid, spent some time on the street? Or was this all some game she'd been pushed into by a first year university project?

You have no idea what it cost to get here.

Sharon had said that. A personal cost. What sort of cost?

Suddenly a buzzing signaled the end of a class hour and the hallways at either end of the one where Griffin stood filled with students.

He should leave. Before he did, though, he had to look one last time at the haunting picture of the screaming girl. Was that girl still out there on the Vancouver streets?

As he stood in front of the oversized photo, Griffin felt someone at his elbow.

"She's very talented, isn't she?"

He turned to see a smooth-skinned man in his forties regarding him closely. The man wore an expensive suit and tie. His hair was neatly trimmed. His eyes slanted slightly at the corners—oriental blood. He had to have just come out of a class in session. Which made him a professor, Griffin assumed. He was far too well groomed to be a mature student.

"Do you agree she's talented?" the man pressed.

"The photographer? I suppose so."

"In picking her subjects, at least, if not in her technical compositions. Mister...?" The man proffered his fine-boned hand.

Griffin's scuzz alarm was buzzing again and he pretended not to see the hand.

"Do you know the photographer?" Griffin asked.

The man gave an oblique smile. "I do. Do you?"

"Yes."

"I see. She's in one of my classes." He didn't offer his name but asked Griffin again, "And your name is?"

Griffin reached the end of his patience and turned to face the man full on. The guy might have been wearing a suit to Griffin's technical running shirt, but Griffin had a good two inches on him, plus at least a decade less wear and tear.

"My name's Griffin Walsh. Now what do you want?"

Again the smile. "Very direct. I imagine she likes that in you."

"Not that it's any business of yours."

"Maybe not, but...a word of advice?"

Griffin felt his tension building. But in this case he knew exactly how he'd *like* to ease it. One quick punch into this man's smirk. "If I let you tell me, will you leave?"

The man chuckled. "Certainly. I have students to meet."

"Then tell me."

"Sharon Dekker is not who you think she is. She's not anything that these photographs can capture either. And what she is should probably be left to itself for at least a few more years. Or perhaps to someone with the proper maturity to handle it."

"Meaning you?"

The man inclined his head in acknowledgment. "Or a good

therapist. Are you skilled in that area?"

"I'm a lawyer."

"Ah. I don't think that qualifies."

Griffin held the man's eyes, willing him to blink and turn away. But he didn't. The man merely returned the gaze with the placid confidence of a snake. Until finally it was Griffin who had to turn.

It made his blood boil. He turned back to the photo of the screaming girl and that didn't help. He studied it anyway as he spoke. "You said you'd give me advice then leave."

"I did," said the man. "I will. But please keep this in mind: Sharon Dekker, for you, can only be trouble. For both your sakes, leave her alone."

When Griffin turned to glare at the man, he was already heading off around the corner. Griffin clamped his mouth closed, gave the whole line of Sharon's photographs one more sweeping look, and shook his head.

Leave her alone? Frankly, he'd love to do that.

Except for the fact he'd missed something huge in their argument today and needed to know what it was or he'd never sleep again.

And the fact he needed three more dates with her in order to seal his deal with Majo.

He looked down at himself. His entire body clenched angrily now in the hall of a university he didn't know, staring at a group of disturbing photographs, figuring how to pursue the crazy and sexually-maddening woman who'd put them there.

He'd expected some challenges starting up his law firm, but not ones like this.

Bouncing a little on the balls of his feet, he turned and jogged out of the hall, hoping he could find his way back down to where he'd left his car.

12

THIS DAY SHARON WAS EARLY TO WORK. And still steaming.

She banged in through the front door of the Red Owl and walked straight to the bar. Lisa wasn't in sight. The waitress Cherie Hart, who normally took over Saturday-to-Monday days, was leaning on the end of it. Henry was pouring a mixed drink for Ling Wa, an old man who came in every Friday afternoon like clockwork. The only other patrons were two women in the back right, whispering together over the table.

"Henry," Sharon said, her voice shaking.

The bartender/owner held up a finger at her without looking at her.

"*Henry.*"

Henry finished pouring and clinked his bottle of rye down a little harder than necessary. "You're early. What's the occasion?"

"Are you going to sell this place to the Hard Riders?"

The blunt-nosed face got suddenly tight, and Henry fixed her with a dark look. "I don't discuss this sort of business with waitresses, or in front of customers."

"Then let's go into the back. Now."

"Are you sure you work here?" he said.

"You want to talk about it out here, or in the back?"

He gave her a long look and must have seen some of the fire that was raging inside her, because he finally nodded. "Two minutes. Mr. Ling, you watch that no one steals my liquor."

"Oh, yes," said the old man, nodding once hard.

Henry nodded at Cherie and gave Ling a heavy glare, then walked through the kitchen door. Sharon followed.

Inside he shooed the Chinese girl and Elrad out the back door and turned to Sharon with a fury on his face that normally would have made her want to cut and run. Not today. The fire inside her was at least as hot.

"Well?" she demanded before her could blast her. "Are you doing business with criminals now?"

"What I do, Dekker, is none of your fucking business! And if—"

"Are you hard up for cash, Henry? Because you know that what they'll pay you with will be drug money. Or money made off the backs of young girls."

"Dekker...."

"And they'll use this place to just do that better—drugs, girls, ruining people's lives."

"Says you."

Sharon stomped her foot. "Open up you eyes! Willful blindness is no excuse!"

"Sweet Jesus." He rolled his eyes.

"Don't do it, Henry. Don't play footsie with evil."

"You're fired, Dekker."

She blinked. "What?"

"You're fired. Don't bother changing for your shift this evening."

A pit yawning open in her stomach sucked out some of Sharon's fire, but not all. "You got cause?"

"Fucking *cause?*"

She stuck out her chin. "You fire me without cause, I get two weeks' pay. Now."

"Fuck you."

"You be stupid and I'll sue you for more. Not to mention calling the cops about serving liquor to kids, keeping this kitchen like a pigsty, and hiring illegal immigrants under the table."

Henry raised a fist, and the fire that had died down a bit in Sharon blazed up so fiercely her face burned.

"Go ahead!" she said. She stepped up to him, face first. "Assault and battery! Go a*head!*"

Henry stared into her eyes, dropped his fist, and turned away in disgust. "Get changed for your shift."

"What?"

Henry walked to the back door and opened it, signaling the Chinese girl and Elrad to come back in. He looked back at Sharon. "Jenny can't come in for the rest of the month. I'm fucking short-staffed. You were going to be it. You *are* it. Spike up your hair. Strip down. And consider this your two weeks notice."

"As if."

He put his hands on his hips. "Or just don't. Give me 'cause' to fire you right now."

Now the yawning pit inside her opened wide, swallowing all her fire but a tiny spark. "This isn't over, Henry."

"Actually,"—he wiped his hands on his bartenders apron—"for you it fucking is. Now get changed and get out there. I got a phone call to make."

~~~

It only took Griffin two wrong turns to find his way back down the path he and Sharon had come up, though his quads were shaking from the unaccustomed strain by the time he got back to his car.

When he got back downtown, it was almost four o'clock. He showered at the Fitness Freaks where he had a membership, changed into the suit he'd brought in his car, and went into work.

He handled the list Jocasta gave him of "urgent" calls, ploughed through some research on a soft-drink company one of his clients wanted to buy, drafted a rough partnership agreement for three tech-heads who were trying to start up a virtual mapping company, then called Majo.

Amazingly, his friend was in.

"Recidivism," Majo said when he picked up.

"Hello, Recidivism. You know who this is?"

"I've got call display. You know why 'recidivism' is the word of the day?"

"Why?"

"It makes it damn hard to feel good about getting people off when you're not sure they're innocent."

"Because?"

"If they're not, you always find out about it."

"Right," said Griffin. "Recidivism. The tendency to fall back into old criminal patterns of behavior. What? Like stealing cars? Mugging little old ladies?"

"In this case, breaking and entering. Nineteen year old perp who has everything going for him. Smart, rich family. Spins a hell of a good sob story. I had him out and walking free for a whole two months before they caught him again. This time he broke into a house when someone was home. Beat them over the head with a frying pan and the victim may have brain damage."

"Oh, man. It happens, Maj. Criminal law. You told me that yourself."

"Yeah."

There was a long silence where Griffin could feel his friend's pain over the line. Finally, Majo said, "I need a beer. You want to come to the Red Owl with me and get drunk?"

An image of Sharon in her waitressing outfit flashed before Griffin's eyes, stirring a pang in his chest. Then an image of her face red with rage and tears, telling him he was a conceited asshole and to just stay away from her.

"I...don't think that would be a good idea right now."

"Why?" Belligerent.

"Nothing to do with you, Maj. Just, I don't think Sharon needs to see me right now."

He heard Majo shift in his chair, probably sitting up straight, smelling blood, the little hound. "What did you do? You insult her? You went out with her, didn't you? What happened?"

Griffin sighed. "We went for a hike together. We fought. She called me a conceited asshole and never wants to see me again."

"Progress! That's good!"

"Uh-hunh." Griffin smiled ruefully and sat back in his chair. "She thinks Lillian's investors, this Coogan Group, are secretly Hell's Angel types. Bikers."

"Are they?"

Griffin played with his pen. "I don't think so."

"Why does she think so? Did you ask her?"

"I... No."

"Because her accusation was attacking your honesty, right, Mr. Righteous?"

"That's not–"

"So you blew her off without even giving her the benefit of the doubt, without checking to see if maybe she was right and you were, in fact, in bed with the mob."

"Who's side are you on?!"

"Sides?" Majo said innocently over the phone. "Justice has sides?"

Griffin said nothing, sticking his pen in his mouth and chewing on it with a frown.

"Come with me to the Red Owl and ask her," Majo said.

Griffin pictured Sharon again, this time wandering the streets of East Hastings, taking pictures of hookers and street kids, kneeling with them in the gutters, getting up close to people who were destroying their lives.

He spat out the pen. "I'm not coming. I think I need to schedule another meeting with the Coogan Group first."

Majo chuckled. "That's my boy!" His voice dropped, energy gone. "I'm still going. I'll give her your regards."

"Majo?"

"What?"

"Shit happens in law. You going to be okay?"

"Yeah."

"You really want me to come with you?"

"Naw. I'm fine. Look, I can always call Brent or Rotty. Later, Griff." He hung up.

Griffin stared at the phone for a moment. Then he clicked it off and dialed the lead man of the Coogan Group.

~~~~

In the Red Owl, Sharon took a second, while Henry was pouring beers, to drag the back of her hand over the sweat of her forehead. The place was bustling and the thick smell of B.O., greasy food, and boozy smoke was like liquid you swam through. A surge in after-work types, including a surprising number of suits, had come in for the TGIF hour. Henry had hired a couple of local kids to put up flyers for it in Chinatown and all up through Gastown. It seemed to be paying off.

Over there three cops from the local shop were putting away the shooters like they had a long weekend ahead of them. No underagers tonight that Sharon could tell.

And finally, Pete and Digger had their usual middle table; tonight with a bunch of buddies, both biker and non. The creepy Hard Riders were absent, but Sharon kept jerking up her head every time the door opened. It was partly to look out for them, partly for a face she'd basically told to go to hell earlier that day.

None of those faces had showed.

As she grabbed her last order and ran it over to the suits at table four, Pete called out to her with his hands around his mouth. "Hey, B-b-booby Girl!"

She whirled towards him with an involuntary scowl. He was one of *them*, after all. Four of them there like some good-old boys club.

Plus two hangers-on. How much were Pete and Digger involved in the drugs and girls? How much did they know about the plan to buy the Red Owl?

She strode over and dropped her face down to Pete's eye level. "Don't call me that again, Pete. Got it?"

The big guy blinked and sat back a little. "Sure, Sh-Sharon. C-c-can the boys and me get six more Heinies? Please?"

"Yeah."

She straightened and was about to go back to the bar when the front door opened with a jingle and a familiar face walked in.

Sharon froze, then her mental slip corrected itself and she saw the familiar face was too short and dark to be Griffin. She allowed herself one of her first real smiles of the evening and walked over to grab his hand.

"Hey, Cruzie. Good to see you."

Majo Cruz gave a weaker smile than normal. "Crowded."

"Always room for you. Up at the bar, far end. Talk loud tonight. Henry's going deaf."

Again the flickering smile and he walked towards the bar.

"I'll come over later!" she called to his back.

She went for the beers for Pete and Digger.

It was almost seven when there was enough of a lull that she could grab the seat beside Majo at the bar. Henry frowned at her, looked around the bar, then went back to cleaning glasses.

"So what's up?" she asked.

Majo, now down to his open striped shirtsleeves, tie gone, turned to her and nodded sloppily. "You should jus' sleep with him, y'know."

"With...who?" Sharon said, though she knew. It was just disconcerting seeing Majo Cruz like this. The lawyer had been coming in ever since she'd started working here, and she'd never once seen him drunk.

"With my friend," he slurred. "Th'one honest corp'rate lawyer in greater North America."

"You mean Griffin."

"Hell, yes!"

"I don't think Griffin thinks of me that way."

Majo looked at her, glassy eyes wide, and burst into laughter.

When he'd finished, Sharon added, "And even if he did, I don't think we're very compatible."

"Cause of this stupid building-buying thing. He tol' me. Henry! Another one!"

Henry sauntered over, looked at the line of shot glasses Majo had polished off and at the man himself. "Uh-unh. You're done for the night."

"Oh, shit!" Majo said and slapped the bar top. But then he sank back onto his stool, did nothing more, and Henry wandered away again.

"You know," Majo said at last, staring at his chest. "Griffin only took that case cause a friend asked him."

"You?" said Sharon, surprised.

Majo shook his head like it was a cement building block. "Lillian Lee." He lowered his voice to a hoarse whisper and wavered on his bar stool. "She thinks they're running a child-slavery thing through here. Figured this development group would put a stop to it."

"But—"

"Why d'you think th'investors are bikers? Hunh? Wass your proof? You think Lillian's stupid? You think Griffin's stupid?"

"I..."

Sharon shut her mouth and stared at Griffin's friend. In fact, she realized, her whole conviction about the matter had come from just two things—Micky's second-hand rumors and Sharon's seeing that mean-looking Hard Rider meeting with Henry two nights in a row.

Could she be wrong? Henry hadn't denied the accusation, but he hadn't confirmed it either.

All of a sudden her whole perception of the afternoon—her fight with Griffin and then with Henry—flipped about in a gut-sickening spin. Had *she* been the one in the wrong? If so, she had been *so* wrong, flinging accusations, behaving like exactly like the drug-crazy prostitutes she was supposed to be trying to save.

The more she tried to get away from it...

"Or y'could be right," Majo said suddenly, leaning her way.

"What?"

He waggled an unsteady finger at her. "Never take things at face value." He narrowed his eyes to focus on her and then wove his glance around the room, coming to a blinking stop on the table with Pete, Digger, et al. "You know them, right?"

"The middle table? Yeah. They're friends. Kind of."

"They're bikers. Ask them."

"You think they'd tell me the truth if they knew?"

Majo's head wove back and forth as he turned back to the bar. He suddenly slammed his hands down flat on the bar top with his mouth all tight and ugly.

"Majo?" Sharon said, waving Henry away.

"Innocent until proven guilty!" Majo said. "But you gotta damn well do your best to find out whether they *are*, right? Are you up for it?"

"Okay, Majo."

"An' talk to Griff!"

"Okay."

"Recidivism!"

13

THIS TIME GRIFFIN HAD THE COOGAN THREE, as he was now mentally calling them, come into the Greene McNamara offices.

As he led them into the conference room at 9:32 p.m., the offices were mostly cleared out. Only because it was Friday. And even so, Jordan Basteran, Jr., and May Phillips both had the lights in their offices still on. No doubt preparing for some big negotiation or court appearance that was going to take all through this night and the weekend to prepare.

Lawyers. Sigh. Specifically young, unmarried lawyers, who strove for high billable hours. Though frankly Gord Tinsdale and partner Marvin Flagg were both married and spent more weekends in the office than home. *And* they rarely left the office before seven p.m..

Which, of course, Griffin knew because he was usually working until eight.

Would that change if he had someone like Sharon to come home to?

Whahhh! He mentally shook himself. Where had that last thought come from?

"Take a seat anywhere, Gentlemen," Griffin made himself say. "Did you bring along the papers I asked you to?"

With some quick looks exchanged between them, the lead suit, Jackson Kilhenny, nodded. He took a seat a little right of center on the long, cherry wood oblong, then reached down to his briefcase. He started pulling out envelopes and files.

Griffin, remaining on his feet, studied Kilhenny keenly.

There was something disturbingly familiar about the short-haired, short-mustached man. He had a hard, mean look about him whenever he thought Griffin wasn't looking. And the "old football injury", which he claimed he'd gotten in college, made him lurch when he walked.

With a shuffle and whumpf, Kilhenny's right hand man, Andre Malovet, sat down...to Kilhenny's right. In his late fifties or sixties, Malovet (he pronounced it in his French-Canadian accent: Mal-oh-vay) sported an even, undistinguished face, and thinning gray hair. He could have been any of a dozen legal counsel Griffin knew. Griffin suspected most of the paperwork came from him.

The last man sat to Malovet's right, almost like the other two wanted to keep him out of trouble. Not surprising as this man, Jamal Bhoja, was much younger than the other two. He had a skinny, hungry look to him. The black burn mark on his upper lip, the shoulder-length black hair pulled back in a ponytail, the darker skin—they all made him look more like some hothead terrorist than a property developer.

All in all, Griffin didn't find it hard to believe Sharon's accusations about these three.

Now it was time to put it to the test.

~~~

At 9:35 p.m. inside the Red Owl things were still loud and thick.

Pete and Digger's other biker buddies had left, and the two non-bikers had peeled off to try to pick up a couple of women who'd managed to snag a table in the right rear of the noisy room. Sharon hurried over to the abandoned chairs before another table could grab them.

She clattered down her tray of empty glasses and bottles and sat.

"Hey, Sh-Sh-Sharon," Pete said with a slobbery grin.

"Hey, Pete. Digger."

Ignoring Henry's evil eye from the bar, she studied her suspects.

Pete, the only name she knew him by, was maybe five-eleven and three hundred pounds. He had an enormous gut, enormous ash brown sideburns on either side of a perennially-stubbly chin, and the sweetest grin this side of Johnny Depp. He hit her with it full force now, like he could cute his way out of his faux pas earlier that night.

Pete's buddy was shorter, full-bearded, almost as big of gut. He didn't talk much. He mostly belched and laughed along with whatever Pete said.

Neither man looked capable of hurting a flea, and it almost hurt Sharon to lean forward to Digger and quietly hit him with her best shot.

"Digger, do you deal in child sex slaves, child porn, illegal immigrants, underaged prostitutes, any kind of prostitutes?"

"Wha–? Bah.... Prostitutes? I...yeah. I been to one."

"Underaged ones?"

"What's...uh...what's the age?"

Sharon shook her head. "Have you ever taken money *from* one, Digger? Have you ever drugged one or made her do something for someone else?"

"Uh...no? Uh-unh."

He looked too brain dead to be lying.

Sharon felt a tap on her shoulder. "Sh-Sh-Sharon?"

She turned. "Same question to you, Pete."

~~~~

"These are the papers you asked for," Kilhenny said and slid over the pile.

Griffin held his eyes as he did, and as Griffin himself pulled out a chair and sat in front of the papers. Kilhenny looked the picture of mild puzzlement.

What Griffin had told him on the phone was that someone reputable was questioning the Coogan Group's bona fides. Kilhenny therefore needed to bring, *urgently*, the corporate filings for the Coogan Group, their development plans for the Red Owl and adjoining two properties, and the operations proposal of the Kelowna group they were bringing in to run the redeveloped location.

Now Griffin looked at the papers, starting with the Group's filing for incorporation, just that month. They listed six directors, Kilhenny as CEO, Malovet as CFO. John Coogan, who Kilhenny said was the key organizer of the group but very private, was listed as one of the fourth director. Everything in order.

As were the development plans. At least they were in accordance with what they'd told him at their first meeting on Thursday.

"You have permits on all the changes-of-use?" Griffin asked.

"They are pending," said Malovet in his French accent, confirming Griffin's guess that he was the paperwork man.

"And what are you going to do with the properties if the permits aren't allowed?"

Malovet looked at Kilhenny on that one. Jamal Bhoja, Griffin noted, was looking back and forth between them with a canny-but-desperate look.

"If we don't get the permits," said Kilhenny, "we'll find some other way to use the properties."

"Some other way. I see," Griffin said.

~~~~

Pete's large, red-cheeked face was jiggling with distress. "We d-d-don't d-do that kind of s-stuff," he said.

"But you're bikers, Pete. You do something like that. Prostitution, drugs, protection, gambling. Or are you going to tell me you're all just a bunch of guys who like to ride big Harleys and get together to say how good that motor feels between your legs?"

"Y-yeah. What?"

Someone from two tables over called out Sharon's name and demanded service. Sharon touched Pete's hand and Digger's. "Both of you don't move. I'll be back."

She grabbed her tray, got the orders from the shouter, then powered around the entire bar, storing the orders like little unforgettable chits in her brain. She floated up to Henry, gave him the order, then ducked into the kitchen to rattle off the food needs. She was back to pick up all the drinks just as Henry let go of the beerpull for the last draft.

"Two weeks, Dekker," he growled.

"Best you'll ever see," she shot back.

Twenty minutes later, all drinks and food delivered and a quick check to make sure Majo was okay, she caught another lull and plopped back down with Pete and Digger.

"So?" she said.

"Y-you gotta underst-t-tand," Pete said. "There's a h-h-hierarchy." He looked desperately at Digger.

The second big man cleared his throat and leaned forward to whisper. "We're pretty low guys, eh? Like, collecting pot and stuff from the grows."

Sharon bit her lips. "See no evil," she muttered. Then, "What about that mean-looking guy with that tiny mustache. The one with the limp."

Digger and Pete exchanged looks. "J-J-," Pete said.

"No names," Digger said. "But he's up there."

"Can he do whatever he likes?"

Pete shook his head and Digger said. "God oversees everything."

"God being?" said Sharon.

"J-John Calibeau," Pete said before Digger could stop him.

"Okay," Sharon said, and took the hands of both men with her own. "Then here's the big question. Is your John Calibeau trying to buy up the Red Owl?"

~~~~

"This group from Kelowna," Griffin said, shuffling through the last file Kilhenny had slid over. "Ace Management. Why do you want them to run the operation once you get it set up here?"

"What's it to you?" blurted Jamal before Malovet could put a hand on his arm.

Kilhenny stroked his short mustache and pushed his rolling leather armchair back from the table so she could stretch out and cross his ankles, straight-legged, between him and Griffin. The action-suited jeans and leather jacket more than the expensive suit the man wore now.

"I've been building some relationships with people in Kelowna. I want them to get closer."

"This is in your capacity as a freelance land developer."

"That's right."

"Who's forming a new corporation just to do this deal."

"With Mr. Coogan. Right."

Griffin held the man's steady gaze, then looked at the still-twitching Jamal and the calm older Malovet. He finally pushed back his own chair and turned it to face the others.

"You have a list of your other deals? Or Mr. Coogan's."

"I can get it."

Griffin half-smiled. "I'm sure you could."

"What's the problem, Griffin?"

"How do you know Lillian Lee?"

Kilhenny raised his eyebrows and swiveled a little to point at Malovet, who said, "I get to know Lillian during an immigration case, eh? A boy I sponsored."

Griffin let another long pause settle in while he studied the churn of his gut, the buzz of his scuzz alarm, the bad smell. If it weren't for Sharon's accusations, he might have just held his nose and powered ahead with this. As it was....

"I'm sorry, gentlemen," he said and stood up. "I don't think I'm the lawyer for you on this."

~~~~

"Wh-why would he want to b-b-b-buy this place?" Pete said, looking honestly confused.

"To run girls from. Or drugs."

"N-not here." Pete seemed sure of that. Digger nodded too.

"You sure? You said you're low in the hierarchy."

"He said we w-weren't getting into here. Too m-m-messy."

"You believe him?" Sharon felt herself scowling and forced herself to stop. "Really, Pete. Think hard. It's important. You honestly believe your gang boss doesn't want to buy into this part of town?"

Pete shook his head without hesitation. "Y-y-you gotta underst-st-stand." He looked to Digger.

"Hard Riders don't run H any more. No injectables. And nothing in this part of town. That's the rule."

"Because?" said Sharon.

Pete and Digger looked at each other like it was obvious. "This part of town's crawling with AIDS. Mr. Calibeau's son died of AIDS three years ago. No way he'd ever want us to move in here."

~~~~

Malovet stood up quickly as well. "Perhaps," he said. *Pehr-aps.* "But maybe you should talk with Lillian, eh? Ask her?"

Kilhenny drew in his legs. "I get the feeling you think we should be something we're not," he said. "We're not a big slick organization. We're not Harvard educated. We're just a few businessmen who want to change one little part of this city for the better. Not with tons of money. Maybe not enough for a really big law firm to work with. But I thought..."—he motioned to Malovet—"*Lillian* thought you could help us anyway."

Griffin just stood there, wishing he had Sharon in front of him now with her certainty.

"Look," said Kilhenny. "You think about it over the weekend, talk to Lillian or whoever. Tell us on Monday, okay? It'll give us time to move ahead with someone else if we have to."

Then they were gone.

And damn it if Griffin was no closer to knowing whether to proceed than he had been before.

He had to see Sharon. Tonight.

14

SHARON FELT STUPID.

As she cleaned up after one of the Red Owl's busiest, messiest Friday nights she could remember, she felt stupid and lost and confused and guilty and probably other things too. She was too tired to figure it out. She'd been elbowed in the back by some jerk in the last hour. Her feet throbbed.

She banged through wiping the tables and chairs, dragging dishes into the back room, eyeing the Chinese girl there and wondering where she'd come from, where she'd end up.

"Dekker!"

Henry was finished cleaning the bar. It was time to do cash out.

As she walked up to him, he wouldn't even look at her. He just pulled the cash from the till, took it to a table and laid it down. He began going through it comparing it to his tallies.

Sharon sat beside him to double-check.

When they were done and she'd scooped out a very healthy two hundred in tips, Henry bundled the rest and walked back to the safe in the back, still not looking at her.

She walked behind him, the bruise in her back smarting. "Henry?"

"Stand back from the safe."

She did. Tried again. "I'm sorry."

He huffed.

"About the accusations I made. I...spoke with Digger and Pete.

My information was wrong somehow. I just... I'm sorry."

He stood, not looking at her. "You want to keep your job?"

"I...yeah. I guess."

Her turned to her with his lower lip out. "No more of this 'Can I buy the Red Owl?' crap."

Sharon wanted to just say yes, fine. Or even, I quit. Then she could go off, finish her degree, get a desk job somewhere.

And lead a half-life? A lie?

"If you *were* going to sell this place, the whole building, how much would it take, Henry?"

He huffed again, but she could see his mind working. "More than you could ever get."

"Eight hundred thousand? Nine?" She hoped she was shooting high. The whole area was a dump. The guest rooms were rarely filled. Tonight's crowd was an exception. She wondered if Henry was even turning a profit on the place.

He narrowed his eyes and looked at her sideways, appraising. "Before the market tanked, I woulda got one-point-five mil."

"Now?"

Another considered pause. "At nine-fifty, maybe we could talk."

"Okay." Sharon nodded her head and tried to look wise. Inside, though, her head reeled. Nine hundred and fifty thousand dollars! And she had corporate pledges so far of what? Seventy thousand?

She turned and went to put on her track pants, fleece, and runners. As she pulled them on, the awful thought struck her that just maybe Henry was pulling her leg.

Or using her to bid-up someone else's offer?

Her gaze strayed to the dishwasher rack and pictured the Chinese girl there. And the one before that. Pete and Digger seemed so sure, and yet...

Out front there was a hard knock and tinkle of bells. The locked front door.

Henry was out to it and opening it before Sharon reached the main room. Her heart went into her throat as she saw it wasn't the mean-looking Hard Rider guy. It was a taller man, dressed in an olive trench coat. Clean cut, strong jaw, serious dark blue eyes that cut across the room at her now.

"I've come to give Sharon a ride home," Griffin said.

"What the fuck?" He turned to Sharon.

"S'okay, Henry. I know him."

"You sure?"

"Yeah."

"Fine. Go."

Double-checking she had her wad of tips safely stashed in her inside fleece pocket, she walked out the door past Griffin. He followed.

The door shut and locked behind them with rough jingle of bells. A moment later the lights went off in the main room so that the only light on her and Griffin now was from the street lamps. Dim sounds of occasional traffic on Hastings. Cold. The sky misted over again and pregnant. Dank, bloody smells from the meat shop next door.

It was the empty fish bowl effect, she remembered. They'd been here like this just a few nights ago. It seemed a world ago, so much had changed.

And hadn't.

His presence still hummed like this incredible beacon beside her. He stood a foot away but she could feel his presence all around her. Like she could run down the street and still be in his arms.

Her mouth was dry. Her heart pounded.

"I'm—" "I just—"

They both tried to speak at once and stopped. He looked at her with a rueful smile and she felt it go straight through her, all the way down to her toes.

"You want me to go first?" he said.

Sharon nodded.

"Your...accusations about these people I was acting for. I honestly had no idea about any of that. So I called them up this afternoon.

Had them into my firm's offices with lots of papers—corporate filings, plans, background stuff. Asked them questions. And when they left I called up the friend who'd referred them to me. Grilled her for a good half hour about where she knew one of them from."

"And?" Sharon held her breath.

Griffin frowned, breathed out a puff of steamy breath. "And...I don't know. Everything they've got in writing looks legit. At least one of them has solid credentials working in the import-export business. But they sure don't seem like the idealists they say they are."

"Not bikers, though."

"I don't think so."

"I see." She pursed her lips and looked down at the sidewalk. "You?"

She cleared her throat, feeling stupid, and told him everything that had happened that night—the fight with Henry, Majo telling her to ask Pete and Digger, the things those two had said, her apologies to Henry, his rehiring of her, her offer to buy the place at around nine hundred thousand dollars.

She laughed hollowly at the last one, then found herself wiping away sudden tears that had formed at the corners of her eyes.

"So," she said and sniffed. "I guess what I was going to say was, I'm sorry. I was stupid. I was misinformed."

"By whom?"

She looked at him, at his handsome, intelligent brow, honestly trying to understand her. And Sharon realized again, with a pain even sharper than the ones in her back and feet, why they could never be together. It was like she'd known on the mountaintop this afternoon. She was fooling herself to think she was of that upper world. She'd never get the street out of her. She couldn't talk for two minutes without it raising its dirty head between them.

"It doesn't matter," she said. "Will you walk me to my bus stop?"

He shook his head, confused. "I've got my car."

"Nuh-unh. I just want to take the bus home. Alone."

"But–"

"Will you walk me?"

She saw him struggle. She could almost feel the electricity flowing from him as he fought not to grab her. Because, like all men, he thought with his little head first. And Griffin's little head remembered their first night together, how they'd joined like wild animals in heat, a perfect match. It saw her body. It probably felt the way she so obviously admired him, wanted him. It conveniently forgot everything else.

Like how he'd carefully taken out the trash with his filled condom in it. If that didn't say no future...

"I'll walk you," he said and Sharon sighed a little death inside.

She nodded and began, her own running shoes nearly soundless on the concrete but for the occasional *scritch*. His dress shoes clicked along in even rhythm.

The reached Hastings, turned right, and reached the stop in twenty steps. No one else there, as usual, though there were still dealers hanging out on the corners, women spaced out further down the street, shapes huddled in doorways. They'd never bothered her—they probably sensed she was somehow one of them—but she still carried pepper spray in her fanny pack.

"I missed the 2:35," she said quietly. "Will you wait with me for the last one at just past three?"

To his credit, he didn't even check his watch before he said, "Of course." He was learning.

After a time, she smiled to herself. "You know what Majo first said to me when I went over to talk to him?"

"What?"

She put on her best sloppy drunk face and staggered a bit as she looked at Griffin. "You should jus' sleep with him, you know!"

He smiled weakly back at her. "Really."

"Sloshed. Drunk. First time I've ever seen him like that."

"He had a case go sideways on him."

"He lost?"

Griffin shook his head. "He won. The guy re-offended, hurt someone. It won't be the last time. Majo's too good. He gets everyone off."

"Oh." After another long pause, she said, "You didn't tell him, I guess, about...that first night."

"No."

"Oh."

~~~~

God, he was going crazy. Every part of Griffin wanted to reach out for Sharon and touch her. Forget being seen, forget the unspoken agreement he'd made with her when he'd agreed to walk her out here.

His entire body jumped with every breath she took, every time she moved her lips.

~~~~

"What about our history?" Sharon said, needing to know. It might be the last chance she got. "Did you tell him about that?"

"Just what you heard. That we were on the same debate team in high school."

She was suddenly aware of his eyes. She could *feel* them looking into hers, then sweeping over her face, her body. "Nothing about...?"

"Nope."

Her mouth was dry again and she chewed her tongue. He'd somehow moved very close to her. "Because, you know..."

"What?"

"If you wanted to..."

"Yes?"

"Tell..."

It was all she could get out before his lips were on hers, his hands lightly sliding around her, finding the small of her back.

15

For an instant Sharon thought she'd resist. Then her lips seemed to open of their own accord, melt into his, feel and slip around his mouth. She leaned into him, her hands sliding onto his hips, pulling her own against him. Even through his trench coat she could feel his hardness and need.

His tongue slipped between her lips and teeth, finding her tongue, teasing it, coaxing it to meet and dance with his. Warm. Wet. And she wanted him to stay like that forever. Crush her breasts against him. She thrilled with the fear that he'd withdraw and that made it even sweeter. Desperate.

Her entire being seemed sucked into him now, wrapped around him. Her scalp prickled. Hot flashes raced up and down her body, caught up in the force of him.

It was *so* right, so perfect, always meant to be. Her and Griffin. Childhood ships that had only bumped together briefly in high school before swinging wildly apart, charting unknown, terrible waters until they finally found each other again.

Her lips and tongue pulled at him, wrapped around his as if she could eat him up.

He was hers! Griffin Walsh was hers! And she his! He owned her, possessed her, could do anything he wanted with her. Anything at all.

Anything?

Suddenly, she couldn't breathe. Like her entire world, the truth of it, the *street* of it, came crashing down around her head.

In sudden fear, she pushed back at him, tried to draw her lips away.

But he wouldn't let her go. His lips followed hers. His hand around her back that had slid in so softly was now hard and demanding, drawing her to him so she couldn't escape.

No!

Panic surged through her like a wildcat and she shook her body side to side, grunting and squealing under his lips.

He pulled back at once, his eyes wide in shock, as she stumbled back from him.

"I'm..." he said.

Sharon panted hard. She wanted to attack him, his big male shape, his dominating muscle, his *evil*. If she'd had nails, she'd spring on him and rake her nails over his face. Punish him. Show he that she would *never* be taken that way again. Never!

A coke dealer from the corner was walking towards them now. She whirled on him and pointed a finger. "Fuck off!"

He backed away.

Then the panic that had crashed around her eased a little. It sloughed off her like sheets of ice. Until she was standing there with her fingers outstretched like claws, squared off again with a Griffin Walsh who looked at her with a stricken face.

Like I'm crazy, she thought.

Which she was. Crazy. Scarred. Irrevocably marked by a life and times he knew nothing about and, if she could help it, never would.

Inside, she was shattering. A thousand pieces that wanted to collapse onto the dirty, cold pavement and sob there until the world just walked away and left her alone.

But she didn't. Because you never did that on the street. Not if you wanted to survive.

And Sharon, while she might never, ever have a normal life, was going to survive. And help others. Save at least a few of them from the hell she obviously still carried inside her.

Taking deep, ragged breaths, she pulled herself more upright, looked down at her still claw-like fingers, and shook out her arms. She reached up hesitantly to touch the spikes of her hair. To make sure she hadn't somehow melted them down with her insanity.

Then she looked at Griffin again.

She almost choked.

The look on his face wasn't horror or disgust, she saw, but frowning concern. Oh, God, no.

"You changed your name," he said.

That, she hadn't expected. "Hunh?"

"From Neal to Dekker. But not by marriage."

She swallowed. "Yeah. So?"

"You wanted to leave something behind. In Vernon?"

The words cut into her, like he knew exactly where to slice. "Dekker was my mother's name," she said, putting him off.

"And..."

"What?"

"You ditched your father's name. Was that part of the personal cost you won't tell me about?"

"What cost?" Her whole body was quivering now with the aftereffects of her panic's adrenaline.

"The one that got you into university with no support, after years away from school. That took a lot of courage."

Why wouldn't he stop? Didn't he see how his kindness was ripping her up inside? "It was just something I did."

"With scholarships. A woman at the university's administration told me. She sent me to your photography exhibit in the art wing of the Academic Quadrangle."

Sharon shut her mouth. She could hardly breathe.

"It was a remarkable show," Griffin said.

Did he know? Had he guessed?

"At first I couldn't figure out how those girls and women would have let you get so close to them. But I think I've figured it out."

He looked around himself, like he was truly seeing the ugly section of street they were on for the first time. The dirty sidewalks. The boarded-up, graffiti-sprayed buildings. The human refuse. To make matters worse, even as he was looking around him, the thick sky decided at last to start spitting water down on them. In under a minute, the spit had become full-fledged rain, and even the dealers on the corner were retreating back to the buildings for cover.

Griffin didn't seem to notice. He just let the rain fall on his hair and face as he turned towards her.

She crossed her arms over her chest and stuck out her chin at him, blinking at the rain. "What do you think you've figured out?"

"They let you get close because you're like them."

She breathed in sharply.

"Because you feel life intensely," Griffin went on. "You look around you here and you really see what's happening. The truth."

Sharon bit her tongue.

"You told Henry *you* wanted to buy the Red Owl," Griffin said. "Yeah, I noticed when you told me. Just didn't understand it. So why do you?"

Sharon looked behind her to see if the damn bus was there yet. It was coming. She could see the lights of it eight or nine blocks away. But her tongue hurt, she was biting it so hard.

Fine. He wanted to know? She'd tell him.

"I wanted to make it a safe house, okay? I wanted at least one place near to the action where these girls could run to and get away from their johns, their pimps, whoever was hurting them. I've got four corporate sponsors so far who'll put up money to buy it if I get enough pledges. I've been calling the government for months to try and get a commitment on a methadone program. Okay? That's one of the reasons I was so pissed off to find you were helping someone buy it. Because *I* wanted it. Okay? Satisfied? Fuck!"

She turned away from him so she didn't have to see the disgust or pity on his face. And so he couldn't see the tears leaking out on hers. Not that you could tell in this rain.

Perfect ending to a perfect day.

"Sharon. Look at me."

Not reaching for her arm, she noticed. He'd learned that lesson the hard way.

"Just look at me."

She made her face blank and turned.

He held his hands out to her. "I didn't know."

"So don't help them."

"They'll just get someone else."

She shook her head, face tight. "That is so lame."

"Let me drive you home."

Turning her head to look for the bus, she saw it was almost to them. Come *on*. "That is so not going to happen, Griffin," she said, looking back. "You and me, we might have worked in high school, but it all went downhill from there."

"What do you mean?"

The bus had stopped with a squawnk on brakes. Its front doors hissed open.

"Thanks for waiting with me," Sharon said, and hopped aboard, her hands gripping the front bar so tightly her knuckles hurt.

~~~~

Then she was gone. Griffin watched the bus's red taillights stop at the next traffic light. Move on.

Gone.

And he should have felt depressed, lost. But he didn't. Strangely, Griffin had a peculiar leaping sensation inside him, like his heart was trying to leap out of his chest through his throat.

It explained so much, this crazy plan of hers. And while everything certainly wasn't clear, he could almost fill in the rest. Sharon had dropped out of school, maybe gotten into drugs, been kicked out of her house?

Then she'd seen friends of hers overdose or get sucked into prostitution. She'd run. Fought. Her reaction to being grabbed suggested she'd been beaten somewhere in there.

And yet through all that, somehow she'd kept her moral focus, managed to get to Vancouver, finish her high school, and get into one of Canada's better universities. Which, for Sharon Dekker, was only the beginning.

Do you know what she's planning to do with her education? the administration woman had asked him. Well now he did. Part of it.

It occurred to him that he should probably worry about her. Her plan was essentially trying to take hookers away from their pimps, after all. Even if she had little hope for success, wasn't it possible one of those pimps might take offense?

Or had she already thought through all that? Had she figured out something which Griffin, if he knew anything about life on the street, should have seen too?

Probably. Because what she'd already achieved showed she had an incredible strength and street smarts. And courage. Man. It made Griffin's own straight-line career path look almost...pedestrian.

None of which meant she was a particularly sweet woman to know. More like a irresistible prickly pear. Maybe more prickly and savage, ultimately, than he could ever be with long term. But short term? Yes. He needed another two dates (since he was sure as hell going to count this one as a date) to seal his deal with Majo.

He brushed his cold, rain-wet fingers over his lips, and marveled at how the memory that stirred gripped his whole being.

He blinked and squinted. From the group of drug dealers huddling by the building down the block, one pale face stared out at Griffin. It was oriental and familiar. The guy from the university, The one who'd accosted him while he was looking at Sharon's photographs. What was he doing here?

Griffin started walking in that direction but the face vanished and the other drug dealers, mostly Latino it looked like, turned towards him.

Griffin quickly altered his route and cut back up the street he'd walked down with Sharon. As he went, he doubted himself. The rain made it hard to see clearly. And what were the chances of seeing someone who'd warned him away from Sharon down here at three in the morning?

He chuckled to himself as he reached his BMW and climbed in. One thing the surprise *had* done was jolt his thinking. He suddenly had an idea how he could help her in her noble, pigheaded quest. It was ethical if he did it the right way round. It was also the right thing to do.

He just wished he'd be there to see her face.

16

SATURDAY, other than getting up to feed Boobo, Sharon could hardly leave her bed. Her back hurt. Her forearms ached from carrying overladen trays the night before. Her feet felt like throbbing grapefruits.

Worst of all, though, was the sick realization that she'd lost Griffin.

Well, given him up, to be precise, but it didn't feel like that. It felt like Daryl Polson had stuck his hard, cruel hands through the years at her, all the way from Kelowna, and ripped her chance with Griffin to shreds. Because, despite everything with her mother and step-father, having to leave home, Sharon had still felt like she'd had a chance before she met Daryl.

"Dink," she muttered, asleep for the fourth time that morning and dreaming about him.

She saw Daryl like he'd been when she met him—tall, broad-shouldered and big-chested like a former football jock should be. Eight years older than her. He'd worn his rusty-red hair long, parted in the middle and curling over the back of his collar. Matched it with a full red mustache like the cowboy he fancied himself to be. His shirt cuffs were smartly rolled up, and the thick hair on his arms matched the curls on his head. All those curls glittered like fire in the hot sun of that Kelowna summer.

Best of all, though—his wallet. Stitched camel leather the color of his hair. He drew it out of the back pocket of tight blue jeans and showed her how he always kept it stuffed with twenties.

Then...yes! He bought Sharon her first real food in days. A teen burger at an A&W, dripping with hot grease and ketchup. Then a vanilla milkshake at Dairy Queen, and after that, fine chocolate, rich and smooth.

She barfed it all up afterwards on the pavement of the parking lot.

He laughed, helped her clean up, and took her home.

Which was a crowded room above a store, over one of the louder, rougher streets of town. Not that Sharon complained. It was inside. No one to beat and rob you. The only people she had to share space with were Dink and three other girls he sheltered—Adele, Carlie, Petra.

Daryl offered Sharon drugs. She refused and he applauded her for it, made her feel like a hero.

Then he came to her at night. A gentle, tender lover. He didn't smell great—Sharon wrinkled her nose in her sleep at the remembered burnt licorice smell that seemed to stick to his hair and come out through his pores—but it was a small price to pay for her safe room and board.

Two weeks flew by. Two weeks to get really comfortable. Then...

Get down there with Adele.

No. Listen, Daryl. Please.

Now! And your name's Breeze *now. Use it.*

His face is bloody with rage, slapping her, dragging her out of bed.

No! No, Dink! Let go!

"Let g–?!"

Sharon jerked up to sitting in her bed with her arms raised like a cross before her. Boobo hissed and shot like a bullet out the bedroom door.

Sharon was alone in her room.

Twenty-six years old.

Alone.

~~~

At three p.m., almost exactly twelve hours after leaving Griffin, Boobo sat on her face and made Sharon drag herself out of bed and into the bathroom.

She stared at the mirror over the sink. She hadn't even washed out her hair spikes last night. Her eyeliner had run around her eyes both with tears and rain so she looked like a sad raccoon.

"Hey, sexy," she croaked.

She stumbled into the shower, washed, dried, dressed in sweats, ate some toast and peanut butter, and tackled her assigned reading for the week.

Her breaks were telephone calls, working her way down the list she'd pulled off the net of B.C. corporations with assets over five million.

Then more studying, a sketch outline of what she was going to write for Professor Tighe for her assignment due Thursday, and fiddling with the phone number she'd found for Griffin Walsh at Green McNamara.

More food at five to fuel up for her Saturday-night shift. She got dressed. She pulled on her still-wet fleece and track pants over her waitressing outfit.

The intercom buzzer rang.

When she hit the button to answer, some young-sounding kid answered. "Sharon Dekker?"

"Yeah."

"I got a couriered envelope for you down here at the front door. You have to sign for it."

She released the button, frowned over that. Finally went down and signed. Her name and address were typed neatly on the front of a large manila envelope. No return address.

She waited until she got upstairs to open it. When she did, out slid a set of ten sheets of paper. The first was a letter addressed to her. She flipped past it to the rest.

There were two photographs, on glossy 8½" x 11" paper, of the Red Owl Hotel. One was in brown sepia tones and looked like it had been copied from an archive somewhere. When she turned it over, she found on the back a scrawled notation with some long letter-number combination and the Red Owl's street address. Date—March 22, 1903.

The second photo looked like it had been taken within the last year or two. She flipped it over and confirmed it.

The only difference with the older one, other than the grainy sepia color, were the buildings around the Red Owl. And the fact there was no gaudy awning advertising the bar. And a wooden sidewalk and dirt road ran by the front.

Behind these photographs was a set of papers with a long list of properties and their addresses. The addresses were designated as heritage buildings. A guidelines sheet explained the restrictions on their development or change of use. Sharon's mouth opened in slow awe as the implications began to sink in.

She flipped quickly back to the letter and read:

Dear Sharon,

I came across these documents in the course of my research. Thought you might be interested.

Griffin

Sharon stared at the letter for a long time. She reviewed the other sheets. She smiled and felt the first lightness she had in forty-eight hours.

Not just because this could work, or at least give her a chance.

No, the real float came from what was said behind the words. However much she knew she and Griffin couldn't work, at least she'd gotten through to him. He saw her as a person with goals, things to accomplish.

Boobo rubbed himself up against her legs and she reached down to pet him quickly before grabbing her fanny pack and heading out the door.

Okay, maybe it wasn't a lot, being seen as a person, but it was something.

It made her smile.

17

G RIFFIN TOSSED AND TURNED on the top of his bed where he'd crashed when his lack of sleep finally caught up to him.

His nightmares involved running naked with Sharon through the court buildings downtown, grabbing Majo, then Lillian, demanding they tell him where to file his papers because Kilhenny was after them!

Suddenly the limping businessman lurched out from the end of the hall, pointed his finger at Griffin and Sharon, and two snorting black motorbikes roared straight at them.

Sharon pointed her finger back at Kilhenny, shouting, "Fuck you! Fuck you! Fuck you!" Griffin joined in.

The bikes mowed them down.

....

On to another dream.

~~~~

Griffin didn't wake up until 8:05 p.m. and realized his sleep schedule was getting totally messed up.

Rather than stew about it, he made himself a sandwich, grabbed his briefcase, and headed for the office. Most evenings there were good for undisturbed work, but Saturday night especially. Jordan Basteran was the only one in. He waved distractedly to Griffin as Griffin walked by his office. Griffin waved back, paused, then kept walking.

Jordan obviously had work to do. Griffin had work to do. Each to his own.

When he looked up again, it was one a.m. and, as if his mind was getting programmed, he thought of Sharon.

Was she working tonight?

Not that it mattered. He couldn't go see her. After the way they'd parted this morning at the night bus, Griffin had decided he'd better let Sharon make the next move. The package he'd sent her with the Heritage Building stuff would hopefully give her a nudge in that direction.

But *was* she working tonight?

He sat back in his chair and grabbed a pen to play with, swiveled to look out his narrow window at the lights of the city.

Was she?

Despite his mini-revelations at three a.m. that morning, Griffin realized he knew almost nothing about her.

She took classes at Simon Fraser University in psychology and sociology, second year, paid for mostly by scholarships. She worked at the Red Owl to pay for living expenses. And she raised money with this quixotic notion of buying the Red Owl Bar & Hotel to make it a kind of hooker's transition house.

Swiveling back to his desk, Griffin recalled one more fact. Sharon had a creepy professor who'd warned Griffin away from her. And who might even have been spying on her where she took her night bus home.

Feeling a bit like friend Brent on one of his quests to ride out and save a pretty damsel in distress, he picked up his phone then looked at the time and laughed.

On the other hand...

He pulled Brent Major's number off his computer screen, dialed, and left a message on his office voice mail:

"Hey, guy. Griffin here. Need a favor. You've used private investigators to shadow people you're suing, right? I need to hire one pronto. Like, Monday. Call when you get this message, okay? Either home or work. Thanks."

18

S UNDAY. Mid-afternoon.

Sharon picked at the remains of her tangy spinach salad and waited for Lisa to show up. Sun glinted off the huge front window of the Glad Rose, an airy tea-and-salad place on Robson. Classical piano music played from the speakers by the counter. Other than the sparse patronage at the moment (Sharon was the only customer), the place couldn't have been more different from the Red Owl if it had tried.

"You look sad," said the young waiter with the slicked-back hair, suddenly at her elbow. "You sure I can't get you a cup of macha tea? It's like a slow, gentle pick-me-up. None of the nerves you get with coffee."

"No. Thanks."

"You sure?"

She nodded.

"Then how about me?" He gave her what was actually a pretty sexy grin for a skinny boy. "I'm done at four, but I could probably beg off early since there's no other customers."

Sharon smiled but shook her head. "Thanks for the offer, but I've got a friend joining me."

"Right. You said that." He nodded and backed off quickly to behind the counter, obviously assuming the friend was a man.

Which, on such a beautiful day, it should have been?

Sharon fought imagining what it would be like to have Griffin sitting across from her. Because he hadn't shown up after her shift last night to walk her to her bus, had he. Just because she'd *told* him to stay away. Just because she'd snarled and beat at him. Jeez. Now he'd only talk to her by couriered letter.

Her quick smile faded as she remembered how she'd actually felt uncomfortable waiting for the night bus last night. Like she was being watched.

She hoped that wasn't some game her subconscious was playing to make her run back to Griffin, try to get him to be her protector. Her record for having men do that sucked.

The door of the Glad Rose opened and Lisa bustled in. She was dressed in a pink sweatshirt and jeans, but her blonde hair, usually back-combed, Texas high, was pulled down and back in a bun behind her head. She wore less makeup than usual, too. All-in-all she looked older than her thirty-some years. Stressed.

She saw Sharon and clomped over. Her feet sported her usual off-work clodhoppers that she liked because they let her, in her words, "kick serious butt. "

"Hi," Sharon said as her friend sat and sagged.

"My butt feels bigger'n a couple of pumpkins today."

"Looks it too."

"What?" Lisa's head jerked up.

Sharon laughed. "Kidding. You want some macha tea? Coffee?"

"Espresso!" she yelled at the skinny-boy waiter. "Strong enough to stand up and talk back!"

Then Lisa sat and collapsed back into herself. Sharon had to lower her face to look into Lisa's.

"So what's up?"

"Baker."

"Who's that?"

Lisa looked startled and raised her head. "Baker Fadden is Danny's daddy."

"And your husband?"

She smiled lopsidedly and Sharon noticed for the first time that Lisa's jaw was a little uneven, her nose long, her mouth very wide. "Naw. We was never married. Never much of nothing, really." Her smile dropped. "But it hasn't stopped him from trying to find me."

"Uh-oh. He contacted you?"

Lisa shook her head but suddenly her whole body trembled. She stopped it before she lost control. "I...got a call from an old girlfriend down in Big Spring. Baker found some jackass-joe did business up here, said he seen me. I mean what're the chances?"

Sharon pursed her lips and shook her head as the waiter-boy showed up with Lisa's coffee. Sharon was glad of the time to regroup because Lisa's story had just sent chills through her.

Fact was, Sharon herself had always figured that changing her last name and appearance and getting the coast mountains between her and Kelowna to keep Daryl away. But really, it was only a few hours drive. And now that she'd started mixing with prostitutes and had two bikers she called friends...?

Except that Daryl-the-dink, unlike Baker with Lisa, had never loved her. Sharon was just one street kid among dozens Daryl had probably sucked in over the years. He'd never bother chasing her out here. He was too inherently lazy.

"You think Baker will come up here after you?"

Lisa nodded, leaning over her brew. "Any time now. His brother works for the airlines. Baker gets this family discount thing."

"So what are you going to do?"

The older woman looked at Sharon with such a longing that she almost didn't have to say it. It was the same kind of yearning look Micky got when she thought Sharon wasn't looking. The same look Adele, Carly, and Petra, Daryl's other girls in Kelowna, had given Sharon the day after she'd first met with the street social worker who eventually got her out.

It was like they saw something in Sharon that she herself never could. Confidence? Hope?

"I guess we gotta move somewhere," Lisa said. "I just...don't know where. Gotta keep running."

Sharon knit her brow and stared at the table until finally the obvious came to her. The pain in her gut that came with probably explained why it hadn't come at once. It involved a phone number she'd only called once a year for the last two years. Like a duty call to a probation officer.

She licked her lips, trying to figure if she really wanted to do this. Then she looked up and saw Lisa's haggard, pleading face again. Thought about Lisa's son, two years old.

There really wasn't a choice here.

She tugged out her cell phone and dialed through all the numbers she'd stored in its memory until she found the one she wanted. Dialed.

One ring. Two. Three. Four. Fi—

"Hello," answered a chirpy voice. "Julia Morrow, Kelowna Family Services."

"Julia? It's Sharon."

"Darling!" Sharon could almost picture the big woman flinging her wobbly arms wide like she could give her one-time spitting, wounded bird, a great big fleshy hug. "It's been so long! How *is* everything out there? How are you doing? What's happening? How are the courses?"

Sharon felt a little flush creeping over her face. She realized she'd told Julia nothing about the Red Owl project, nothing about her contacting prostitutes again. It was trying to help those prostitutes, of course, but she felt like Julia would fear the worst. What was Majo's word (that she'd finally gotten around to looking up yesterday)? Recidivism. Backsliding.

"I'm doing well," Sharon half-lied. "But what I'm calling about today, is actually a favor for a friend of mine. Can I put you on speaker?"

"Certainly, darling."

Sharon laid the cell phone in the middle of the table and pressed the speaker button. "You hear me?" she said.

"Fine and clear."

"Julia, I've got a friend with a two-year-old son and an ex-boyfriend stalking her. She needs to start a new life."

There was a pause and Lisa looked at Sharon. Then Julia's voice crackled out. "Is she on drugs? Working the street? In trouble with the law?"

Lisa leaned over the phone. "None of those things, ma'am. I'm just not too smart with the men I choose. You know, you buy me books and you buy me books and I just chews on the covers."

Julia voice cackled at that. "Texas girl?"

"Yes'm."

"Sharon, give her my number and we'll see if we can work something out. Now pick up the phone, darling."

Sharon did, switching off the speaker. "Okay," she said.

"Sharon, I've been meaning to call *you* for some time, but things have just been so busy. Cutbacks and all."

"About what?"

"Oh, everything. But you remember your former 'manager', Daryl Polson?"

Sharon felt an icicle plunge straight through her neck into her chest. She couldn't breathe. "He...He's been asking about me?"

"Why no. I doubt he even remembers you. No, it's just I thought you'd find it interesting to know that he's managed to muscle his way to be top boss of the Bad Machine biker gang, the same one that tried to take all his girls, including you, away from him way back when. The worm turns."

"I...guess."

"Wait, darling. That's only half the story. Kelowna's new mayor has pledged to drive the Bad Machine out of the city. He's publicly committed to cut off all their sources of revenue and arrest and try every member of the leadership by year's end. Which means your man, Daryl, is going down. That's the ultimate end of every creep like him. I thought you'd want to know."

There was a long beat while Sharon tried to mentally remove the ice from between her shoulder blades. She managed it enough to breathe a quiet, "Thank you."

"You're welcome, darling. Now don't forget to give your Texas gal my number. And call me soon, okay?"

"I will."

Julia hung up and Sharon hit END.

As Sharon pulled a pen out of her fanny pack and grabbed a napkin to write Julia's number, Lisa started falling all over herself to thank her in colorful Texas style.

When that was all done, though, the number in her possession and thanks shining in her eyes, Lisa sat back with her coffee, winked at the waiter-boy who'd been watching the ladies with interest, and said loudly, "Now, at last, I want to hear all about that hunk you picked up in the bar last Wednesday."

~~~~

Griffin's ears were burning red. He swiveled back and forth at his office desk and swiped at them, annoyed. Must have been the tuna fish sandwich he bought down the street and brought up to keep him company.

Not that he was alone in the Greene McNamara offices this sunny Sunday afternoon. Oh no. He estimated fifteen lawyers were in, if you counted both floors. He'd even shared a ride in the elevator with Burt Lester coming up. Everyone striving to get those high cost, stick-it-to-the-client, billable hours.

And Griffin?

He lifted the Coogan Group documents again and tried to find what it was about them that troubled him so much.

It was partly the directors, of course, suspicious characters all. He confirmed with Lillian that she'd met Andre Malovet during an immigration hearing where Malovet was sponsoring a young

Honduran man to come work in an accounting firm Malovet owned. Lillian had nearly chewed Griffin's ear off when he'd suggested a young Honduran male in Vancouver often meant drug dealing.

Griffin wasn't going to get anywhere on that front. As far as Lillian was concerned, this deal was legit and had to proceed.

On impulse, he pulled over the yellow pad where he'd been scribbling things for Brent's P.I. to check out for him. Brent had called him with the name this morning. The P.I. hadn't been in, but the voice mail said he be back Monday.

Already on the list for the guy to check out were:

- *Sharon Dekker's class schedule, work schedule*
- *Unusual attentions shown by any of her professors*
- *Background of her oriental-looking male professor(s)*
- *Bkgd of Coogan Group directors (attach list & info)*
- *Bkgd of Kelowna group, Ace Mgt, and its principals*

To these he now added:

- *Current occupation of Honduran immigrant sponsored by Andre Malovet last year.*

Then he stared at the list and tapped his pen on the Ace Management item. Something about that one...

Suddenly his conversation with Sharon on their Friday hike came back to him. She'd mentioned she'd spent time in Kelowna, but then refused to say another thing about it. Just maybe, if Brent's P.I., or whoever he subcontracted in Kelowna was already looking into Ace Management there, they could also do a quick scout around for anyone who'd known Sharon.

He added it to the list.

19

Prostitution," said Professor Tighe, "is another example of Canada's liberal approach to social policy. Unlike the United States, for example, it is not the act of prostitution itself which is illegal but the act of soliciting for sex and 'living off the avails' of prostitution.

"And!" He stopped here in front of the very middle of the class and Sharon just knew he was going to look straight at her. Even though she'd come in quietly, on time, and sat directly in the middle of a bunch of girls dressed more wildly than her.

"And!" His eyes locked on hers. "In Canada the legal age of consensual sex used to be only fourteen! Now it's all of sixteen! Would someone like to comment on the power dynamic that sets up?"

Hands shot up all over the class. Tighe kept looking at her.

"Yes, Ms. Dekker."

All heads turned towards her expectantly. The whispers made it evident that those who'd missed Wednesday's little confrontation were being filled in.

Sharon chewed her lip, then said, "I...don't have anything to say at present."

"No opinion?" Tighe pressed.

"I didn't say that."

"You just don't want to share."

"Not right now. That's right."

"Are you afraid we'll laugh?"

He spread his arms out a few inches, palms up, and smiled as he said it. A few of the students did titter, maybe out of tension as much as true amusement.

Sharon looked down at her lap. *Let it lie. You've got nothing to prove*. She looked up. "I'm afraid that whatever I say, you'll try to twist into a joke, Professor. And that would just be obscene."

There was another hush. Tighe never took his eyes off her or let his smile so much as twitch. The hush dragged on.

Unable to stand it, Sharon picked up her books and backpack, stood up from her seat and began awkwardly walking out past the other students' legs towards the exit door.

"You'll remember the assignment I gave you, Ms. Dekker. Due Thursday morning after class. My office. Eleven a.m. sharp!"

She didn't look back as she slammed out the door. Outside it, though, she took a great gasping breath, like someone had been trying to choke her. Then, breathing and gasping, she stumbled down the hall towards the cafeteria. She needed to collect herself.

She heard the door of Tighe's class creak open behind her and looked back to see another student slipping out, looking her way. A nondescript Japanese guy. Come to commiserate? Cheer her up? Ask her out?

She sure hoped not. She felt pawed-over and dirty already.

Shaking her head fiercely, she began to run and didn't stop until she was outside, away from the Academic Quadrangle, and sure no one was following her.

Ironically, she found herself standing on the same triangle of grass she'd stood on when she'd blasted Griffin for quite innocently taking on a client a friend had asked him to.

She wished he were here now and that she had a do-over. But life didn't give do-overs, did it? All you could do was make your stupid mistakes and try to do better next time.

At least she'd done a good job on the application to get the Red

Owl declared a heritage building. When the clerk at City Hall had asked why she seemed so anxious about it, Sharon created a story about Henry's renovation plans that was so outlandish and yet so convincing, that the clerk winked and whispered there were ways to expedite these things.

Which meant her plan was still possible. So she should skip class and run home to do more phone-call fundraising?

No. Julia's face and, oddly, Griffin's both rose up before her, expecting better of her.

She turned around and went back to the cafeteria. She still had two more classes today.

So it wasn't until almost four o'clock that she finally hiked down the mountain and into the front of her apartment building where she found the letter someone had hand-delivered to her mailbox. The words inside were handwritten in dark blue, flowing ink.

> *Sharon,*
> *Your turn again. I'm waiting for you to call me.*
> *Griffin.*

~~~~

Sharon didn't work Mondays or Tuesdays. Those nights she sometimes went out with Lisa to a movie, or the two of them took Danny somewhere fun—Crash Crawleys, a skating rink, the playground at Second Beach.

But Lisa was busy getting ready to leave and didn't want to go out with her. Soon she wouldn't be there at all.

It made Sharon realize just how few friends she had in Vancouver. Despite her classes, her boisterous work environment, she had mostly kept a high wall around her private self so no one could see the dirt that lay hidden there.

Griffin?

143

Sharon sat in the little window box of her apartment's main window, Boobo purring contentedly on her lap, and looked out at the street. There were lights up and down it. Too much light to see the stars above. Big blackness that was Burnaby Mountain over to the right. A small trail of lights that looked suspended in the sky over in the north—Grouse Mountain.

And her, alone here. Wishing. Knowing it just wasn't possible, but wishing anyway.

She took out the letter he'd sent her. Handwritten. *I'm waiting for* you *to call* me.

Foolish. Pompous. Clueless.

And God, the sweet taste of his lips.

It was almost midnight when she finally pried herself out of the window box and staggered into bed.

~~~~

Tuesday went by in a haze. Solid day of classes but no work that night.

She made a few more fundraising calls, then forced Lisa to take her in for dinner. Julia had already nailed down a few places Lisa could stay in Kelowna or in Peachland, Lisa said. So Lisa would be leaving within the week. Sharon cried with her and lied about that being wonderful. Then she played with little Danny, helped Lisa pack, went home late.

~~~~

Wednesday, Sharon felt lost and restless. She'd given Lisa her shift as it was going to be Lisa's last and Lisa needed the extra traveling money. To distract herself from her friend's imminent departure, Sharon threw herself into more fundraising calls when she got home.

It almost made her miss the call from the City Hall clerk who'd given her the wink.

Sharon's application for the Red Owl had been fast tracked and approved! The Red Owl owner had been notified. He was apparently not happy. (Sharon smiled. Henry was probably screaming and bashing the phone against the wall.) All applications to sell or modify the structure now had an additional twenty kilometers of red tape to cut through first.

"It's *very* time-consuming," the clerk whispered on the phone. "Weeks to *months* time-consuming."

Sharon laughed with her and marveled at how easy it was to emotionally connect with a stranger. All you had to do was create a reality the other person could really understand.

Create a reality...

Twenty minutes after she'd hung up, her buzzer rang. It was the same courier boy who'd brought her the original heritage building papers. This time it was just a letter. She took it up to her window well and sat down before she opened it to again see the handwritten, flowing blue ink.

> *Sharon,*
> *Congratulations. My clients are fit to be tied.*
> *I'm waiting to be asked.*
> *Griffin*

He'd scrawled both his business and home phone numbers under his signature. Sharon stared at them and the reread the message as often as she had at his last one, even with Boobo trying to butt and swat it out of her hands.

Should she commit to creating a false reality for Griffin too? But what did he even want? Sharon the hot slut? Sharon the incorrigible dropout? Sharon the hooker photographer? Sharon the courageous come-from-behind kid?

Anything but who she really was.

Tears welled up inside her and spilled onto the paper, absorbing and spreading the ink. Blurring the words.

At six-thirty, she managed to rouse herself enough to eat dinner and type in a postscript to the assignment for Tighe. Just two notes. On about how much money she currently had pledged from corporate sponsors—$185,000 now, and a probable $60,000 more from a group of five women's retail fashion stores. The second note about the heritage building designation and how she'd pulled it off.

All was fair in politics and war.

~~~

11:42 p.m.

Sharon turned off the TV, whose programs she watched too rarely now to follow or care about. She paced to her second-hand computer and thought about turning it on, but she had no games on it and no net access. What was the point? Prowling aimlessly around the living room, she kicked at her couch, making Boobo dive off and run to the bedroom to hide under the bed.

The air felt close. The brief break of sun they'd had Sunday through Tuesday was giving way to more seasonal drizzly skies.

Pregnant skies.

She stopped by the window and looked out.

Vancouver's rain, after the almost desert climate Sharon was raised in, had always seemed symbolic of the city's fecundity. Later, as she got to know East Hastings and the misery there, the rainy seasons spoke of bloat and rot. Sometimes it could never rain hard enough to wash away the stink.

Did Griffin experience any of that? Other than driving through the area, or standing with her briefly Friday night at the night bus stop, did he have the slightest clue what went on there?

None of the professors or students in her classes did, she was sure. It was all an abstraction to them, info for an exam, a joke Tighe told to lighten a Monday or Wednesday morning.

Her co-workers and friend-customers at the Red Owl, Pete and Digger, didn't seem to. They just skirted the fringes.

Even Julia Morrow, who worked those trenches day-in and day-out never *felt* them the way Sharon did because she'd never *lived* there.

Which left Sharon even more alone.

She turned and stared at the dingy walls of her hard-won apartment. Her freedom. She wanted to scream.

Then her eyes fell on the last letter Griffin had sent. She'd set it down on her eating table where she always dropped her backpack and fanny pack with cell phone when she came home. As if a part of her had always known she'd call him. Had to call him.

12:04 a.m. He'd be sound asleep.

She walked to the table, spread open the sheet of paper, retrieved her cell phone, and dialed.

20

1 2:30 A.M.
    As Sharon walked him around the dark chainlink fence
of Needle Park, pointing out shambling bodies she recognized or
describing the code of what was happening, Griffin felt like he was
in a netherworld. This was half on Earth, half somewhere else. Hell
maybe.

It was after midnight. Would he be doing this regularly if he
let himself follow his gut attraction to Sharon? Prowling the city's
festering boils while all normal people slept?

At least the rain was holding off and she'd warned him to dress
down.

And at least Sharon, even dressed in a hooded sweatshirt with the
hood pulled up so that her face was shadowed and almost sexless, had
called him! He'd had to slap himself out of bed, roar out to pick her
up at her place, and then drive them both back downtown. She'd made
him park on Dunsmuir and walk with her here. Her own voice never
rose above downbeat and depressed.

But she'd called him!

In fact, her taking him here with her was probably an important
act of faith on her part. It was ironically similar to how it would be
when he finally took her to meet his law school buddies or parents.

"How are you holding up?" she said and turned to him.

"Barely functional. You?"

148

"This is my normal awake time, remember? Welcome to my world."

There was something beneath the words he knew he'd missed, but he didn't care. He was too caught up suddenly by the shape of her lips as she moved. How could he have thought them sexless? And her eyes, heavy and sad as they seemed tonight, were still dark and expressive. Despite his semi-conscious state (or because of it?), Griffin felt a growing need to kiss those lips, stir the passion he'd seen blaze in those eyes before. He would. Soon. Tonight. It made his sluggish pulse speed up as he thought it.

They were at the corner of the park, facing east.

He leaned towards her. "Sharon..."

"Let's go this way," she said and started walking without waiting for him to agree.

He skipped faster to keep up, impressed by the length of her stride. She led him past a crowd of five or six people brazenly speedballing in the middle of the sidewalk. Griffin could smell the sweet stench like burning rubber. One woman started screeching as they passed and struggled out of the crowd as the others literally tore the clothes off her. The woman staggered away in her bra and panties, giving them all the finger and screaming something so unintelligible Griffin thought it was another language until he caught the words "Piss on..." and "... you can't do..."

He stepped after the woman, but Sharon grabbed his jacket sleeve and tugged him on. The woman disappeared, still screeching, down an alleyway.

"Aren't there shelters?" Griffin said. "Needle exchanges places?"

"At this time of night? There aren't even toilets."

He felt stupid, then noticed she'd frozen on the next corner, her eyes darting back and forth, scanning both sides of the street. "What is it?"

She shook her head. "I just thought I saw.... Nothing." She smiled grimly. "Come on. The girls I want to help usually hang out on the next block or two."

What was the expression? In for a penny, in for a pound? Griffin nodded and crossed the street with her.

He felt her pace increase and had to almost run to keep up. She'd seen someone! That dark-haired woman up ahead, leaning into the window of a dark Accord. As Sharon and Griffin approached, however, the woman opened the passenger-side door and got in. The Accord pulled out and drove down the street, running the red and disappearing around a dark corner ahead.

Sharon stopped and Griffin, stopping beside her, felt her tremble.

"There's still someone there," he said quietly and pointed.

A second woman—no, girl—was watching them from back in the shadow of an unlit wall. She ducked her head as Sharon looked, like she didn't want to be recognized. Then her skinny frame coughed. Again. The girl got caught up in a full-blown hacking fit that sounded like she'd leave her lungs on the pavement.

Jeez. Such a wonder that the Accord driver picked the other one.

The girl stopped, wiped her mouth and threw back her mousy brown hair as Sharon stepped up to her, Griffin following.

Griffin's heart got stuck somewhere in the churn of his stomach. The kid looked barely fifteen, seventeen tops, though it was hard to tell because she was so emaciated. Her nose and cheekbones were sharp enough to cut paper on. An addict? Or just sick? AIDS? Hepatitis? What were the symptoms? Griffin was sure Majo, or even Lillian, would know. This was *not* his area of expertise.

It made his skin crawl.

Sharon, though, shook her head with compassion in her eyes. "Micky said you'd been taking your antibiotics."

The kid turned her face and had another coughing fit. Turned back, resentful. "I was. Lost the bottle. Or someone stole it."

"You shouldn't be working."

"Right." She hacked without turning her face. "Tell it to Jamie."

Then she looked at Griffin and his skin crawled again. He'd never been sized up so carnivorously. He felt like this walking cadaver had stripped him, measured his penis, and counted his money. "Who's he?"

"Griffin Walsh," Sharon said before Griffin could speak. "Corporate lawyer. He's working for the people trying to buy the Red Owl. But he's not letting them. He's my secret weapon. I'm still going to get you your safe house."

"Jesus!" Griffin said, turning away from them and walking to the curb. He couldn't believe she'd just said that. To a prostitute! Very trustworthy, he was sure. And the way she'd put it—his whole reputation as ethical counsel had effectively just been thrown into a Dumpster.

Of course maybe no one would believe this young streetwalker, Rose. But if Sharon was so free about twisting his actions this way to her, who else was she telling it to?

And was this the only reason Sharon had called him after all—to use him in her fight?

Like you're using her to get Majo on board with the new firm?

That was different.

How?

"I'm not frigging with her career, for starters," he mumbled.

"With whose career?" said Sharon, suddenly at his side, her eyes bright.

He whirled on her and spoke with ferocious intensity. "*My* career! What you just said. You believe that? That I'm consciously sabotaging my clients' chances of buying the Red Owl?"

"Aren't you?"

"No! I'm giving them the best ethical advice I can on what they need to do to make their deal work. The fact is, I came across some freely-available public documents and I passed them on to you. End of story."

"Ah." It seemed to take a bit of the flame out of her eyes. "Well, it probably doesn't matter anyway. I doubt Rose will mention it to anyone else."

Griffin snorted. "Of course not, because she's such an discrete, upstanding member of society!"

"She's a girl. Just like I was girl once."

Again there was something in her voice, but Griffin was too angry to figure it out. "There's a difference! You got kicked out of your house. You got beaten too, right? But you steered clear of selling yourself like a slab of meat! She didn't. And I'm just not that comfortable turning my career over to someone who's shown that basic weakness of character."

Sharon's face had gone even paler, or else the street lamps were changing spectrums. "Basic...weakness," she said.

Griffin glowered back over his shoulder at the hunched figure of "Rose" by the wall. "Okay. That's a little harsh, probably. I know you're trying to help them pull themselves out of it. I just..."

He gathered himself up. How to communicate this sense of destiny he had about himself? Especially since the beliefs he'd held about the value of obsessive work had all been seriously shaken this week. By her.

"Don't say anything more," said Sharon. Her voice was like stones down a deep well. "I need to say goodbye to Rose, then I have something to say to you."

~~~~

Just what words she'd say, Sharon didn't know.

As she turned and walked back to Rose, Sharon's ears were ringing, her vision was cloudy, she couldn't feel her feet.

The grand finale of this evening was to have been her telling Griffin about her past, her days as a prostitute. In her need, she'd decided that Griffin's persistent wooing of her meant he could take it. And then she wouldn't have to keep pretending with everyone. Griffin would be her shield. His decency would spread around her like a magical cloak. It would make *her* decent.

But Griffin had failed the test. Failed!

Because, when you came up hard against it, guys like Griffin Walsh did not end up with girls like Sharon. She'd known that. Even in high school she'd known that and it was even more true now.

If he knew what she'd done in Kelowna, he'd never speak to her again.

She worked this out in the fifteen steps it took her to get back to Rose. And as Sharon she said goodnight, forced herself to breathe, to see, and turn back to Griffin, she decided one more point.

Sad as it all was, true as it all was, she wasn't going to let Griffin go. Because she had a right, moral weakness and all, to be happy. And if it couldn't be an honest, complete happiness, then she would take what she could get.

Really, it was the nameless civil servant woman who'd laughed with her on the phone about the heritage building designation who'd reminded her how it was done. Give people the illusion that you're what they want and they'll believe because they want to.

But isn't that just like...?

It was *not*. She wasn't selling her body; she was giving it. She wasn't asking for money in return; only companionship. And it wouldn't be with some nameless person who chose her; it would be with Griffin Walsh.

Bought with a lie.

Yes. So?

Before her nagging self could utter another doubt, Sharon reached Griffin and faced him square on.

"You wanted to say something to me?" he said.

She met his eyes. They were so lacking in guile, yet still burning with anger. Or was that lust for her? Or both?

"No," she said with a smile. "But I do want to show you something. Follow me."

~~~~

Griffin's hand felt incredibly warm to Sharon as she led him to Main Street then south to Pender.

"Hey," he said. "This is...."

"The Red Owl Bar & Hotel, four buildings in on your left. One hour left until closing."

"What? You can't get enough of the place?"

He sounded peeved and Sharon turned to him with a smile. Her innocent smile. Her reel-them-in smile that Daryl had pounded into her, and that she'd sworn she'd never use again in a million years.

For full effect, she pulled down her hood, revealing freshly-washed hair that she'd left soft, feathered around her face rather than spiked up with gel.

"It's not the bar we're going to check out this time," she purred. "I want you to see what all the fuss is about—the rooms of the Red Owl."

He obviously finally got the change that had come over her, because she could see him thinking quickly. He looked at her. He looked up at the six double-hung windows that fronted the building. Only one had lights on, but it was impossible to tell if the others were occupied.

"We'll ask Henry first, of course," Sharon said. "I'm not going to walk in on some exhausted tourist who's crashed here for the night."

Griffin still hesitated. "Are you saying you want us to...check in?"

She opened her eyes wide. "Oh no. I just thought you'd want to see where it is I want to shelter my girls, where it is that your clients are trying to buy up and run as...who knows what. Are you up for it?"

An odd look crossed Griffin's face. "That expression—'Are you up for it?' You use it much?"

Sharon smiled and cocked her head at him. "No. But Majo dared me with it on something the other night. It sounded right."

"I see."

"So? Are you up for it?"

"I guess we'll find out," he said. "Lead on."

21

THIS PLACE AGAIN.

To Griffin's nose, it reeked. Sticky, greasy, smoky, sour. Especially this late at night, early in the week. Probably fewer bar checks on Tuesdays, so the sour-looking bartender Henry just let whoever wanted to light up and puff to their cancer-ridden content.

Still, there was that something...sexy about it. Waitresses in tight clothing. He remembered Sharon in that outfit.

While Sharon padded over to take with Henry, Griffin waited by the door. The waitress on duty tonight, a petite blonde with a broad, suggestive mouth, leaned back against the bar and looked Griffin up and down slowly. The fact that there were only four customers left in the bar this jumping Tuesday night probably meant she had nothing better to do.

By the time Sharon had come back with three old-fashioned keys, the waitress had licked her lips and rolled her hips at him. After coming from Hastings, and the bodies for sale there, he was starting to feel sex was everywhere tonight. It was an item on a supermarket shelf, waiting to be plucked down.

"Two semi-permanent lodgers, two guests, only two free rooms," Sharon said, holding up the keys so the barrels clinked together. "Who'da thunk?"

Griffin ripped his eyes away from the other waitress's come-ons. "But you've got three keys," he said.

Sharon looked back to the waitress at the bar, then to Griffin. She smiled. She pointed to the door between bar and hotel stairs, then held up a key distinguishable from the other two by a thicker barrel.

"Ah," said Griffin.

He followed her over and stood behind her as she bent over, fiddling with the lock. He could feel the eyes of the waitress still on him, as well as the sour barkeep and the three drinkers—two men and a woman. As if he was reading their minds, he saw himself reaching forward to fondle Sharon's bottom, tug down her sweatpants, run his hands down between....

He shifted uncomfortably. He'd grown hard as a tire iron inside his jeans.

"Is this is the only door?" he said under his breath. "You don't get in or out except through the bar?"

Sharon finally got the lock to click and straightened and turned with a smile. "Controlled access. That's right. Exactly what I'd want for a safe house."

"Uh-hunh."

"Come on," she said, and pulled him through the door, shutting and locking it behind them.

They actually stood in a narrow hall that led to the back of the building. From there a narrow set of stairs headed up over what would have been the kitchen of the bar. As Sharon walked to the stairs, Griffin readjusted the pressure in his pants and followed.

At the second floor, there was a narrow hall with two doors and a fire alarm pull on the wall, no doubt added during a modern re-licensing of the premises.

"One here," Sharon said. She went to the door on the right and tried both keys.

The second key opened the door and they walked in together. Sharon found the lights and Griffin saw the room was done in chintz and old lace. Homey, but a sour, smoky smell said it hadn't been scrubbed down recently. Still, with Sharon so close, even that seemed to be transformed in his nose. Maybe if—

"This room stinks," Sharon said. She raised her nose to sniff, which raised her chest, which drew Griffin's eyes there.

"Let's check out the one on the fourth floor," Sharon said.

Griffin just nodded. It was like she had him by a very tight leash that tugged him along by his zippered fly. Where she went, he went.

The thought made him shake his head as he climbed the stairs. If he was reading this wrong, if this was just the result of wishful thinking and the lateness of the night, he was going to shoot himself. Which might be better. He'd handled his last sex with Sharon so poorly. The kiss three nights ago had been even worse.

Maybe he should just back out and call an old girlfriend? Or even the waitress downstairs?

His penis flagged so fast at the thought he almost laughed. Apparently not. His lust was very person-specific. It had to have this prickly, baggy-sweats-clad woman sashaying up the narrow stairs ahead of him. In fact his erection pricked right back up as he watched that sweet bottom sway. Back and forth, back and–

My God, when had he become an ass man?

Answer: when he'd discovered Sharon Dekker had one.

"Here we go," said Sharon, reaching the top and stepping to the door on the left.

This time she knew which key it was and opened it smoothly. She reached in, flicked on the lights, and waved him in.

~~~~

She would have giggled at his obvious arousal had it not been for the way her own heartbeat triphammered in her chest. Her face felt flushed, her muscles tingly.

Sweeping into the room behind him, she sniffed at the air, relieved that this one didn't have the acridness of cigarette smoke seeping out of every joint and piece of fabric. As much as she still felt cravings, she'd learned to recognize that old smoke simply stank. And she wanted *this* room to be perfect.

Give him the reality he needs.

"The upper rooms in these old places were where they put the non-smokers, even way back when," she said.

"Really," he said.

She could feel his whole body focused on her. If she touched him now, she'd hear a sizzle.

Shivering deliciously, she turned from him and walked to the window. "One of the nice things about these rooms?" She reached up to the pull cord she'd found when she'd first scoped out the place. With a tug, she pulled down a heavy, solid white blind.

"Solid locks on the doors, too," she said.

She walked back, shut it, and turned the key on the inside, plus the sliding bolt up higher. She turned and smiled at him.

"Thick doors. Thick walls. Your own private hideaway."

His eyes narrowed on her. She could feel him undressing her with his eyes and relished the power. The power and...something more. A completion. One only he could give.

"Henry won't come up looking for us?" he asked.

"Not for another hour at least."

"An hour."

"It will have to do." She tilted her head at him, a final invitation.

This time he didn't need to be told to take it. Closing the distance between them with two strides, he reached for the bottom of her hooded sweatshirt and she started to raise her arms.

But then he stopped, smiled, and shook his head.

"What?" Sharon said, trembling from head to toe with frustration.

"First..." he said, and slid his right hand up to her chin.

He took it so gently between his fingers that she barely felt it. It was like a whisper of warm wind. But it compelled her too, drew her towards him, tilted her lips up towards him.

And though fear rippled through her body, she closed her eyes and urged his lips down.

I won't run this time. I won't scream. I won't fight. Please, oh please. Kiss me.

He did. Just brushing her lips at first, as if he was scared as wall. Then not scared, just teasing, running his dry lips back and forth over hers. He brushed them up her right cheek, over her eyelids, her forehead, down her nose to the one scar Daryl had sloppily left on her. Hovered there.

As he did, his fingers left her chin and ran up either side of her face, tracing its outline, smoothing back through her feathery, un-gelled hair.

Oh my God. His hands around the sides and back of her head. He held her like a child, with total possession, total love.

His lips slid down onto hers and the feeling changed to something hotter, more demanding. Yet he still didn't force her. Instead he nuzzled at her lips, asking. Urgent, but asking.

She opened, waiting for the panic she'd felt last time.

It didn't come.

She sucked in his tongue, wrestled it with her own, knowing that any second her past was going to jump up inside her like claws of terror.

It didn't come.

So she let her own hands rise up now, under his sweatshirt. She felt the ridges of his stomach muscles through his tee-shirt, the ribs, the solid mounds of his chest.

Remembering that *she* was in control this time, she found his nipples with her fingers through the thin cotton of the tee. She tweaked them and was rewarded with a groan. Again.

Suddenly his hands were reaching down over her back, grabbing handfuls of her hoodie. He drew back his lips from hers and pulled the hoodie up, forcing up her arms, dragging the hoodie up over her head.

She laughed and let him, and opened her eyes so she could grab the bottom of *his* sweatshirt when he'd thrown hers aside. Up and off.

Now he would be the wild man Griffin again, the one with the blank face, the almost feral sexual drive. She ran her fingers back through her hair, took a step back from him, and braced herself.

And...he spoke.

"Hello, Ms. Sharon Dekker," he said, breathing hard. "This time *you* undo *me*."

For a moment Sharon couldn't move. Literally couldn't. It was as if someone had frozen every limb of hers solid. She'd been able, the last time, to take Griffin rushing at her. She'd been able, despite the nightmare basket of memories tied to every inch of her body, to let him take her completely. She'd even let her body respond, to feel, to rush at the heights and explode there as she never thought she would with a man ever again.

But this, what he was asking her to do...

"Come on," he said. He kicked off his running shoes, pulled off his tee-shirt, and kicked off his jeans. He stood wearing nothing but a pair of medium white briefs, a lean hunk of muscled male. Wanting her.

In a near daze, Sharon followed suit, kicking off her runners, dropping her sweat pants, whipping off the long-sleeve top she'd worn.

Now she too stood in only her underwear, thankful the room was warm. Something in her had obviously expected this, because the underwear was one of her better sets. The bra was a skimpy, sheer black number from La Senza. The lower half was a matching thong, its stretched triangle barely covering her pussy.

"*Very* nice," said Griffin, looking her up and down with tight flicks of his eyes. His erection had throbbed so large, the tip of it was sticking out of the top of his briefs.

"Come on," he repeated.

Which meant walk those two steps to him, tug down his briefs, take his erection in her hand or mouth or both, caress his balls, maybe even insert a finger into his anus when he began to come and massage his prostate to increase his pleasure.

She'd done it a hundred times before. Or was it five hundred times? Once Daryl had taught her the technique, it had become her favorite, her way to get repeat customers because she was so very good at it.

She couldn't move.

"You...don't want to?" said Griffin.

Give him his fantasy!

"I do." She forced a smile. "I just wanted to admire the view a bit first."

Then, internally whipping and shouting herself onwards, she took a step forward. Two. She placed a hand over Griffin's hot, throbbing erection through its cotton restraint. She pressed the bare skin of her torso up against his, her cheek and lips to his shoulder and chest. She heard his breath—deep shudders, in and out. She felt his heat. Smelled his sweet musk.

And somehow all those intimacies made it easier. Or maybe it was just the old habits coming back.

Because next thing she knew, she'd dropped to her knees, stripped his underwear off him, and sucked his penis back to full tumescence. He tasted clean, at least. He must have showered before coming to see her.

When she finally rose up, she unclipped her brassiere for him, then stroked his center as he explored her, first with his hands, then his mouth.

The electricity of his fingers and tongue on her nipples shot through her, but it was only something happening *down there*, down with her smiling, moaning body. The real her, the one she couldn't tell him about, hovered up above them somewhere, watching this handsome couple making love in the top west room of the Red Owl Bar & Hotel, a heritage building, the future transition house for the whores of East Hastings. The real her coolly studied Sharon's technique as she laughed Griffin into retrieving a condom from his wallet. She watched

Sharon take him to the lace-covered double bed and push him onto his back. She watched Sharon mount him and ride him languidly like an innocent girl out for a stroll in a sunny meadow. She applauded the convincing way she panted and yelped when he bucked under her and thrust faster and faster as she used her vaginal muscles to squeeze him until he finally came...undone.

Then, at last, the real her zoomed down into herself to reap the fruits of the work.

~~~~

Griffin's breath, shuddering with hot sighs, blew over her left shoulder.

After he'd pulled out of her and disposed of the condom, she dragged him back to the bed, made him lie down, and lay on top of him, burrowing her head against his chest, fingering his downy chest hair. She could hear his heartbeat in this position. A strong, regular beat.

"Thank you," he murmured and his fingers stroked her hair.

"No, thank *you*," she murmured. She tweaked his nipple.

He jerked but didn't kick her off him. "How long do we have now?"

Sharon looked around as much as she could without moving her head but couldn't see either her watch or his. "No idea."

He laughed with such a warm rich sound that she reached up to feel his mouth, how he did that. She felt him raise his left arm.

"It's 1:35. They close downstairs at two, right?"

"Mm-hm." She ran her hands up and down the biceps of his arms, burrowing her head more firmly against his chest.

"At which point Henry will come up to look for us?"

"Probably."

"You don't think we should get dressed?"

"Soon."

Her hands tightened on his arms, feeling the strength and pulsing blood. She wanted to suck him into her, join with him somehow. To not be alone.

His hands went over her back and strained down to cup her bare bottom, feeling it, fondling it as if he, too, wanted to suck in this moment and her presence. Make it last.

Finally it was time to go.

He pulled her up his body until he could slide his arms under hers and around her back. Pulling her hard against him, he kissed her once—long, slow, and deliberate.

When he finished and Sharon's heart was pounding hard in her chest with an ache she couldn't put her finger on, he said, "I'd like to do this again sometime."

Sharon swallowed and dipped her face down to one side to nibble his ear (and hide her eyes). "I'm not sure Henry would let us do that... without paying."

"Then we pay. Or I go to your place. You come to mine. I don't care."

But she heard the little hesitation in his voice. He did care, of course. Girls like Sharon didn't end up with guys like Griffin.

"My place." She crooned it like it was what she really wanted.

"When?"

"Not today. I have classes. I have to turn in, and probably defend, a special report I did to keep from flunking out of Social Psych."

"That doesn't sound good."

She heard the take-charge sound creeping into his voice and drew back to look into his eyes. "It's just a thing. But I probably should get home. I'll need at least a few hours sleep before then."

"Okay."

He released her and watched her with open admiration as she rolled off him to retrieve her sheer bra and thong. Would he have that same look if he knew how many other men had seen her body?

She shook off the thought and gave him a cute smile. Griffin never *would* know. So it was alright to let him admire a bit. Kind of nice, actually.

Fighting the urge to throw herself back onto his chest to kiss him again, she pulled on her considerably-less-sexy sweat pants, top, and hoodie. She turned to face him.

Still lying naked, up on one elbow now, he grinned at her.

"Well?" she said.

"I just want to admire the view a bit first."

She rolled her eyes, scooped up his underwear and jeans, and threw them at him.

~~~~

This time Griffin led the way, whistling softly and still tucking in his shirt under his sweatshirt as he tromped down the stairs. He could almost hear Sharon gritting her teeth behind him, willing him to be quiet.

Because this was her place, where *she* had to account for who she was seen with.

And she believed Griffin was just a passing thing. He knew that, however much she tried to hide it. He'd sensed the distance in her lovemaking even as he'd been totally carried away. She thought she had him figured out, pegged, slotted, written off as a stiff, stuck-up, corporate slave.

And there was some truth there. Things about her—this insane determination to save the hookers of the world, for instance—still made him uncomfortable. That was why, despite this being officially their third date and just one shy of passing Majo's little test, Griffin wasn't ready to present her as his serious love interest to the people who really counted—his friends or family.

Did that mean Sharon was right about him?

Maybe.

Or maybe, he thought as they walked through the door from the

Red Owl Hotel into the Red Owl Bar, he just needed time.

He ambled to the door to the street while Sharon returned the keys to Henry. Then Griffin drove Sharon home.

Little talk. Quick goodnight kiss. No invitation up, which was just as well.

He wanted to be well-rested the next time he saw her.

22

SHARON AWOKE OUT OF A DEEP-BUT-TROUBLED SLEEP to find that she'd slept right through the start-time of her Thursday morning Social Psych. class.

She lay in bed, staring at the ceiling with feeling of profound dread pressing in around her. Professor Tighe was going to be pissed.

Why was she sure of this, when skipping class at least a few times per semester was considered *de rigueur*?

She was sure because her reawakening hooker instinct told her so. She just had to run over the conversation she'd had with him in his office. Or the way he'd insulted her in class on Monday. Even the brief glimpses of his face downtown that she was suddenly sure weren't just her imagination.

Nuh-unh. Her prof had the hots for her to the point of stalking.

Even worse, he knew Sharon had once been a prostitute. He must have found out where she worked and followed her from there to where she'd checked up on Micky and Rose. What sick fantasies had Tighe conjured up after seeing her walking that strip? How likely was he to act on them?

Not much, she hoped, because calling the police was out. Tighe would just point out Sharon's background and call her delusional.

Would it help to get Griffin to hang around with here on campus? No, that might just make Tighe jealous and stupid.

Sharon lifted her head and slammed it back down against her

pillow. Again. And again. *It—just—doesn't—end*! However much she tried to put her mistakes behind her, they kept coming up. Either it was men smelling her fear—first her father-in-law, then Daryl, then Micky and Angel's pimp, Jamie; now Tighe. Or it was her own body remembering and freezing up on her like it had with Griffin. Or it was just the lying, being someone she wasn't.

Basic moral weakness.

Guys like Griffin never ended up with girls like–

Oh, get over yourself!

Rolling out of bed, she trotted furiously to the washroom, washed up and did her makeup, had some juice and cereal, then grabbed her backpack with the printed-up report on her Red Owl safe house project, and headed out the door.

This, at least, she was going to push through, whatever it took. And Tighe was going to help her.

He was just a man, after all.

She knew how to deal with men.

~~~~

"So what do you want me to do?" said the light tenor voice on Griffin's office phone.

It was Ken Tanaka. Griffin had been trying to reach him all morning and the P.I. had finally called Griffin back. At last!

Griffin had been surprised at how young Brent's PI had been, but Tanaka seemed to know his stuff. He hadn't finished the Coogan Group and Kelowna stuff, but he had delivered a report on Sharon's Simon Fraser schedule.

Also a list of her professors, pinpointing one professor who fit the profile Griffin had laid out. Colm Tighe. He was a psychologist who'd been quietly "removed" from private practice because of complaints to the College of Psychologists of BC. He'd become a political wonk somehow, working with an earlier form of what was now the Ministry of Families and Children to research street kids and drug abuse. Somehow he'd gotten a professorship at Simon Fraser U. Not tenured, but it looked good on his CV.

"Drop everything else for this morning and get up to the university," Griffin said. "She's has to turn in something unusual, and maybe defend it orally. I'm betting it's Tighe."

"Because?"

"Gut sense. The way he talked to me about her. It was like he thought he had some kind of special relationship with her. Romantic maybe."

There was a silence on the phone. "That fits," the voice said at last.

"What does?"

"I didn't put it into the report, but one of Tighe's colleagues let slip a comment about Tighe chasing tail on East Hastings. I wrote it off as professional jealousy, but maybe there was some truth in it."

"I still don't follow," Griffin said.

"Sharon Dekker works in the Red Owl in that area. That fact was documented in her records."

"How did you–?"

"If Tighe actually *is* 'chasing' a woman there, it could be Sharon."

There was a long silence as Griffin's hands grew tight on the phone. Here he'd just been worrying about her angering some faceless pimp somewhere...

"You'll get to the university?" he said.

"On my way."

~~~~

"Come in, Ms. Dekker."

Tighe, standing in his tie and shirt sleeves at the ornate teak bookshelf that rose up to the right of the matching desk, smiled as he waved her forward. He looked like a man who'd just been told he was wonderful or who'd finished a deliciously satisfying meal.

"I have...uh..." She waved her report.

"The report. Yes. Come in. Have a seat."

He looked so ebullient in the mid-day sunshine through his window that Sharon's earlier fears seemed foolish. She walked forward slowly, slung her backpack off her shoulders, and took the nearest chair. The metal creaked as she sat down.

Tighe smiled and waved a beckoning hand to her. His emerald-green tie flashed in the sun. His oiled-back hair glinted. "So let's see it, shall we? You're plan to save the sexually challenged women of Vancouver one at a time."

Sharon frowned a little at his odd terminology, but handed it over. She'd even photocopied the pictures, old and new, of the Red Owl and stapled them to the back of the report with a summary of her success getting it declared a heritage building.

Still smiling, Tighe took the papers like a precious offered gift. He sat behind his desk and immediately began to read.

"May I...?" Sharon half stood, indicating the door, but he waved her back down without looking up from the papers.

Pompous control again. It rankled her. Everything about this man rankled her. But she needed this class credit and she *wanted* his help with the Red Owl.

She sank back into her chair and watched him read. He had to see, even speed-reading like he was doing, how valuable this project was.

Five minutes passed. Ten.

Sharon played with the side seam of her jeans and wished like heck that just this once she could pull a tall Export 'A' out of her fanny pack, light up, and puff away her building anxiety.

He made her feel like a child. Helpless. She hated that feeling.

When Tighe looked up, he had a fixed smile on his face. He no longer looked happy. Shit.

"This is a dangerous game you're playing, Ms. Dekker," he said.

"What do you mean?"

He lay her papers down on his desk and spoke to her slowly, like she was hard of hearing. "Drug-addicted prostitutes with an Arab pimp who's keeping them that way. And, oh yes, who likes to beat them. That's what you wrote."

"I said his name was Jamie," Sharon said, her face growing hot. "He doesn't speak with an accent. He was probably born here, like you."

"And you."

"I wasn't born. I was hatched."

Shut up, Sharon. You need his cooperation.

"Ah. Angry humor. Learned on the street, no doubt." He leaned towards her and templed his fingers. "Is that what's going to keep you safe when 'Jamie' comes after you?"

"I don't—"

"And what of this other group that wants the Red Owl? Do you think they're going to just sit idly by while you do everything you can to *frustrate* and *oppose* them?"

He almost spat the words at her. His sudden fervor caught her by surprise.

"What, exactly, do you think they might do?" she asked.

Tighe stood up. "That would depend on who these men are, wouldn't it? How they're used to dealing with people who get in their way or don't do what they want?"

~~~~

There was a knock on Griffin's office door and Jocasta stuck her head in.

"Sorry, Griffin. One of your clients is out in the lobby and he's apparently demanding to see you right—"

"Right now!" said a rough voice, and Jackson Kilhenny pushed his way in past her so that Jocasta stumbled forward with a gasp, her face suddenly pale.

Griffin stood slowly behind his desk, restraining himself. So it had come to this. Whatever it was about the Coogan Group, he'd figured it would come out first in Kilhenny. He was obviously right.

He nodded to Jocasta to go.

"Do I get security?" she said.

Griffin shook his head tersely. "I don't think we'll need them."

She skittered out and Griffin fixed his gaze on Kilhenny, who was still trying to look threatening but suddenly not quite sure how to carry it off in the small office. He wore the same blue business suit he'd worn last time which made Griffin suspect suddenly that it was his only one. Without Andre Malovet backing him up, he looked out of place in a business setting.

"Sit down, Jackson," Griffin said.

The man, probably eight or nine years Griffin's senior, shrugged his shoulders as if figuring whether to go along with the request.

Griffin waited. The man was a cheap bully. Griffin had learned to deal with bullies in the second grade.

Kilhenny tugged back a chair and sat. "Listen, Walsh," he began in his soft, intense voice. "I found—"

"Stop," Griffin snapped and Kilhenny did, his face screwing up in surprise. Doubly so as he realized that Griffin hadn't sat down himself but was leaning forward, both hands flat on his desk, glaring down at Kilhenny.

"I'm going to give you five minutes," Griffin said slowly. "But only because I promised a friend of mine to help your group. And only because I realize you're upset at the delays in your deal. Your behavior—stomping in here and manhandling my assistant— is unacceptable. You do this one more time and our relationship is terminated. Understood?"

It had the desired effect. Griffin had home court advantage, height advantage, total confidence. Kilhenny opened his mouth to say something. He stopped, chewed on it, and nodded.

But as Griffin straightened and prepared to sit down, Kilhenny stood. The man picked up the three-dimensional magnetic sculpture of an office building that Griffin kept on the left side of his desk to play with when he got bored, which meant never. But it was his.

Griffin glared at Kilhenny until the man met his eyes. A small sneer curled under Kilhenny's mustache and his eyes shone coldly back at Griffin's. The look might have cowed some, but to Griffin, preoccupied with what was happening with Sharon right now and the snags he'd just been handed this morning in the Shiptite deal, it mostly just annoyed him.

"Put it down," he said.

After a pause, Kilhenny did.

"Now sit down," Griffin said, "or get out."

For a second, Griffin thought he had him, but then Kilhenny winked. It was an unsettling thing, more a fluttering twitch than anything normal. He turned, and ambled back to the door. There he paused, one hand on the door handle, and turned back to Griffin.

"You didn't tell us you had a girlfriend who was trying to buy the same property we were," he said.

Griffin narrowed his eyes so that the man didn't see how that shook him. "Care to elaborate on that?"

Kilhenny's mouth twisted up slightly. "You just pass on to her that anything she could set up there wouldn't work anyway. Better to let a professional management team handle it."

"Ace Management."

"Right. Ace Management. Calm, competent, professionals."

He opened the door and left.

~~~~

Tighe was oozing around his desk towards Sharon, obviously fighting to contain himself but not doing a good job. All of Sharon's internal danger alarms, made hair-trigger from her years on the street, were going off.

"How do you think they'd feel, Ms. Dekker, if they found out you'd been sleeping with their lawyer?"

23

H<small>E KNEW</small>! How did he know?

Sharon gripped the rough cloth armrests of her chair to keep herself still as Tighe wove back and forth. It was obvious, wasn't it. Tighe *had* been following her, spying on her. And researching Griffin's background?

Despite her embarrassed rage, Sharon tried to focus on the issues at hand. The Red Owl project. Getting Tighe's help with government contacts. But even before that, getting him to explain the veiled threat he'd just made. Were Griffin's clients the sort who'd hurt her to get what they wanted? Or hurt Griffin?

They were Hard Riders, Micky had said. They weren't, Griffin was sure. Calibeau would never let the Hard Riders touch East Hastings, Pete said.

"You tell me," Sharon said. "What would 'they' do?"

Tighe chuckled and his hand ran back and forth along the edge of his desk. "Oh, you can do better than that, Ms. Dekker. I'm sure you can."

The sleeze. He was taunting her. Dangling little hints of information. Pretending he knew so much.

And what was it she'd thought this morning when she'd first realized what he was? *He's just a man, after all.*

Taking a deep breath, Sharon used her foot to shove her backpack a little more to one side. Then she turned her upper body towards the professor, clasped her hands together lightly in her lap, and arched her back.

She'd worn a baggy champagne-cotton sweater over a polo top today, but the action still had the desired effect. Tighe stopped his oozing scorn and stared at her chest.

"Who's 'they', Professor?" Sharon said.

Snapping out of his lust-induced haze, Tighe drew himself up straight beside his desk. He straightened his emerald tie and smiled meanly at her. "You'd really like to know."

Sharon unclasped her hands and ran them lightly back and forth across her thighs. Tighe's eyes followed.

"Do *you* know?" she pressed.

"Oh, yes."

But then, rather than keep his eyes where she was trying to direct them, his eyes jumped up to hers.

"I do get the feeling, Ms. Dekker, that this project of yours is almost as important to you as your grades."

"It's...yes, it's important." Control. *She* was to be the one in control.

"How important?"

Sharon's hands stopped moving on her thighs, feeling the power balance shift radically under her. Her mouth went dry. No! She was supposed to be subtly tempting him, playing off his obsession. He wasn't supposed to jump right to the chase like this.

Because that's what it was. He'd just baldly asked her how much her body was worth to her. How much did he have to give to get a piece?

A wave of nausea flooded through her and she reached down beside her for her knapsack. No, she wasn't going back there. Not even for the Red Owl or to protect Griffin.

"It's not that important," she said quietly and began to stand.

"Pardon me?" said Tighe.

He lunged directly in front of her, preventing her from rising all the way. She dropped back to sitting.

She could see the bulge in front of his expensive slacks and stared at it in awful fascination. From the streets of Kelowna to here. Four hundred kilometers, six years, three jobs, three semesters of university. And it was like she'd never left.

"I said no," she said more loudly.

"I heard you." His voice was almost a croon as he reached down to her chin. His fingers were soft and delicate, the touch almost as gentle as Griffin's had been last night, but this one made her recoil in loathing.

The fingers grabbed her chin more firmly and she squealed.

"Now, now, Ms. Dekker. Sharon. Breeze."

He said it lightly, sliding it over his tongue and smiling widely when her head jerked up in horror.

"The name you wore for a special period of your life. Breeze. No, it isn't in your school file. You managed to keep your original high-school records out. But as you pointed out last week in here, I do have my resources in government. Including people who can access change of name records."

"They couldn't..."

"Oh, yes," he said, stroking the side of her chin. "There's nothing in our modern world that can stay hidden for long. No secrets. No histories. No...hidden talents."

His calculating eyes slid all over her again.

"Please don't," she said, weaker now as she wondered if she were somehow responsible for this. Did she somehow think she deserved it? Her eyes were starting to leak. "Please."

"Now, if you still want to know who your Mr. Walsh is representing in his Red Owl bid, and if you want to pass your course with me and maintain your scholarships, I think it's time you shared a few of your gifts with me."

So saying, he ran his fingers back through her hair and grabbed her short curls around the back.

Bam!

Tighe's head jerked and his fingers released as a young man—the Japanese student who'd followed her out into the hall Monday?—burst in through Tighe's office door. He was holding a book in front of him and grinning with excitement. "Professor Tighe! Profess—"

He stopped when he saw Sharon's face. And Tighe's.

"Oh, I'm sorry. Um...I could...come back at another..."

"Yes," said Tighe coldly. "Yes, you could."

But the break had been enough to snap Sharon out of her helplessness, and now she shoved back her chair quickly and stood. "Actually, I was just going. I think we're done here, right, Professor?"

"No, Ms. Dekker, we're not!"

"Yes, we are!"

She grabbed her backpack and strode to the open door, insides quaking. But she stopped for a second when Tighe said, "Do you want to fail your course?"

She wavered. Without looking back at him, she said, "No, I don't. And I'll work very hard to make sure I don't."

"You need the weekend to think about it? Fine. Report back here at three o'clock Monday afternoon," Tighe said. "We'll review this paper of yours and decide whether you really know the meaning of that word—'work.'"

"I..."

"Yes, you want to pass? Or no, you won't be there?"

Her body was shaking, literally trembling from head to toe. But he was talking about four days from now. So much could happen in four days. She could get Griffin's help. She could call in the university harassment committee. Four days.

"I'll be there," she said.

"Good. Now get out."

As she stumbled quickly out into the hall, she heard the Japanese student ask Tighe something. Tighe yelled something. Then the student ran out the door. The door slammed after him.

Sharon looked at the boy. Blinked. Her breath was coming in tight little gasps from high in her chest.

"Hey," he said. "You need help? You don't look too good."

She forced herself to slow down, forced her breaths to deepen. It was four days. And she had Griffin in the interim.

"I'm okay," she lied. "Just fine."

She turned and walked quickly away.

~~~~

An hour later, standing behind the chair in his office, Griffin watched as Ken Tanaka stuck a flash drive into Griffin's computer and uploaded the audio file he'd recorded through Tighe's office door.

"I was there too late to get the first part," Tanaka apologized as he pulled them up onscreen in the media player and cranked up the volume.

There was static, then the muffled voice of the smug man Griffin remembered from the hall of Sharon's photos: "How do you think they'd feel, Ms. Dekker, if they found out you'd been sleeping with their lawyer?"

Griffin's body tensed. He looked over to double-check that the door to his office was closed. Tanaka's face, he noted, was studiously blank. Griffin looked back to the wavy lines of the screen as Tanaka boosted the gain. Now they could hear the scuffle of footsteps, the creak of a metal chair.

Tighe began pressuring Sharon. Griffin almost couldn't listen. This sort of evil was why he'd never even considered criminal law. It made his gut twist and his hands sweat.

When it was done, Tanaka pulled up the file directory of Griffin's computer. "I've copied this onto your local hard drive, not the office LAN," he said. "The folder's named Dekker."

"Thank you."

"I also copied the photos I caught with my book-cam as I came through the door. Two came out fairly clear."

Tanaka brought them up in one of Griffin's presentation programs. The first showed Tighe trying to press Sharon's face to his crotch. The second was Sharon looking towards the cameraman, her face stricken, Tighe roaring angrily in the same direction.

It was nothing compared to the roaring in Griffin's own head.

"I'll kill him," he said, his eyes fixed on the screen.

"I wouldn't recommend it," said Tanaka. He glanced back over his shoulder at Griffin. "You could probably get him fired, though. They've got good harassment policies at Simon Fraser University. Only..."

"What?"

"You'd need her to file the complaint. And if you're going to submit this evidence, she's got to know. Something my father told me? The people who hire you to spy might do it for the best of reasons, but the people spied on still hate them for it."

Griffin's eyes traveled from Tighe's shouting face in the second picture to Sharon's stricken one. "That's really...wise, Ken. Thank you."

"Hey." Tanaka shrugged and pulled out his flash drive, packed it into his shoulder carry-bag, and worked his way out of Griffin's chair. "I sat in class with the woman. She's got a hell of a spirit. I think it deserves respect."

"What do you suggest?"

"Professor Sleaze gave her until Monday at three. I'll have you a report about your Coogan Group and probably Ace Management by then. Relieve that end of the equation."

Griffin swung his chair out and sat down. He brought himself into his desk and angrily clicked off the computer screen's pictures. "And what if she hasn't decided to do something by Monday?"

Tanaka edged his way a little nervously to the door. "You're the boyfriend. You figure it out."

~~~~

At four o'clock, Griffin got back from what he hoped was the final meeting on the Shiptite matter.

Jocasta handed him his message slips, including one from Sharon Dekker. He dialed that one first and reached her as she was preparing to go to work.

"You're working? Tonight?" he said

Something in his voice must have betrayed him because she waited a second before replying, "Why wouldn't I?"

Because you've just been virtually raped. "Because...I wanted to take you out to dinner."

There was another pause. "Somewhere private, I bet."

He hesitated just long enough that he knew he'd confirmed her suspicion about him—he'd only take her where they couldn't run into anyone he knew. No! Well, yes. Her life was very messy. But...he didn't *want* to be so stiff about it.

"Anywhere you like," he said.

"I have to work. I have to live. Unless you want to rent me an apartment and keep me as a mistress? Don't answer that."

Her voice was flat and Griffin couldn't get out of his mind the stricken look she'd had in Tighe's office. Almost like she'd been the guilty one.

Damn that prick!

"Then...how about tonight," Griffin said gently. "I'll drive you home?"

Another pause. Then her voice came back very small so he had to strain to hear it. "I'd like that."

She hung up before he could boom out, *It's a date!*

24

S O BEGAN THREE DAYS IN THE TWILIGHT ZONE FOR SHARON—pleasant but painfully, achingly unreal.

During the day, she was on her own to do her Friday classes, make fundraising phone calls, visit Lisa to help her pack her final boxes. In the evening she worked at the Red Owl Bar. At night...

Well, at night, Sharon entered a place she'd never known before or really even imagined. It was...companionship. With Griffin.

Bought with sex. Yes, of course. She understood it had to be. And even though her body thrilled and trembled now when he even looked at her that way, in her mind the sex was the payment; the snuggling afterwards the reward.

He tried to talk deeply with her on Friday night, draw her out with questions about her childhood, or what she remembered about her mother. Sharon froze it out by giving only monosyllabic responses and outright lies that she said were lies.

Next he ironically tried to warn her away from Professor Tighe. The man had approached him when he was checking out her photography exhibit and warned him away from her. It had led him to check the guy out and he had a bad feeling about him.

If he only knew.

Sharon shrugged it off, though. She'd decided not to tell Griffin about Tighe. She couldn't handle it if a confrontation led to Tighe spilling her secret.

Which was also why she'd chosen not to get the university's harassment squad involved. If they discovered she'd been a hooker before going to university, who were they going to believe? Her?

No. She had to find a way to handle it on her own. Somehow.

In the meantime, she brushed off Griffin's concerns the same way she did with his questions about her childhood.

Until finally he asked her only about her night, and the things she was studying, what she planned to do with her degree. Social worker! Yes, she told him that. She told him how she was learning so much about how people functioned and thought, why they did things. Which was a good thing because, to her, it had always seemed people did things for so many inexplicable, stupid reasons.

The same thing on Saturday night, but it was Griffin talking. Sharon listened and burrowed down against his muscly smooth chest, and occasionally tweaked his nipples to let him know she was still awake.

Which sometimes led to more sex. Which was okay because her body liked it and it always led to more snuggling, and fatigue so deep she could sleep without dreams.

Then came Sunday....

~~~~

Sunday in the Red Owl was, unlike more suburban bars, usually almost as busy as Fridays and Saturdays. Whether the drinkers were desperate to wipe out thoughts of the coming work week, or whether they just had some of their Friday paychecks left, the people poured in. And tonight, the more who poured in, the louder Henry turned up the eighties and nineties rock—The Clash tonight, and The Cars, and The Police. Almost made Sharon think Henry had a sense of humor.

By eight-thirty, the beer and shooters were already flowing full force, the tips were pouring in. Despite her feet and calves and forearms hurting from the strain of the previous two nights, Sharon was loving it.

Pete and Digger were there. Just them, not the meaner members of the gang.

As were Majo and two of his law school buddies—big Brent Major and a decadently handsome new guy with hollow cheeks covered by a short blond fuzzy beard. Over the hubbub and music, Sharon thought they called the new guy "Rotty."

"Scotty?" she said, bending down to hear.

"No! Rotty!" Majo called to her.

"To Snotty!" the newcomer said and raised his glass of draft.

Sharon smiled, shook her head, and went to the other tables.

Part of her unaccountable good spirits, she guessed, was the possibility that Griffin might show up while his friends were here. And be with her. With her around them.

Girls like you never end up—

Oh, piss off!

From the bar, Henry was calling to her. She dropped off the round of shooters she'd brought to bowling league guys crowded six to a table on the side, and hustled to the bar.

"In the back!" Henry said and pointed with his thumb, then wiped off his hands like he was going to follow. "Denny!" he called to the Red Owl's sometime-bouncer who'd been called in tonight as insurance when they'd topped the fire safety numbers.

Denny looked and Henry pointed down—*Here, boy!*

When Denny got his bulk close enough, Henry shouted, "Watch the bar!" Then he pushed at Sharon's back to shove her to the kitchen door and through it.

What? She was in trouble? She was–

"Auntie Share!" shouted a two year-old voice, and little Danny jumped at her legs, wrapping his arms around them. "We going big twip!"

Then his mother, Lisa, was there, wrapping her arms around Sharon and bawling and swiping at her nose, something she'd apparently already been doing with Elrad and even the Chinese dishwasher girl.

And despite the over-the-top corniness of it all, Sharon found herself swept up in it. She hugged Lisa back, feeling like now, when she was just starting to understand companionship, she was losing her best friend of the last two years. Fighting tears, she pulled back to look Lisa in the face. Sharon grabbed a rag from the nearby counter, found a clean corner, and wiped Lisa's nose for her.

"Now *you're* gonna take care of *me*?" Lisa said and laughed, sniffled, and laughed again as Sharon laughed and sniffed with her. "Lord, ain't we a coupla cows in the house."

Lisa turned to Henry. "And you too, boss-man. C'mere."

And only because she was Lisa and could do things like that, she stepped over and wrapped her arms around the Red Owl owner/barkeep and gave him a big tits-to-the-chest squeeze that left him open-mouthed.

"There you go!" Lisa said when she released him.

He spluttered, Danny giggled down by Sharon's legs, and Henry finally pulled it together. "Okay. You're done. Goodbye, Lisa. I got a bar to–"

"Wait!" Lisa held up her arm with a drink can she'd pulled from somewhere. "I've got one can of...Sprite...here." She showed it around and indeed it was. "With which I want to propose one last toast—to the Red Owl and to each one of you...."

~~~~

Outside the front door of the Red Owl, Griffin paced back and forth, huffing in frustration and clutching a stuffed manila folder. When someone entered or left, he looked in through the open door briefly before getting out of the way.

In this way he'd seen Sharon bustling about, obscenely happy. And he'd spotted his friends at Maj's usual table in the left rear.

Griffin needed to talk with his friends, with Majo at least. Or with Sharon. He tugged on his ear. He couldn't handle dealing with both at once.

It was the manila folder—Ken Tanaka's report on the Coogan Group and Ace Management. It was so painfully electric that Griffin wished he could drop it and kick it into the gutter, pretend it didn't exist.

But that wouldn't make the facts go away.

Fact 1: Jackson Kilhenny was an officer high up in the command chain of the local biker gang, Hard Riders.

Fact 2: Andre Malovet was an accountant, originally from Montreal. He'd apparently been brought to B.C. by Jean Calibeau in 2002 to help the Hard Riders with their bookkeeping. He now ran a separate general accounting practice as well. The illegal immigrant he'd helped get refugee status, with Lillian's help, was a Honduran teen named Helio Torrez who'd been arrested and given a probationary sentence last year for dealing drugs out in Port Coquitlam, a known Hard Riders territory.

Fact 3: Jamal "Jamie" Bhoja was a local with a long rap sheet, covering everything from living off the avails of prostitution to armed robbery. Five convictions. Two of them gave him jail time.

The others in the Coogan Group, including John Coogan himself, were non-entities, untraceable. Tanaka suspected they did not exist.

Like it mattered. The three existent Cooganers who were Griffin's clients were a criminal nightmare. Worse, Sharon had told Griffin about them and he'd ignored it. Worse, he'd denied it to her face, denied his own scuzz warning instinct, and let himself get thoroughly enmeshed with them. He broke a cold sweat now when he replayed his little confrontation with Kilhenny in his mind. Nothing like telling a supremo biker to shut up and sit down to help your career move ahead with quiet grace.

Not to mention the way he'd helped Sharon put a wrench in their plans.

The Ace Management Group was just as bad. They were a second-rate biker gang known as Bad Machine, led by a guy named Daryl Polson. The new mayor of Kelowna was apparently putting so much heat on them that Polson was looking for a way out. He'd therefore arranged with Kilhenny to move to Vancouver, likely to take over the East Hastings operation, using the Red Owl as their clubhouse.

What was it Kilhenny had told him about Sharon? *Anything she could set up there wouldn't work anyway.* Well, no shit. Not with two bike gangs pissed at you.

And Tighe! How did he fit into this? He'd basically told Sharon he knew who Griffin's clients were and told her they wouldn't be happy about her sleeping with their lawyer. Something that Tighe had confirmed.

How had Tighe known? What was his role?

Oh, and one last point? One of the people Tanaka's sub-contractor in Kelowna had questioned seemed to remember a "Breeze" Neal who'd sometimes answered to Sharon. More name changes. But this Breeze Neal had hung out with Daryl Polson in the days before Polson joined the Bad Machine. So if Breeze was Sharon, she was the one-time girlfriend to a biker boss? Delightful. According to the report, Polson was a big, mustached, redheaded guy who like to beat up women.

The door of the Red Owl opened in another burst of rock music and laughter. Three guys wearing bowling shirts stumbled out.

Griffin scooted right up to the door and caught it as it closed, holding its sharp edge with just long enough to scan the room.

There! Coming out of the kitchen was the barkeep, Henry, followed by a teary-eyed Sharon. On top of everything else, her distress made him want to rush in and demand she go home with him right now.

But it was barely halfway through her shift and—Griffin's gaze swept left—Majo, Brent, and Rotty showed no signs of being ready to leave.

He couldn't face being humiliated in front of them, revealing how stupidly he'd handled this whole thing. Which would be doubly awful when Majo saw how he'd botched things with Sharon, screwed up any graceful retreat with Lillian's contacts....

Shit!

Griffin let the door jingle closed and stomped back to his car. He had to just drive around, maybe go back to his office, maybe call up Ken Tanaka and pick his brains, find some kind of solution here, *something*, before coming back at two a.m. for the end of Sharon's shift.

He sank into the smell of his Beamer's leather, started the engine, and roared away from the curve, praying for inspiration to strike.

~~~~

Inside the Red Owl, pounding music and hubbub continued apace, but Sharon Dekker stood just in front of the bar and felt like every little thing in her life had just grown smaller.

First Lisa's departure. When she'd finally gone, tugging little Danny behind her, Sharon had emerged from the back room, crying.

Then, as if in answer to some cosmic prayer, she'd seen someone holding open the front door of the bar. Griffin! Here early. Just who she needed. She was almost ready to simply quit right there and fly to him, let him wrap his arms around her, tell her he'd been foolish all this time to look down on her. He'd take her whoever she was, whatever she'd done.

But he'd been looking to Sharon's right, towards his table of lawyer buddies, she realized. And as she'd watched, heart breaking, he'd backed out and let the door close all the way.

Embarrassed, she knew. Her already-wet cheeks flamed and her mouth filled with something like sawdust. Griffin Walsh was embarrassed to be seen coming after her.

Which, given what she was facing tomorrow with Tighe, was perfectly understandable. Griffin had good judgement. He sensed the truth about people—his Coogan Group clients, for instance. Or Professor Tighe. In both cases he'd known if they were good or bad, while she...

"Dekker!"

She turned to see Henry glaring at her, red-faced. He jabbed his forefinger out towards tables two, six, seven, and nine. "Move it!"

She nodded, chewed her tongue a little to moisten her mouth again, and tried to put that little extra jiggle in her walk as she set off. At least she could earn a few extra tips before Griffin showed up to take her home and screw her brains out. Earn tips and fuck well. She knew how to do those things at least.

Girls like her....

25

TWO A.M..
  Sharon was still piling empty glasses and napkins, coasters and peanut bowls, onto her tray when Denny hustled the last few reluctant drinkers out to the cold night. Before Denny shut and locked the jingling door, though, he let *in* one body.

Griffin.

And damn it if Sharon didn't feel her heart quicken at the sight of him. Even distracted and frowning as he seemed now, there was a regal set to him. His back was always straight, his movements crisp and decisive, his jaw firm.

For some reason she flashed to that old Katherine Hepburn and Cary Grant movie, *The Philadelphia Story*, or its remake with Grace Kelly and Bing Cosby, *High Society*. In both, the hero tells his princess-like ex-wife that until she gains some sympathy for human failings, she'll never be a complete woman.

Except in Sharon's life, it was Griffin who was near perfect and Sharon who was chock full of failings.

He saw her and smiled. It looked forced.

"You almost done?" he said.

"Ten minutes." She turned to Denny. "Goodnight, Den!"

"Later, Share."

As the bouncer left, Sharon dumped off her final dishes in the back and came out to power through the wet rag wipe-down of the

190

tables at twice her normal speed. The last few days, she'd never been comfortable having Griffin watch her work, but she wouldn't let him help either.

It was just...scut work. She was the scut. Or slut. Both.

She didn't even have the excuse of saving Micky and Angel and Rose these days. That last visit with Rose, the one Griffin had been there for, had shaken her. She'd had two panic dreams of that pimp, Jamie, since then.

And she'd stopped gelling her hair into spikes. For Griffin. Because she liked the feel of his fingers running over her scalp.

That, the dreams, her old hard confidence gone. He'd made her feel more vulnerable in too many ways.

Now, as she finished the wipe-down, she hurried into the back to change into her runners and grab her fanny pack. She hadn't even worn her sweats and fleece these last two days because it had been warm, and Griffin had been driving her home.

"I'm ready."

Henry was already at the door, scowling at them as he unlocked it, let Sharon and Griffin out, and locked it again behind them.

~~~~

My God, but she was ravishing.

Griffin wanted to grab her the second they were outside the door, away from Henry's gaze. That waitressing outfit. On the others it looked good. On Sharon, the high-cut shorts and skin-molding top made her look nearly naked.

But getting busy with Sharon right now would just be avoidance behavior, wouldn't it. Taking her home, stripping off that stretchy top, reenacting their first night together but without the part at the end where he left...

Nuh-unh. Not until he dealt with the things he'd painfully thought his way through over the last few hours.

First, he wasn't going to show her Tanaka's report about the frigging motorcycle gangs Griffin was representing. That was Griffin's professional mess to clean up. Quietly. He'd drop Kilhenny et al. as clients. Spread the word about them throughout the real estate and business legal communities. Majo could tip off the police about the Bad Machine's intentions.

Second, he had to get Sharon to back off her plans for the Red Owl. Period.

Even if the bikers were kicked out of the running, Griffin didn't see Kilhenny just letting her peacefully walk away with it. Like he said, even if she won, she lost.

And then there was whoever was pimping the girls Sharon wanted to rescue. If it was someone like Jamal Bhoja of the Coogan Group, for example, he'd come after his girls *and* Sharon.

Finally, Colm Tighe, however he fit in. Unless Sharon could convince him she had a solid plan to deal with–

"Where are you parked?" Sharon asked impatiently.

"Hm?"

"Your car? Or were you thinking we'd walk?"

"Down there." He pointed south. "I was just–"

"Admiring the view? Right."

She didn't sound any happier than he felt. Because of her meeting tomorrow with Tighe? Good. Hopefully it meant she'd put something in place to deal with him. But why hadn't she told Griffin?

He opened his mouth to ask as they walked under the harsh street lamps, but shut it again. He wasn't supposed to know, he remembered. He was supposed to let *her* raise it. To respect her spirit, as Tanaka said.

They reached the car, got in, roared up to Hastings and east, and almost made Boundary before Griffin decided that his decision to say nothing was stupid. Sharon wasn't talking. Someone had to.

"So what do you have on tomorrow?" he asked as the streets flashed past.

She shot him a frown. "Classes. Why?"

"Just classes?"

"Yeah."

"And?" he pressed.

"A broken heart maybe."

"What?"

"From my friend Lisa moving out of town. And from my sometime boyfriend being a dick."

The car swerved sharply as Griffin whipped his head sideways to look at her face. She was staring straight ahead. "Your sometime..."

"You, Griffin. Though maybe you don't call yourself that. Maybe you just consider yourself someone who spends every night at Sharon's place fucking her."

"Whoah," he said. "Whoah!" and slowed, pulling over towards the curb.

"Keep going," she snapped and pointed. And he did.

After a few blocks of silence, the street and traffic lights washing over them in a kind of slow thrum, Griffin said, "I'm being...a dick. How?"

"You're ashamed of me."

"I'm...ashamed...?" Griffin shook his head. It was so far from what he'd been planning to talk about that he couldn't even understand her words.

Sharon shot out her right palm and slammed the heel of it into the dash. "I *saw* you outside the Red Owl earlier tonight! You looked in, saw your lawyer friends, and decided not to come in. You were too ashamed to greet me in front of them!"

Griffin's face reddened and he shook his head.

"See?" said Sharon, looking at him. "It's true!"

"No, it's not."

"What? You weren't there?"

"I was there."

"And you came in then? I must have missed it."

"I didn't come in." He screeched on his brakes at a red light even though there were no other cars driving for six blocks in any direction. He turned his face to her. "And I *was* embarrassed. But not because of you. I was embarrassed because I'd just discovered something really stupid that I'd done professionally. I wanted to share it with you. I did *not* want to share it with three of the four people who may become my new law partners."

She stared back at him. Her lips were as tightly compressed as his.

The light changed and he turned back his head to squeal forward. He quickly raced past the speed limit, needing to get to Sharon's place. Take her upstairs. Explain everything. Share it. Get her opinion on it. Except he couldn't, of course. There were too many things he couldn't tell her. It made him insanely frustrated.

"Share it with me now," she said finally.

Of course. Of course she'd say that.

"I can't," he said.

She said nothing but hit his dashboard again, making the glove compartment pop open and spill out the neatly arranged owner's manual, licensing documents, flashlight, Kleenex, and chewing gum.

She grabbed the manuals and paper, shoved them back in and slammed the compartment shut again, pointedly ignoring everything else that had spilled out on the seat and foot well around her.

"Look!" he said, running a red light. "When I decided I couldn't come in, I went driving. All over Vancouver, Stanley Park, back to my office. I worked out what I had to do with my problems. Then I got started on yours."

Sharon breathed out disgustedly. "Mine?"

He explained his fears about the girls' pimps first and got only a cold stare. "And then there's Professor Colm Tighe."

"Pardon me?"

She leaned forward as she said it, looking at him as if he'd just grown an extra head. Or psychic abilities? He heard Ken Tanaka's words: *People who get spied on usually hate the ones who ordered it done*. Griffin was grateful he was driving and had an excuse not to look at her.

"I told you about meeting him at your photography exhibit, checking him out afterwards. I worry about whether he's looking at you as just a student or something else."

She didn't say anything for a minute after that and Griffin took that as a good sign. She was thinking. And they were almost to her place at last. He wanted to pull up, park, and assure her, face to face, that he cared.

"He is...a problem," Sharon said quietly. It was almost lost over the hum of the engine and tires.

"What kind of problem?" said Griffin.

They were there. The wall of blackness that was Burnaby Mountain rose up before them at the end of the block as Griffin parked and turned to Sharon.

"A personal kind," she said, looking down. But then she raised her eyes defiantly to meet his. "But I can handle it."

"That's all you're going to tell me?"

"Until you tell me about yours."

He thought about it, looking into her blazing eyes, feeling the warmth of her, seeing the clear outline of her breasts through her white top. Even of her nipples. And the long stretches of white legs below that joined together in such a sweet hidden patch at the top.

He knew he shouldn't be thinking of that now, knew she'd consider him crude. But some kind of stimulus-response, to use the behavioral jargon she'd been using in bed the last few nights, had been conditioned into him lately.

He sees Sharon. He wants Sharon. Pop, goes his penis.

It was sure popping up now.

"Tell you what," he said at last, blood pounding. "I'll tell you just as soon as I take care of a few things, okay? A few days tops."

"Fine," she said evenly. "And I'll tell you how I handled Tighe.

In a few days, tops."

He grimaced and shook his head. "You sure you don't–"

"Goodnight, Griffin."

She opened her door and climbed out onto the curb. Griffin had learned enough not to grab at her to pull her back, but he jumped quickly out his side, shut the door and beep-locked it. He caught up to her as she walked quickly to the front entrance of her apartment building.

"Can't we talk a bit?"

"I'm cold and tired."

"Can I come up, then?"

"Not tonight." She'd reached the door and retrieved the key from inside her fanny pack. Keyed open the door. "I've got...a busy day tomorrow."

"Just one thing then!"

She stopped and turned to him. Before she could ask what the one thing was, he grabbed both sides of her face and brought his lips to hers.

There was no time for finesse, so he just gave her the heat pounding through him. He ran his hands back through her hair, felt its softness, smelled the smoky mango of her skin, tasted peppermint on her lips.

At first she resisted, keeping her lips stiff, but then she got caught in the familiar stimulus-response thing too and melted into the kiss. He felt her hands on his hips, then around his back, then her body melted against him. She opened her mouth to meet his tongue with her own.

Oh, sweet Lord, yes.

When he pulled back with a long, wet sucking sound. He smiled down into her eyes then let her see some of the real frustration he'd been going through. "I don't want to be a dick," he said.

"Just so long as you *have* a dick," she answered. She pushed against him. "And if feels like you do."

He groaned. "So...can I come up and show it to you?"

She dropped her forehead forward against his neck and breathed hotly against his skin.

"Yes," she said.

26

THIS WAS HOW SHARON FELT THEIR SEX:

She was a body, and she was a brain. Most of the time the two were perfectly joined and the brain ordered the body around, felt what the body felt, and was also driven by the body's needs. Like when she had to pee, or eat, or rest, or was so full of energy some days off that she had to go out and climb Burnaby Mountain just to settle down. In all those times it was her doing and feeling and thinking all at once.

But with sex, there was a disconnect.

Not always. Sometimes, when Griffin just forcefully *took* her, she could let her whole self get swept into the deep throbbing chasms of blood and passion that whipped her to an orgasm and left her shaken to her toes.

But when he wanted reciprocity, some kind of civilized give and take like he did this night? Then she was Breeze the hooker again. There and not there.

Unlike with all those tricks she'd turned back in Kelowna, she objectively knew her body was turned on and fully committed. Griffin did that to her. In the privacy of her apartment he seemed to really care for her, took his time with her, respected her, and had a hell of a hot body himself. Her body liked that.

So when he peeled off her top this Sunday night and unclipped her bra, she felt, in a distant way, how her nipples sprang out for him, taut and ready.

When he tugged down her shorts and thong and played his finger and tongue in her dark curls, down on his knees before her, she knew her clitoris stretched out for him, hard as a little rod in her folds of flesh, throbbing full of blood.

It was almost herself that finally grabbed him up and pushed him back to the couch where he'd first taken her. Herself that tugged down his pants and briefs together then stroked him, single-handed, to a staff hard enough for her to sit down on. Which she did, guiding him inside her and riding him backwards and forwards until her own private lips tingled in delight and her clit felt the rough slide of this interloper against it like banana on chocolate, like wind on a whistle, like tongue on tongue.

Then Griffin rose up under her faster and faster, bucking at her, squeezing her ass and tits with his hands, moaning and thrashing in a way her body liked. So she squeezed her legs around him, squeezed her cunt around him, grabbed the skin of his chest with her fingers and thumped as hard against him as he did against her, with a series of grunting cries that sent Boobo darting frantically around the apartment like a thousand mice had been let loose.

While Sharon's head...detached and watching...analyzing... wishing...rode and shook and waited for the end.

It came this time only after Griffin held himself back—held, held, held, held, while she rode, rode, and fingered herself, and he fingered her and squeezed her, and then...together. Double-header. Cries to the ceiling, to each other. Together.

Over.

Amazing.

Done.

Good, said the head, and rejoined the body.

~~~~

Later, lying together with her head in its usual snuggled position on his chest, listening to his breathing, feeling the regular *ka-thump* of his heart, he spoke.

"I know you're not all there during this," he said.

"I came."

"That's what is very weird. I think you really did. But it was almost like you hated yourself for it."

Sharon felt herself tightening up, breathing faster. "I didn't. That's not true. I..."

"It's okay." He stroked her hair and ran a hand softly all the way down her spine. She shivered. His hand slipped to the side and he grabbed the top sheet and blanket and flipped them over both of them, pulling it up around her shoulders.

"Can I sleep here tonight?" he said. "With you?"

It was a first. Usually he wanted to be back in his own bed for the start of a work day. Which seemed to mean every day for Griffin. Sharon looked over at her bedside clock. It was just past three a.m..

"You can stay," she said and cupped her hands just a little tighter around his arms.

Which is how she fell asleep.

But later, maybe 3:30, she slipped back into awareness as Griffin shifted his head to press his lips into her hair.

"I'm not ashamed of you, you know," he murmured. "And I love your hair."

Her dreams were sweet.

27

SHARON WOKE UP NEXT MORNING to the smell of frying chicken breast and coffee.

She rolled sideways in her twin bed, hugging one of her pillows, and smelled his scent still on her sheets. Mmm. Warm and delicious. It wrapped around her like that half-remembered thing he'd murmured to her last night.

Not ashamed of you.

From anyone else it would have sounded condescending. But from Griffin Walsh, he of the daunting mind and perfect career path, it was almost...affirmation.

She'd known since their first meeting that he was drawn to her. And since their hike up the mountain, and especially since their roll in the sheets at the Red Owl, she'd felt him trying to get closer, to actually know her, to share some of who he was.

Then his words last night. It was like he'd seen pieces of her, both good and bad—her scary photos, her classes, her swearing, her goals and attitudes—and pronounced her worthy.

Not if you added in her history as a hooker, of course. But he was never going to know that. She was going to take care of that this morning.

Rolling out of bed, she padded to her closet and grabbed a tee-shirt and panties, pulled them on, and went out to the kitchen.

There he was, her very own Chef Griffin, bare from the waist up, humming some tune she didn't recognize as he fried scrambled eggs in one pan and thin-sliced chicken breast strips in the other.

She goosed him on either side of his waist and he jumped, turned, and smiled. He leaned down to kiss her once, deeply. Her heart seemed to be sucked right up to her throat when he pulled back.

"Hope it's okay to use the chicken from your freezer," he said. "You didn't have bacon."

"I don't eat bacon."

"You're not Jewish...?"

"Slim and want to stay that way."

"Ah."

He grinned and flipped the chicken strips. They were a crispy brown on one side. Lightly greased in olive oil. He put away the pale green bottle of Bertolli's as she watched. And wiped the counter, washed the bowl he'd mixed the egg in. Sharon heard her stomach rumble, hungrier for breakfast than she had been in years.

Minutes later Griffin had her sitting at her eating table with the chicken, eggs and glass of freshly-made orange juice before the coffee. It tasted almost as good as it looked and smelled. He wolfed his down. She lingered over hers, chewing and savoring.

"One more thing before you and I head out to fight our respective dragons," he said and pulled his chair over so that he sat almost knee-to-knee with her.

She put down her cutlery, swiveled towards him, and licked her lips to prepare for a toe-curling kiss. Instead he took her hands in his and said, "I want to introduce you officially to my friends. If that's okay."

Her mouth dropped open. "You're sure?"

He smiled and leaned over her, kissing her once lightly on her forehead then once on either cheek. "For luck and protection. I care about you, Sharon Dekker."

Sharon's eyes welled up instantly and she looked down so he wouldn't see, touching the gift lightly with her fingers. "Thank you," she whispered.

She felt him check his watch. His whole being changed from lover to lawyer and he hurried to the bedroom for his clothes.

"Sorry to leave some of the clean-up," he called back to her. "I have a ridiculously difficult morning ahead."

As did she, Sharon thought with a fatalistic shiver. As did she.

~~~~

Tighe had said noon, Monday. At 11:46 a.m., Sharon stood outside his office on the third floor of the Academic Quadrangle. She wasn't able to wait any longer.

She knocked.

The door didn't open at once. Sharon shifted her knapsack to her other shoulder and looked around.

Muted conversations from other offices floated out into the hallway around her, but the cream-tiled floors momentarily held no one other than Sharon. She was alone. Then a door opened three down and a mixed group of students with one older woman, probably their professor, came scrambling out. They were laughing and elbowing each other. Probably heading out for lunch together. Joking. Respectful. Down to the windows at the corner.

Gone.

Tighe's office door suddenly opened and Tighe stood there, staring at her with no expression.

He'd dressed much as he usually did, in carefully pleated wool slacks, a crisp, pale green, button-down shirt that he'd probably had dry-cleaned, and a floral aftershave that was definitely coming from him, not his office. Somewhat ominously, he wore no tie and had the top two buttons of his shirt unbuttoned. *To make things easier?*

He waved her in and she went. The office's vertical blinds were drawn. She heard Tighe close the door behind her with a click and latch. Thunk. Locked.

Sharon's mouth was dry. She unconsciously touched the three

spots on her face where Griffin had kissed her for protection. She stopped before Tighe's desk and slung her knapsack down to the carpet.

This time she *had* packed pepper spray in the backpack she carried with her. She hoped she wouldn't have to use it.

"Well, Ms. Dekker," he said as he walked around the room past her. "You're early. A little eager?"

His inscrutable face looked worn, his cheeks sunken like he hadn't slept much since last Thursday. Maybe waiting for the axe to drop? For the harassment committee to call? Good.

He stopped only halfway around his desk, though and let his eyes flick casually over her, taking in the hiking boots, long corduroy pants, black baggy turtleneck. And he slowly smiled.

Bad.

"I doubt you used to dress like this on the streets of Kelowna," he said softly.

Sharon felt her face getting hot and fought the reaction angrily. "I'm not there anymore. That was a long time ago."

"But maybe not so long that you'd be willing to share it with all the new people in your life?"

She winced and a spark of victory danced in his eyes. He'd figured her out. He knew why she hadn't gone to the harassment committee or called the police or even turned to Griffin. Even more than her grades, or information he had about the other group wanting to buy the Red Owl, his knowledge of her past was her weakness. And he now knew for sure.

"I didn't think so," he purred. "Because we all have secrets, don't we? We all have little sides to us that we wish to keep private. That's perfectly normal."

He'd started to move towards her and Sharon jerked up her hand. "Stop."

He did, and gave her another slow smile. "How would you like to play this then...Breeze?"

"Sharon."

"Alright."

Sharon licked her lips and cleared her throat. "It's like this, Professor. We're not going to play at all."

He seemed almost to have been expecting it. "You think so? I don't think you've been paying enough attention in class then... Sharon. Humans are highly social animals. Given enough need to fit in, they'll bend their personal standards all over the place. And you do want to fit in, don't you."

He stepped forward again and Sharon stepped back, bent down to her knapsack, and came up with the pepper spray aimed straight at Tighe's face.

"Come now," he said, pausing but apparently not shaken. "I wasn't going to *force* you."

"Glad to hear it, Professor. Now I want you to hear me." She took a breath. "You're right I want to fit in, but not if it means being touched by a piece of human filth like you."

"Ms. Dekker." Tighe narrowed his eyes. "Your grade. Your scholarships."

"Screw my grade. I dropped out of your class this morning."

"Ha." Tighe's head tilted like she'd hit him. "It's a core subject. Or did you change your major as well?"

He leaned toward her and she shot a quick spritz of pepper spray at his body in warning. A wet stain appeared on the pale green cotton and spread. Tighe looked down in horror.

"And my admissions folder?" Sharon said. "The one with my history all spelled out in my own handwriting? Since I'm already *in*, they don't need it anymore, so a friend in the admissions office gave it to me. You'll never see it again. You try to tell people what was in it, I'll deny it and I *will* call the harassment committee on you. You'll lose your job."

Tighe looked up with his narrow teeth bared like a piranha. "I made copies."

"Not likely," Sharon said, raising the pepper spray to point at his face until he backed up. "My admissions friend said you had the file for just over half an hour. "Your photocopy key wasn't used during that time. You barely *had* any time that day to do it that day between picking it up, reading it, sexually harassing me with it, and getting it back to the office."

"I scanned it onto a disk."

"You're lying. And you're not very good at it."

He snapped his teeth at her and began circling wide. "And you're a little whore, *Breeze*! A slutty, teasing whore."

He'd put himself between her and the door.

But Sharon's own anger was up now, boiling hot inside her. That this *embarrassment* would try to force her back to her own life just when she was starting to believe she had a chance with Griffin. A chance to really live.

She waved the pepper spray in front of her to keep her arm from locking. Her breath was high and quick.

And in a jarring *déja vu*, the door behind Tighe banged so loudly it sounded like someone was trying to break it down.

"Campus Security!" bellowed an unfamiliar voice. "Open the door now or we'll break it down!"

Tighe's face had gone white. His clawlike hands froze. His face whipped towards the door, back to Sharon, towards the door again.

Sharon made it easy for him by lowering her pepper-spray can down by her side. He saw it and turned to the door just as the huge voice started bellowing, "One! Two!"

Tighe fumbled open the lock and jerked the door in.

In the doorway stood two men. The huge voice obviously belonged to the bigger of the two, a bluff tower of man who reminded Sharon of the Red Owl's bouncer, Denny, but wasn't. "Brent Major," she said.

The other man was, of course, Griffin.

28

GRIFFIN TOOK A GOOD LONG LOOK at Tighe's confused, angry, helpless face, drinking it in. Then he shoved roughly past him. He scooped up Sharon's knapsack and turned to her.

"I think you're done here," he said.

Surprisingly, she didn't look happy to see him. Her face was flushed, her eyes burning. Without saying anything, she grabbed her backpack from him, slung it on her back, and stomped out the door.

Shrugging, Griffin hurried after her. He paused just outside in the hallway, and whispered to Brent, "Have fun."

Then he jogged after Sharon since she was almost to the stairs heading down and out.

He caught up with her and had to keep moving to match her strides as she leapt down the stairs three at a time, using the handrail for balance. She didn't stop at any of the landings or even at the bottom, but slammed out the exit door and into the middle of the quadrangle.

Only then did she spin around at him, so fierce he instinctively raised his hands.

"How dare you!" she said.

"What?"

"How *dare* you! I was handling that! That was *my* fight! And I...." She stopped and frowned, looking down at the grass, then back and forth, eyes looking for something other than the damp grass from the brief morning rain.

She looked into his eyes with her own very narrow. "How did you know to be there right then? Or even that I was seeing Tighe today?"

"I...um..."

"That kiss of protection this morning. You knew even then, didn't you? How long?"

Oh, boy. Here was where the spying hit the fan. He dropped his arms to his sides. "Since last Thursday," he said.

"Last Thursday. Right after I saw Tighe?"

"Within about an hour."

"How? No, wait." She looked down intensely then back up at him. "The Japanese student who burst in."

He nodded, admiring but careful not to show it. "Ken Tanaka. He's a private investigator I hired to check out a bunch of stuff."

"About me."

"Mostly about the Red Owl and the people interested in it, but you were definitely part of that."

"And Tighe."

"Maybe. We'll know soon."

She looked at him with a look so threatening Griffin just threw up his hands. "Look, when Tanaka broke in on you, he got recordings of the last half of your conversation. And very incriminating pictures when he burst in. Brent will be showing those to Tighe right now and pointing out his options to him."

"His...options."

Griffin frowned and stepped forward. Sharon looked like she was going to pass out. He caught her gently by the shoulders as she swayed.

"Sharon? What is it?"

"I was *handling* it," she said, half to herself. Griffin saw her eyes were brimming now. She looked up into his and her eyes overflowed. "I was. You should have just let me."

Griffin's heart squeezed so painfully he had to gasp. What had he done? What, other than try to protect her?

Or were her tears now just the aftershocks of Tighe, a kind of reverberation of trauma?

"It's okay," he said, rubbing her shoulders up and down, scared to draw her in because he didn't understand what she needed. "Really. Brent won't be more than twenty minutes or so. I said I'd meet him in the coffee shop we saw coming here from the car. And you were early at the meeting, weren't you? On the tape he demanded you be here at noon. You were already inside when we arrived. We had no idea how long you'd been there. We just heard Tighe spitting at you. He sounded like he was going to attack."

Between the talking and the rubbing of her shoulders, he managed to bring her back a little to herself, enough to follow him out of the quadrangle and northwest—she slapped violently at his hands when he tried to take her backpack off to carry it for her—to behind the administration building he and Sharon had argued in front of what seemed like ages ago.

They found the coffee shop and sat. It had picnic-table-style tables and a cafeteria run where you slid your tray along a metal counter, picking up food as you went. Griffin got Sharon an herbal tea like the ones he'd seen in her apartment's kitchen and brought it back on a red tray. With much encouragement, she removed her backpack and put it between her feet under the table. Then stared at the table top, her mouth clamped shut.

Brent took a full forty minutes to arrive.

"Well?" Griffin said as the bigger lawyer squeezed into the bench across from him and Sharon. He'd picked up a full twelve-inch, tuna submarine sandwich on his way over.

"She okay?" Brent said, trying to catch Sharon's eyes.

Sharon still stared at the table, sipped her tea, and wouldn't look up.

Griffin shook his head at Brent. "What happened?"

Brent picked a stray bit of tuna up with his fingers and popped it in his mouth. "Basically I showed him the stuff, told him he'd never see Sharon alone again, ever, and that he had the option to either resign at once or face both a harassment hearing and a civil law suit with lots of press."

· Sharon looked up at the big lawyer with such horror that Griffin worried she was going to throw the rest of her hot tea in his face.

Brent was unfazed. "Ms. Dekker, this is all bluff at this point, okay? It's going in hard and fast to rattle him. The fact is these cases rarely get beyond the harassment hearings and settlement. Details are kept quiet. We always get publication bans on the names of victims."

"What did he say?" Sharon said, her look of horror still there.

Brent shrugged, one hand on his sandwich. "He said go ahead. Then he started spouting the most desperate, laughable accusations about Sharon that I'd ever heard."

"Accusations," Sharon repeated.

"Like?" Griffin said with a frown. It wasn't until Sharon turned her horrified eyes on him that he realized how that sounded.

Brent waved his free hand in the air. "You don't want to know. Ask Majo sometime what you hear at every sexual assault trial of any degree. It's the deviant's way of justifying his behavior. Never provable." He couldn't resist any longer and picked up half his sandwich, took a large bite and chewed.

"You told him that?" Griffin pressed. "That it couldn't be proved?"

Brent nodded, still chewing.

"And?"

Brent swallowed and dabbed at his mouth. "He folded. He gave up. He'll turn in his resignation on Monday."

"Good," Griffin said.

"Oh, and him knowing about you and Sharon? And about the Red Owl thing?" Brent shook his head. "Nothing. He's just a bit of a sex addict. Likes to hang around prostitutes, talk with them, hear their gossip. He saw her on the strip with you, followed you both, put it together."

Brent took another bite and closed his eyes as he chewed. The guy liked his food.

"So it's all wrapped up, then," Griffin said. But when he looked sideways at Sharon, he saw the horror hadn't left her eyes. "Sharon? Did you hear? We still need to get you drawn out of the Red Owl purchasing thing, but *this* part of your problem is over."

She turned her head and looked at him like she was seeing him for the first time. "You really think it's that easy?"

Griffin glanced at Brent, who shrugged and chewed.

"It's done," Griffin repeated. "Tighe's gone."

"I dropped out of his course."

"What?"

"I dropped his course. And I did some other things to make sure he wouldn't bother me. Then you two step in, knowing nothing about anything, and pull a super-lawyer shtick on me."

Brent swallowed and leaned back, suddenly very unhappy. Griffin shook his head at him again to say sorry and turned to Sharon with his eyes hard. "We did pull a super lawyer. You just got one of the best, in fact. And he just got you a pro bono result that was pretty near perfect. If anything, you should be telling him thank you."

She turned to Brent and said, "Your arrogance is going to catch up with you."

Brent dabbed at his mouth, grimacing and looking at Griffin in disbelief. While Griffin twisted up inside and clenched his teeth. This was why Griffin hadn't wanted to introduce Sharon to his friends. This was *exactly* why.

"You should apologize to Brent," Griffin said to her now.

"Why? For messing up?"

"For cleaning up a messy situation.

"It's not cleaned up," Sharon said, voice rising. "You don't know that. You don't know how far it's spread."

"What would you have done? Pepper-sprayed him?"

"Maybe. *Maybe.* Got a little dirty. Slugged it out. Maybe that's what it would have taken!"

"'Slugging it out' is never the—"

"You don't *know* that!" Sharon said and jumped to her feet, struggling out from the bench. "You don't! You think everything can just be whitewashed and papered over! Kept neat and tidy! Follow the rules! It's not that easy!"

She took a deep br eath and seemed to be fighting for control. Her lips pursed together tightly. She closed her eyes. When she opened them, she turned towards Brent and bent her head forward in what might have been an act of humility if Griffin could have believed she knew what that meant.

"I know you did your best. For a friend."

That was all she could manage before she tugged her backpack out from under the table seats with her foot, picked it up, slung it over one shoulder, and walked for the door.

Griffin watched her go with his head literally pounding. Who *was* this woman? Was she insane? Was this all some kind of elaborate fear-of-intimacy thing that was making her shit upon the man who dared to get too close?

He started struggling up from his seat.

"I wouldn't, man," said Brent, picking up his sub again.

"Because?"

"Because the woman's not rational right now. She just had a scary encounter with a sexual deviant, right? Give it time. Besides...." He took a bite. "It's probably that time of the month."

Griffin turned and looked dumbfounded at Brent's grinning face. And Griffin had been worried about his friend's reactions to *her?*

~~~~~

Sharon was shaking head to toe as she hurried away from the admin cafeteria.

She felt like she was standing on the edge of a very long drop, but she wasn't sure which direction she had to step to reach safety.

Griffin had spied on her! He'd somehow missed the revelations of her past in Kelowna, barely, but then blithely stuck his nose into the cesspool that rose up from it.

Like Tighe, who might now be angry enough to spread her history all over the university.

Or like Sharon's contacts on the strip. How many prostitutes did Tighe talk with? How many knew about Sharon and her plans for the Red Owl? She'd been careful to limit her dealings to just Micky and Angel and Rose. But if Tighe had been spreading her name, Sharon might as well have been wearing a big bull's-eye on her back for every pimp down there to read. They'd know her background. They'd know how to get to her.

And Griffin thought this was finished?

Without consciously meaning to, she'd walked out to the north side of the campus. The Academic Quadrangle was behind her. The road that looped the mountain top of study halls, residences, laboratories, and sports fields ran left and right in front of her. If she just walked left, crossed over, she'd find the path that she'd taken with Griffin that day.

The damning file she'd retrieved from the admissions office, the one with her entire sordid history in Kelowna, crackled like a cut live wire in the pack on her back. She should skip the rest of her classes, go down the mountain right now, find a metal garbage pail or the sink in her kitchen, and set the file on fire. Burn it to ash.

But even as she was thinking it, a vaguely-familiar car screeched to a halt on the far side of the road. It was a low-riding Acura Legend. Silver. With an old-fashioned car phone antenna rising up from the rear window.

From the driver's side window, the face of Professor Colm Tighe glared out at her, his face twisted into something hardly recognizable.

Then he gunned the motor and set off down the road, presumably down the mountain, then to...where?

With a dry mouth and pounding heart, Sharon turned back towards the academic building. Up here, at least for now, up on this mountain, she was safe. Elsewhere.... Well, elsewhere were a whole lot of very long drops.

Oh, yeah, Griffin, this was so over.

29

T HE CALL CAME DURING HER LAST CLASS—Behavioral Psychology.
Sharon was sitting five rows back in a flat-floor classroom, concentrating fiercely to distract herself from the hovering sense of dread. She'd put her cell phone on vibrate and stuck it into the front right pocket of her cords. When it went off, she yelped and jumped, knocking her books off her desk and whacking the girl beside her.

At the front of the class, Professor Goggin turned around from the blackboard where he'd been drawing dogs, boxes, and electrical shocks, and grinned foolishly around the class before he located her.

"I know this stuff is startling," he huffed. "Or do you just need to go to the bathroom?"

"Um...cell phone. Sorry."

Sharon stuck her hand into her pocket and started to turn it off. Then had a sudden fear it might be Tighe, or Griffin, or even Julia Morrow with news about Lisa. There were too many things in her life right now that she could not miss. Too many long drops she had to keep track of.

Gulping and apologizing to the girl beside her and to Goggin, she grabbed her notebook, pen, and backpack, and fled the classroom.

She flipped open her cell just before it was ready to switch the caller to her voice mailbox and jammed it up to her ear.

The voice was Micky's. Micky gasping like Sharon had never heard her do before. "...God. Oh shit. Oh fucking Christ."

"Micky!" Sharon snapped, putting a finger to her opposite ear to shut out a group of laughing students walking by. "Stop! Tell me what's happened."

A sob. "She's hardly breathing. Oh, fuck. I think she's... I think...."

"Who, Micky. Talk to me. Who's hurt? Is it Angel? Rose? Where are you?"

"Ph-phone at Jackson and Cordova. It's Rose."

"An overdose?" Sharon started scrambling through her backpack one-handed as she talked, pulling her notebook back out, and a pen. Jotting down the address. Glaring away the students who'd stopped to watch her.

"No. It was Jamie. Fuck He just went crazy on her for some reason. Started *beating* her... I gotta go."

"Stop! Micky, look. Have you dialed 9-1-1?"

"No way! No cops! No ambulance! She's so cranked they'd never let her out. She's fucking fourteen, Sharon! Fourteen years old. And I can't...can't take her back where Jamie..."

"Okay, Micky. Okay." Sharon was thinking furiously. "Listen, do you have any money at all? Cash?"

"Y-yeah. Rose did a quickie before Jamie showed."

"Take that cash, wave it at a cab, and bring Rose to this address. You listening?"

"Yeah."

"Duthie and Pandora. That's near Burnaby Mountain. You got it? Duthie and Pandora."

"Yeah."

"Micky, you gotta trust me on this. Get the cab and come. I'll take care of you. I'll take care of Rose. Okay? Say the address."

"Duthie and fucking Pandora."

"Right." She heard Micky's heavy breathing. "I'll meet you there."

Click.

Sharon folded her cell slowly, then quickly stuffed it and the notebook and pen back into her backpack. It looked like it was time to leave the mountain.

~~~~

It had started drizzling again when the Yellow Cab pulled up on Duthie just before the stop sign. Sharon, soaked from both her run down the mountain and her wait in the rain, ran over and helped Micky pull Rose out of the taxi.

"They pay you?" she called to the East Indian driver.

"Oh, yes." He bobbed his head. "This girl should be in a hospital."

"I know."

"You want I should take her?"

Sharon shook her head. The cabbie shrugged his shoulders and drove off.

Sharon finally took a good look at Rose. She did indeed looked cranked, or tweaked, or stoned. Who knew? She smelled sick and ripe from the streaks of vomit on her clothes. Her eyes were glazed. Staring. Vacant. Her right cheek had a massive purple bruise that spread up in blotches of black and red around her right eye. The other eye looked punched too, already swelling shut. Cuts and scrapes along her jaw line and down her bare arms, ugly bruises up and down her legs, all suggested that Jamie had gone mental on her.

Sharon trembled inside. She'd been through beatings like this with Daryl, though her big cowboy pimp had usually been careful to stay off her face. That would have been "marking up the merchandise" as he put it.

"I'm just down the street here," Sharon said. "Let's get her inside."

Micky, who looked wet and wasted herself, nodded. With each of them hooking one of Rose's arms around their shoulders, Micky and Sharon walked her to Sharon's building. There, Sharon fumbled her key out of her pocket.

If she'd been any less soaked, traumatized by the day, or desperate to just get Rose inside and lying down, taking these two hookers from the mean streets of Vancouver into her building would have clanged through her like some portentous cymbal of defeat. It was her past shambling into her present. It was proof she could never get away from it. It denied everything she'd worked so hard for, all the new hints of life she'd been finding with Griffin.

But it was necessary.

Rose started moaning and mumbling nonsense syllables. Sharon got her and Micky into the elevator and pressed the button for her floor.

"Sixteen," Micky said and wiped her nose. "We're moving up in the world.

The doors closed and they rose.

When they got out and finally into Sharon's apartment, Sharon could almost feel the way Micky sniffed at the air, sucked in the sights and shape of the place, quickly ticking off the value of the space, the furnishings, the artwork, the computer. It was instinctive. The hooker's survival skill. You did it to assess danger and figure out how much you could take your trick for. Blaming Micky for it would be like blaming her for breathing.

"Into the bedroom," Sharon said, and pointed.

They walked Rose in, lay her down, and carefully stripped and cut off her clothes while she grunted and thrashed languidly. Fourteen? Jesus. Sharon could see that now that Rose's scrawny body was peeled. The breasts were mere buds and even they had been brutalized, like Jamie had pushed her to the sidewalk and just started kicking her until he ran out of energy.

Sharon sniffed and tried to find again the toughness she used to have. "Let's get some washcloths from the bathroom," she said. "And some Polysporin and bandages. At least clean her up and cool her down too. She's burning up."

Which they did together, Micky showing such tenderness that Sharon knew she was right about the short hooker with the heavy makeup and red streaks in her hair. Micky was Rose's surrogate mom. Adopted her either before or after Rose came to live with Jamie. Probably taught her the ropes.

"You know she might have broken a rib or something," Sharon said. "She should get x-rays."

"Uh-unh," Micky said, shaking her head hard.

"At least we'll have to stay with her. If she throws up, she could choke on it."

"Yeah." Then, "Don't you got work?"

"I'll call in sick."

"Yeah." Then Micky screwed up her face like she was thinking hard. "No. I mean, you don't need to. I mean, I know you don't know us much or nothing, but...like, we're not going to go anywhere."

She wasn't looking at Sharon now but was blushing red from the tips of her hair roots all the way down her neck.

And Sharon had been there. Only last week she'd been there, with Griffin to her face lumping all prostitutes into a pot as having a basic moral weakness.

As Sharon stared, Micky glanced at her and obviously saw the same thing there that she'd seen in Griffin's eyes. "Forget it," Micky said. "I just, like, thank you for taking us in."

She got up and went to the washroom with her cloth. Came back with it cleaned and wetted down again, and began another slow wiping of Rose's body.

Sharon rose and walked into the living room, closing the bedroom door behind her. She looked around. What was there, really, to steal? She didn't own much. The computer? It was an outdated piece of junk. But she needed it for school and didn't have the cash to replace it.

Chewing on her lips and looking back towards the bedroom, she quietly knelt and unplugged it from the wall, unplugged the monitor and keyboard and mouse from the main box of the system. Then she picked up the monitor and lugged it out the door and to the next door down where she knew her neighbor, Mrs. Dewdney, was always at home at this time, cooking for her two kids. Sharon followed it with the rest of her computer stuff, including her boxed computer programs and operating system.

"Just for a day or two," she promised.

Then it was back to her apartment. Micky was still in the other room, humming some sort of off-key lullaby now. It was nearly five o'clock. Sharon was about to march in and say she was leaving for work after all, when she spotted her knapsack. With her admissions file inside.

She couldn't take it to work. There was no way she could watch it there.

She couldn't burn it now. Not without too many questions.

But she couldn't just leave it out in the open either, trust or not. No monetary value or not. Nor could she leave it with Mrs. Dewdney.

Looking around quickly, she pulled the admissions file out of her backpack and walked to the couch. It sat on the edge of the thick old area carpet she'd laid to cover the apartment's wood floor. As quietly as she could, she moved the couch. Then she lifted the carpet and slid the file as far under it as she could reach.

When she replaced the carpet and slid back the couch, there wasn't even a ridge to show where the file lay.

Feeling satisfied, if less than noble and trusting, Sharon walked back to the bedroom.

Micky looked up from her gentle stroking of Rose's hair. "I heard you moving stuff around," she said.

"A bit," Sharon said. "I decided I'm going into work after all. You help yourself and Rose to whatever food you can find for dinner. Just don't start a fire, okay?"

Micky looked too tired to grin. "Okay."

Sharon held her eyes a moment longer, then went out, readied her fanny pack, and ran to catch the bus to the Red Owl.

~~~

10:00 p.m..

Sharon had begged off early from work because Jenny had decided she could show up after all and wanted the extra tips anyway. So Sharon rushed home, rushed up in the elevator, rushed to the door with her keys, and...

The door creaked open before she could stick her key all the way into the slot.

With a sinking feeling, she walked in, looked around, and started to cry.

"Micky!" she called. "Rose!"

But of course they didn't answer. Because they weren't there. Nothing was. The place had been virtually stripped.

She wandered through the entire apartment, assessing their parting gift—pictures pulled off the walls; the fridge and freezer open, contents gone; her bedside clock-radio missing; all her dressy clothes missing along with a good swath of her underwear; her microwave oven; her television. How had they even managed to carry it all? Had Angel come by with a car? Had they done multiple trips?

Swiping at the tears running freely down her face, Sharon walked into the center of her living room and slowly collapsed to cross-legged sitting on the floor.

It wasn't the stuff. It was the betrayal. The final betrayal of her trust and hope.

Or maybe it wasn't even that. It was the *inevitability* of the betrayal. Because of the basic moral weakness that Griffin described. It just didn't go away that easily. It was strong in Micky and Rose. It was probably still strong deep inside Sharon. That was why she'd attracted Tighe to her. That was why she hadn't been able to hang onto Griffin. There was just—

She blinked. The...couch. It had been moved.

Surprised to find that her gut could sink any further, could actually become a vacuum of sucking bile, Sharon scrambled over to the edge of the carpet, pushed the couch the last inch out of the way, and rolled the carpet as far as she could towards the center of the room.

The admissions file was gone.

She couldn't breathe. Couldn't think. But somehow all the ugly visions she'd had up on the mountain, right after leaving Brent Major and Griffin, came flooding back to her. The long drops. The pimps all over East Hastings knowing everything about her. The information spreading through the whole east side, through the Red Owl, through Griffin's shocked ears, through all of Vancouver. She could see it like stop-motion photography. Click. Click. Click. Click.

And she knew, even before she could formulate exactly the reasoning behind it, what she had to do.

She had to go after her file.

30

I T'S YOUR FAULT, YOU KNOW," Griffin said as he paced Majo's office.
The pacing had a short turnaround, since the room was not only shorter than Griffin's, but had multiple stacks of files on the floor in front of the bookshelves. These were all related to one major appeal that Majo had been dragged into recently by his firm's senior partner. "I do the research. He gets the glory," Majo had explained. Which also explained why Griffin had finally had to come here to find him tonight.

"Hm?" Majo said now.

He didn't look up. He hadn't finished reading the Tanaka report on Kilhenny, Malovet, and Bhoja which he had spread out before him on his desk atop the appeal file already open there.

"You made me go after someone crazy," Griffin said.

Majo finally raised his head. He looked like he hadn't slept in a day or two. "You're talking about Sharon Dekker?"

"I'm talking about Sharon Dekker."

"Va-va-voom Dekker."

"Brent tell you what happened?"

"He did."

"Well?" Griffin pushed.

"Maybe you two should have let her handle it."

Griffin stared at him. Were *all* his friends going crazy now? "You think I should have let her take on a sex addict professor by herself.

While I had the evidence I needed to hammer the guy."

"Sometimes people have to fight their own battles, Griff."

"Come *on*."

"She's just a high school friend, right?"

"She was in trouble. She's still maybe in trouble."

"So?"

Griffin stared hard enough at him that Majo sighed and waved a hand at all the files stacked in the bookshelves around his office. "All these people are in trouble. Talk to Brent or Lillian or Rotty—God, especially Rotty—about their files. Everyone in the world's in trouble. I thought you were one of the smart ones who made a career of helping people who were relatively okay. Just money goals and money issues. La-di-da."

"Screw you."

"Like you've been doing with Sharon? Is that what this is all about? You're sleeping with the woman so now you have to be there to wipe her nose every time she sniffles?"

"No!" Griffin exploded. "I have to be there because if anything happens to her, I—feel—pain!"

Majo looked calmly back at him. Griffin realized he'd planted his fingers on Majo's desk and was leaning over it like a rabid bulldog.

After a long, silent pause, Griffin took a deep breath and let his head hang. "Jesus, she's got me, hasn't she."

"By the short hairs."

"So what do I do?"

Majo snorted and stuck one finger up to rub a bloodshot eye. "You're asking me?"

"Yes!"

"Okay, okay. Phone her. Beg her forgiveness."

"Beg."

"And this?" Majo indicated Tanaka's report. "I assume it's a copy?"

Griffin nodded and straightened up.

"Okay," said Majo. "I'll pass the word. And...uh...let *me* talk to Lillian about your dropping Kilhenny et al. as clients, okay?"

Griffin nodded again and turned for the door. He was already working through what he was going to say to Sharon as he walked out.

"Keep it simple, Griff!" Majo called after him. "Don't be stiff!"

Unfortunately, Griffin thought with a rueful smirk, "stiff" was the one thing he could always count on being around Sharon Dekker. He punched the call button for the building's elevator.

Maybe it was time to change his approach.

~~~~

Sharon's cell phone dingled for the third time on her thirty-five minute bus ride to Jackson and Hastings. Her caller I.D. showed it was Griffin again so she didn't answer. Again.

She turned off her phone and leaned her head against the cold rumble of the window glass. It was stupid. She would have so loved to have Griffin there with her right now—his masculine smell, his strong shoulders, his sense of absolute confidence that anything could be resolved with a little application of intelligence and tact.

But not everything could. And if it couldn't, well, she doubted Griffin would be able to handle the Sharon that was going to emerge on this night.

All those rotting, graffiti-covered buildings sliding past...

Yes, she could feel herself fitting in here again. It wasn't that different from Kelowna. She was a little older, a little cleaner. But she could feel the same sense of hopelessness in the air, flowing through her. The anger and malice. The venality in general. Really the street was all about the weak against the weaker—that's what she would have told Tighe if she were in his class right now.

The bus stopped and Sharon swung herself up to her feet. She clomped off and jumped to the curb in her hiking boots. Zipping up her fleece over her turtleneck, she looked around to get her bearings, then she headed east and a block north to Cordova. Two buildings up on the south side was the hole where Micky had taken her just over two weeks ago. To see the place she and Angel and Rose called "home." To ask whether Sharon could truly help them.

The doorway was lit only by the nearby street lamps. The outside light had burned out. That was good. It made it less obvious when she paused and considered the lock on the old lever-style front door handle.

Taking a chance, Sharon just squeezed the handle down, jiggled it a bit, and gave the door a good shove with her shoulder.

It opened.

She stopped and listened.

There were the usual spooky creaks and groans of an old building. The place was heated by hot water, Micky had told her. Every time the heat kicked on, it sounded like a legion of the dead were banging around in the walls. Sharon wrinkled back her nose as the old urine smell hit her too. The dead were probably just trying to escape the smell.

Footsteps. Muffled voices. Banging that sounded like someone at a door.

It was early enough that most of the street-lifers would still be outside. But unless Rose's injuries had been some phenomenal act on her part, she, at least, would be at home.

And Sharon only needed one girl to tell her where the file was.

Sharon went to grab the handrail, decided against it when she thought of the other hands that had done so, and walked up the stairs as quietly as she could tiptoe in her boots.

She passed one man on the way. He was bustling and muttering so loudly to himself that Sharon doubted he even saw her.

Then she was up, down the hall. No mistaking the door. Micky had sniggered over the crude giant phallus someone had scratched into it. She thought Jamie had probably done it.

And if Jamie were in there now?

Well, she had her pepper spray and she'd already had some experience using it, so she knew it worked. With that thought, she reached back to her fanny pack, unzipped it, and pulled out the pepper spray. The slim bullet-shaped can felt good in her hands.

Then Sharon quietly turned the knob of the unlocked door and stepped inside.

~~~~

It hit Sharon all at once. The same dirty floor with plates and food strewn about. The same four filthy bed sets that must have given the room its sour smell.

Even the emaciated girl in the bed by the window was the same. Rose. Mousy brown hair, bad color.

Only this time, Rose had bandages and gauze pads all over her chin and on her arms and legs. And the plates on the floor were china, not paper. They were Sharon's plates. Smeared with leftovers of Sharon's food that had been cooked in Sharon's microwave oven, now sitting on the floor in the right-hand corner.

On a chair by the window, with an extension cord that had probably also come from Sharon's apartment, sat Sharon's television.

Micky stood between it and Rose, fiddling with it, banging it, trying to clear up the static.

"Micky," Rose hissed.

The short woman spun around, saw Sharon, and her heavily made-up face went into a grinning spasm while her eyes darted back and forth, finally resting their gaze on Sharon's hand holding the can of pepper spray.

"Oh, fuck," Micky said and rushed over to the foot of Jamie's bed to fumble in a clatter of plates and cutlery left there. She came up with a steak knife, an orphan from Sharon's hodge-podge collection, and waved it at Sharon.

"Stay back," she said.

"Give it a rest, Micky," Sharon said, taking one pointed step forward. A second one. "I'm not going to attack you." She jabbed a finger at the TV, the microwave, the dishes. "You know, these don't do you any good here. You know why? Because *you* are still here."

Micky worked her mouth around, shooting glances at Rose.

"And as long as you and Rose and Angel stay here,"—another step—"your lives are shit, your futures are shit, and when you end up beaten to death or O.D.'d somewhere, you'll be tossed out with the trash."

She was suddenly at Micky, holding her pepper spray can up to Micky's left hand side. As the woman's eyes shot that way, Sharon grabbed her hand with the knife and wrenched it down, twisting with all her anger.

Micky cried out and dropped the knife. Sharon kicked it away and shoved the smaller woman over towards the bed where Rose cowered.

"Owww. You broke my fucking wrist!" Micky wailed.

Sharon stepped over in front of her. "Shut up!" Micky did. "Now look," said Sharon, her whole body tensed. "I don't care about the TV or the microwave or clothes. But I care that you two did more than just grab some things and run. You *scoured* my place. It was a set up, wasn't it?"

Micky was breathing hard and trying to look anywhere but into Sharon's eyes. Rose saw it and was shaking her head back and forth. "C'mon, Micky," she whined. "We don't have to listen to nothing she says. We don't—"

Sharon shot out a hand and caught Rose around the jaw, making her squeak. "All the bruises and scrapes. Did Jamie really do them or was that all a lie too?"

"F-fuck you." Rose burst into tears.

It made Micky come back. "Wasn't Jamie," she said, not looking at Sharon. "It was one of my regulars, a guy who hates you. Wanted Rose to be you. Would have killed Rose if Jamie hadn't a come."

That rocked Sharon back. "What?"

"It was *his* idea we use it, okay? He said you had a thing you'd stolen from him. He wanted it back. Said he'd pay Jamie all this money."

Sharon felt that old familiar feeling of ice burn down through her veins. "The file," she whispered.

"The thing under the rug. Yeah."

"And this 'regular' who wanted it...." Sharon said.

Two sets of footsteps clumped to a stop behind her. A familiar, smooth voice she was most used to hearing in a Simon Fraser lecture hall said, "He was thinking you wouldn't be here for at least another hour or two. But then, you have shown a tendency to be early for appointments recently, haven't you."

Sharon turned with a bone-aching slowness to see Professor Colm Tighe standing in the doorway. Beside him was the girls' pimp, Jamie Bhoja.

31

STRANGELY, Bhoja, even dressed in the same tee-shirt and cheap sports jacket he'd worn that last frightening time, almost didn't register with Sharon. Not with Tighe there, a man capable of thrashing a fourteen-year-old as a sick substitute for Sharon.

Her former professor held up the file of Sharon's admissions papers, then tossed it forward so it fluttered apart, the papers drifting separately to the floor.

"This time I made copies," Tighe said. "Enough to paper the entire university, if I need to."

"Very mature," Sharon muttered.

"What did you say?" Tighe's face turned a sudden crimson and he strode forward with his hand raised.

Sharon scrambled backwards and whipped up her pepper spray can, aiming it at his eyes.

He jerked to a halt and his face twisted in an ugly red smile of hate. "Oh yes. And do you have your backup troops ready to burst in too?"

He said it lightly but twitched his head around to the door. Then back to her. "You don't, do you? Not this time. Because they wouldn't come? No. Because you didn't tell them. Yes. Do you know how predictable you are? How very easy to manipulate?"

He'd moved in close enough to her that she could see the dilation of his pupils. She tightened her finger on the pepper spray button and he stopped. His eyes flicked sideways towards Micky.

"Slut," he said, "please get me a knife or something to attack this girl with."

Sharon held her breath, scared to look away from Tighe for a second. Or from Bhoja, watching with casual menace back by the door.

"No," said Micky.

"*What?*" said Tighe and turned to her with his lips pulling back.

"You're just a trick," Micky said with a scratchy voice and ran a hand shakily over Rose's bruised forehead. "You don't own me. Bastard."

Tighe took a half step that way, then, seeing Sharon tightening her hand on the mace can, reconsidered. "You're right," he said smoothly. "*I* don't own you. But Jamie does."

Then he gestured. The greasy pimp shook back his long black hair and began to walk with his sideways gait towards Micky and Rose on the bed.

Sharon shuffled quickly sideways so she stood in front of Micky and Rose now, pointing the pepper spray can first at Bhoja, then at Tighe. Her breath was high and quick. Any second now. Any second.

But Bhoja had already stopped, shrugging and smiling. There was something cold behind his smile, something hidden, but no immediate threat. She turned her full attention back to Tighe.

Tighe laughed, an ugly sound. "You've got nowhere to go, *Breeze*. Your secret's out. Your pathetic little dream of a normal life here is done. Face it. You're back to being a cowed little whore who knows it's better to give in and live, than fight and get beaten."

It was true, Sharon thought, all true. And it ran that river of ice through her veins. But as she glared back at Tighe, she realized something else was true. The pact she'd made with herself when she left the street five years ago still held and it was time to prove it.

She was never going to "give in" again.

"*You*, 'Professor' Tighe,'" she said slowly, "are a pathetic joke of a man who's spent his whole life puffing up his academic pretensions to hide the fact he's got a tiny penis. You want me to cite the *DSM-IV-TR* pages that cover your condition?"

Tighe's face went pale and he lunged towards her only to drop back screaming as she blasted him in the eyes with the pepper spray.

"Self-defense, in case you're wondering, Professor!" Sharon shouted at him, dancing forward like she was going to kick him, her adrenaline pumping full bore. "Now why don't you go find a washroom for your sorry ass!"

"Yeah!" shouted Micky, though Rose was still trying to hide.

Sharon's words seemed to reach Tighe, his eyes squeezed-shut, the skin around them bright red, because he stopped his desperate grunting just long enough to site on the door. Then he ran for it and disappeared.

Sharon swung the can towards Jamie Bhoja.

The dark-skinned pimp hadn't moved. He just smiled at her, the goatee and black burn mark on his upper lip making it look obscene. His eyes glittered.

"I think my girls might like to go to work now outside," he said in his disconcertingly girlish whisper.

Sharon felt both girls strain behind her but neither got up from the bed.

"With a little nanoo to make it easier?" Bhoja said and tugged a small baggy of brownish powder out of his inside jacket pocket.

Rose was out of her covers and almost falling on her face as she crawled over her bed, tearing her arm away from Micky's grasp. Then Micky was after her, catching her off the bed, finding her some clothes and helping her pull her pants and long-sleeve stretch top on over her bandages and bruises, while Bhoja just smiled at Sharon and Sharon trembled inside for the two women.

"Micky!" she called to the older of the pair as she grabbed a lighter and spoon and scrambled about on her knees by the bed for a syringe to use with Bhoja's little baggy.

Micky stopped and turned, the eyes looking out from the thick eyeliner torn between despair and eagerness. Then her fingers found a used hypodermic and she scrambled to her feet and out the door, grabbing the baggy and Rose as she went.

"I haven't given up on you!" Sharon called after them.

And they were gone. There's was just her and Bhoja.

He stood silently staring at her, Sharon still holding up the pepper spray can until her right forearm began to ache. "So?" she said.

"You are more pretty than I remembered," he said and touched the bridge of his nose.

Sharon resisted the urge to reach up and touch the scar that Daryl had given her there the day he'd finally lost control. The turning point.

Her right arm was starting to tremble with the strain of holding the pepper spray can so tensely for so long. She lowered it quickly, transferred it to her left hand and shook out her right.

"For a whore," Bhoja qualified his last statement. "A whore under a man like Daryl Polson."

She couldn't stop the involuntary jerk as her gaze flew to the admissions papers still scattered on the ground between them. She'd never written Daryl's name anywhere. How had he known? Or had he guessed? Was Daryl some kind of big shot pimp in Kelowna now?

Bhoja tongued the black burn mark on his lip and smiled again. "You know I get into this deal with the Red Owl because of you, because I know about you and I tell the bikers I can keep watch on you. I can tell them what you are doing to try to take the Red Owl away.

"Then I meet the boss of the Bad Machine Motorcycle Club. From Kelowna. Daryl Polson. This guy, he is going to be the one to actually run the Red Owl. He finds out I run girls and don't want to lose them, yes? And he says he never lost a girl except this once. This *one time*. A girl who would not do drugs. A girl who always fought when he fucked her. She got to be crazy, yes? Because he's really strong. And she got away! Years ago!"

Bhoja paused in his breathy little speech, stared hard into Sharon's eyes, and touched the bridge of his nose again.

"You know what the name of this *one girl* was?"

He reached the toe of his dirty running shoe to the closest of the admissions papers and gave it a little shove, drawing out the moment for her benefit, looking to see the trembling that was in fact threatening to overwhelm Sharon at any second.

"Sharon Neal."

Sharon took a big breath and wished she could solve this by striding forward and spraying pepper spray into this slime's eyes, his nose, his mouth. She remembered his grip as being strong like iron the last time. But the last time she'd been scared and had so much to lose.

Now what was there? The whole city could know who she was come morning. Certainly the university and Griffin and Griffin's friends. The people who mattered.

And Daryl-the-Dink?

"Who have you told?" she said. "Tighe?"

Bhoja shook his head. "He does not know Polson."

Sharon thought about that, standing there in that sour-smelling room with her stolen appliances, clothes, and dishes scattered around like they (and she?) belonged here.

"What do you want?" said.

"I tell you what," Bhoja said in his breathy little voice. "Other than you trying to steal my girls, I got nothing against you. You back off, save some *other* girls, I could maybe help you. I say nothing to Polson. I get rid of these." He bent down and sidled around quickly, sweeping up the scattered papers of Sharon's admission file. "And we hurry, I get you the others. I know where Tighe parked his car with all the photocopies. Then no one knows Breeze or Sharon Neal any more."

Sharon's heart had begun racing as he spoke with a heady spurt of hope. All the papers gone, her secret only with people no one would believe. Except Daryl. But if Bhoja would, actually, shut up and not talk to Daryl, and maybe he was making it up about even meeting Daryl, then maybe....

You back off. Meaning abandon Micky, Angel, and Rose like most of the world had abandoned Sharon for four years.

The hope in her heart died away. She couldn't do that. She couldn't abandon them. Not and live with herself afterwards.

Bhoja must have seen it on her face. Maybe he'd even been expecting it. He waved the gathered sheaf of papers back and forth under his chin.

"There is another way," he said.

She probably looked like a fish gasping for air as her chin jerked higher. "What?"

"My girls, they're not going to leave me. They are too addicted. But you are not. And...to have the one Daryl Polson could not, just once, no fighting. That would be worth it to me."

His tongue was licking at his burn mark again and again. His eyes were somehow not as sure and cocky when he looked her over. Even his bony hands, so still and confident before, were twitching beside his skinny legs. He...wanted her? He did. But....

"You do not know if you can trust me, yes?" He stepped back into the hall and listened. She listened with him and heard banging and splashing sounds. Tighe! "Come."

Still clutching her pepper spray, she followed behind him, running to keep up as he went thumping down the stairs. With a limp, she realized. That sideways gait of his. At the bottom, still carrying the gathered papers of Sharon's file, he ran outside and ducked left. Sharon kept her distance as she followed.

Almost a block back, pulled into what looked like an abandoned lumber store's back parking, was Tighe's silver Acura Legend, the old-fashioned car phone antenna rising from the back.

Jamie Bhoja was looking around, then bent down and came up with a rock twice the size of his hand. With one heavy swing, he cracked the passenger side glass. Four more blows knocked enough out that he could reach in and open then door, then pop the trunk.

Sharon looked nervously around but no one seemed to be coming. She hurried to the trunk as Bhoja pulled out what looked like fifty clipped stacks of her admissions file. He put the original stack on top of them, then turned and handed the whole package to her.

"All yours," he said, like a suitor handing her a bouquet of flowers.

She could smell him. His unwashed stink. His craven meanness. What kind of failure, she thought not for the first time, lives off renting out women to other men just as desperate?

And what kind of women gives in to him.

"We have to get back, yes? Before Tighe comes. I will show you where you can hide these, burn them later."

Solicitous. The anxious lover.

Sharon was growing sicker by the second as he turned from her and began jogging back, but turned a corner in the middle of the alley. When she caught up, he pointed to a dumpster and helped her lift the lid, dump in the copies of her handwritten past.

Then he reached out a hand to her, there by the giant garbage can. "We will go to a different room I know," he said. "Where Tighe will not know."

Where the world wouldn't know?

Where he could do anything to her and she would let him because it would be the last time? The very last?

She gave him her hand. Bhoja grabbed it with his bony fingers that were suddenly vise-like. His smile was hard and glittering as he said, "Come."

32

MONDAY AFTERNOON, driving down from Simon Fraser campus atop Burnaby Mountain, Griffin tried Sharon's phone number again. And, like the previous twenty times or so he'd tried over the last few days, he got her voice mail. "The person you are trying to reach is currently unavai–"

He hung up. Trees flashing by on either side.

Sharon hadn't been into work since Thursday, when she'd left early. She hadn't attended her Friday classes and hadn't shown up for classes today.

Of course Colm Tighe wasn't in today either. He hadn't announced his resignation like he'd promised. He'd apparently just called and cancelled his classes.

All of which was rapidly confirming Majo's assessment of Griffin's and Brent's work last Thursday—a mistake. It might have gotten Tighe off the radar, but it had vanished Sharon, too. She'd gone into a depression, obviously, or some kind of major snit where she just cut everyone off and tried to figure out her next move.

Or had she done none of that? The woman was so complicated sometimes it made his head spin. She could be in her apartment right now, just a few blocks from the bottom of this parkway, or she could have moved out of the province.

Which would kill you.

Yes.

So?

Damn it all anyway. He jumped on the brakes and did a squealing turn onto Duthie. A minute later he was parked in front of her building and punching the call button on the outside phone. No response. An old woman pushed by him with her groceries and Griffin followed her in. And up the elevator, the old woman staring at him suspiciously.

"Who do you know in this building?" she said, but he reached sixteen and slid off with a smile and wave.

At Sharon's door, he knocked lightly, then loudly. Put his ear to the door and listened. Heard nothing. Knocked again and called her name.

The door down the hall to his left opened up and a kid of five or six ran out, made a face, and ran back in as a woman, obviously his mother, plump and a little frazzled, stepped out and looked at Griffin.

"Are you a friend of Sharon?" she said.

"Yes. Is she–? Has she been home much lately?"

"I don't think so. She left her computer with me on Thursday and hasn't come back for it."

Fifteen minutes later, Griffin finally convinced the building superintendent to let him into Sharon's apartment. One look around and his heart sank.

She'd moved out. For some reason she'd left the odd knick-knack, but everything else including the cat and the cat's kitty dish, was gone. And the computer?

"It's very old," the neighbor Griffin now knew as Clara Dewdney said. "None of my kids' games would run on it."

"No forwarding address," grumped the super, wiping his nose.

Griffin nodded at Clara, nodded at the superintendent. "Let's not jump to conclusions here," he said.

But already his logical mind inside was rapidly constructing a scenario to patch over the hurt. She'd been harassed by Tighe maybe far more than she'd said. She'd finally concocted a plan to deal with him. Griffin and Brent had interrupted, killing her plan, maybe somehow making it worse. And Sharon, crazy when he first kissed her, prone to emotional outbursts, unwilling to talk about her past or anything that would give her connecting threads to follow, just takes off. Just like she did from high school.

Like a...breeze.

Was that why she'd chosen that name for a time?

"So do I keep the computer or can I sell it?" said Clara Dewdney.

"A few more days, at least," said Griffin evenly. "Is that okay?"

But he walked away before she'd even given her answer.

~~~~

Tuesday it rained.

Griffin tied up the last Cross-Shiptite problem and sent them a revised bill.

He considered and rejected for the fortieth time the idea of hiring Ken Tanaka to find Sharon. If she really ran away that easily from things, he'd have to commit to chasing her for the rest of his life. It made no sense.

Majo called and invited him to drinks. He declined.

~~~~

Wednesday it rained harder. Forecasters still kept their fingers crossed for a dry Halloween in another week.

Burt Lester personally came down to hand him the file on the son of his brother's second wife. The boy had set up a small import-export business dealing with Hong Kong and had just landed his first big import, a toy that was all the rage in Mainland China. He needed help negotiating with five investors who wanted in.

"Family," Lester said with a wink. "No padding this bill."

~~~~

Thursday the rain stopped. The sun came out sporadically.

Majo called again for drinks. Griffin turned him down again.

"The Hard Riders I know claim ignorance of any attempt to buy the Red Owl," Majo said. "But they've heard of Daryl Polson's group. Heard he's been run out of Kelowna completely. They're waiting to see where he turns up."

"I don't care," Griffin said and hung up.

~~~~

Friday. Rain again.

Griffin stared out at the drizzle, bothered that all he could see was what Sharon's face looked like with mist and raindrops lining her nose. Smiling lips. Sad eyes. All he could smell was that mango body lotion she liked to use sometimes. And that peachy kind of shampoo she'd started when the gelling stopped.

His hands, if he held them out in front of him and closed his eyes, could remember what her hands felt like. And her hips, both clothed and naked. Her belly, her breasts...

"Griffin?" said Jocasta's voice.

He popped open his eyes and spun around. "Yes?"

"You were going to see Burt Lester's nephew at two," Jocasta said.

"I was. I am. You have the file?"

She handed it to him with smug little smile, he bowed his head to her, took it, grabbed his suit jacket, and walked out the door.

Remembering he hadn't eaten lunch, Griffin grabbed some takeout pasta salad from the eatery in the lobby, and only discovered once he was in his car and driving out with the salad balanced on his lap that the thing was loaded with oregano and garlic.

He ate it anyway and made it to Lester's nephew's place down on 41st Ave. by 2:20.

Wallace Lester jerked up his head in surprise when Griffin entered but when Griffin introduced himself, Wallace ushered him in with such enthusiasm that Griffin found himself smiling for the first time in days.

"Happy Flap?" Griffin asked, indicating the row of identical, anime-styled clowns. They sat in delirious lime green, candy purple, and florescent orange. Their hats were so large they fell to one side on the shelf and threatened to take their clowns with them.

"They're gaudy, right? But kids go crazy, absolutely crazy!"

"Just for these?"

"Uh-unh. Check out the back room while I go upstairs and dig out all the offers. Sorry. It'll take me a bit. For some reason I thought you were coming by next week."

"Take your time," Griffin said. What else did Griffin have these days but time?

Smiling morosely, he wandered around the front counter and into the back storage room.

There he couldn't help but goggle at the enormous array of Happy Flap merchandise stacked neatly in boxes on the floor and on shelves running along the walls of the room. More shelves ran floor-to-ceiling to the right as he came in. Under the long banks of florescent lights, the gaudy green/purple/orange combo screamed from everything— noisemakers, hats, kickballs, plastic underwater gear, remote control cars and submarines....

Griffin had just wandered to the end of the first row and picked up a Happy Flap propeller beanie in a sealed plastic bag, when the door through which he'd entered the storeroom suddenly closed with a thunk and locking sound.

He turned quickly. Her. Wearing an ankle-length cloth coat, she leaned back against the shut door and looked at him from under lowered lids.

"Sharon," he whispered.

Her face looked darker somehow, changed, but even with all the questions racing through his mind, he was almost instantly distracted as she shrugged off her coat and let it fall. Underneath it she'd worn little more than hotpants and a cut-off black tee-shirt, with apparently no bra beneath.

Now she lifted her left hand, drawing it up her body and way over her head until it pressed back against the door at full extension. The motion exposed her full midriff and the bottom of a bare breast. Every curve of her body popped at him.

What was she doing? Did she think she could vanish for a week, make him think she was gone forever, then just show up and expect him to pant after her like some horny teenager?

Yes, panted his voice inside as his little head below bobbed and nodded and swelled in agreement.

"Hello, Griffin," she purred. "That beanie would look good on you. You could put it on any time you had to meet a big client. They'd come in. You'd reach up and give it a little spin."

She demonstrated with her free hand, squeezing her breasts together as she reached up. Griffin swore he could feel a few more liters of blood rush away from his head to help pound out his growing erection.

"How did you find me?" he said.

"I called your office. Your assistant helped me out."

Griffin frowned. "She told you exactly where I was?"

"I think she knew you missed me."

"Missed you...."

She arched her back towards him, forcing his gaze to the bumps of her erect nipples through cotton. "Didn't you?"

This was foolish. Griffin shook his head angrily at her lack of apology. How could she treat him like some kind of game? Was that all her university education had been to her too? And her plans to help those prostitutes? Damn it, Griffin had been ready to take a very foolish step with this woman, *invest* in her emotionally because he thought he'd seen depth! Had he been totally blinded by the sex?

"We need to *talk*," he said.

"Sure," she said. "But wouldn't you rather do that with your sausage warm in a bun? Hm?" She licked her lips and looked pointedly at the bulge in his pants.

"No."

"Are you sure?"

She eased off the door and walked toward him, sliding her hand suggestively along the side of the inventory shelves as she came. He could feel her emotional heat coming at him like blast furnace, trying to burn up his defenses, burn up his intellect and reason.

She reached him and slid her arms softly around his neck, so that the sweet mango smell of her filled him and made him want to forget everything that had happened...to forget...

"No," he said. He reached up to take her hands away.

But she locked her fingers together behind his neck. "Yes," she said and bit her lips together, a whole other emotional field leaping across her face.

"Sharon, whatever it is, you know you can talk to—"

"I don't want to talk!" she said fiercely. "I want to fuck! Now!"

It shook him. "That's not—"

"Oh, shut up, Griffin. Just fuck me! Fuck me now! Right here! No words! You fuck me now or you won't see me again for a very long time."

33

HER EYES WERE STARTING TO FILL but Griffin knew she wasn't backing off. That core of steel he'd felt in her at times was blazing hot. What she said, she meant.

And while his reflexive self said, *Great! Toss her out just like she was ready to toss you.* That part of him that had just started to blossom with her before she'd vanished came struggling back and shut his mouth.

Instead, he reached for the bottom of her tee-shirt and raised it up. He paused while Sharon, breathing hard, released her hold on his neck. Then he whipped her shirt up over her head and off her long skinny arms.

He barely had time to drink in her bare breasts before her fingers were at his suit jacket, tearing it off him as his arms came down. She tugged it free and threw with almost feral disregard at one of the boxes by the wall shelves. Then she was at the tie on his neck, tugging and pulling at the knot until her fingers whipped it free. Griffin saw her eyes blaze in triumph as she threw it away, attacked his buttons.

Helpless to stop now, Griffin grabbed her hips and pulled her bare belly in against his groin. He ground himself against her even as she reached the bottom of his shirt and tugged it free of his pants.

"I'll do it," he said, and stepped back.

He undid his cuffs and tore off his shirt, tossing it after his shirt, with just a slight twinge over whether it and the suit had landed on any oil or grease spots.

Then Sharon, who'd torn off her own shorts and panties so she wore just her black running shoes, came at him again.

Like a wild dog. A bitch in heat. She'd been the aggressor in their love making before, but only when he'd asked, and then with a vacant look in her eyes that said she was only half there.

Now, as she attacked his belt and pants, he could feel how present she was, how aroused and needy. It was like she wanted to rip him apart, ravage his skin, suck out his marrow, climb into his being.

As she unclothed him and grabbed his hard cock, engulfed it with her mouth, Griffin's knees went weak and he had to reach for the wall shelves to steady himself. His hand landed on a box of Happy Flap cars instead and sent them crashing to the ground. With his pants still tangled around his feet, Griffin stumbled off-balance and jerked out of Sharon's mouth with a sucking pop. He crashed down on top of the cars, hearing crunches and not caring. Because Sharon was rocking on her knees, watching him, mouth wide in silent laughter.

Griffin grabbed his wingtips and tugged them off. Then his pants. Then, naked and raging with both lust and anger at her for leaving him, Griffin did his own imitation of a raging bull as he stomped to Sharon, grabbed her under her armpits, and lifted her bodily off the floor and back to the far wall.

"You want me to fuck you?" he said hoarsely, pinning her there.

"Yes. Fuck me. Fuck me so hard that I know I'm yours. *Fuck* me."

The words barely registered. Only the nod, the assent.

He reached down with his left hand to find his raging center, then, with his right hand, *her* center, hot and wet. It opened as she stood on her tiptoes, spread her knees, and thrust her middle towards him. Her ran his fingers roughly around the slick lips of her, thrust them in and out, making her shudder, then ran the head of his cock in the same pattern, around and around. Finally...*in.*

She shrieked.

He didn't stop.

~~~~

Oh God, it was like being impaled.

And she wanted more.

Sharon wished his cock could ram right up through her, through her chest, through her heart, through her head. So she wouldn't have to feel any more. So she wouldn't have to remember who she was and what she'd done. So she could just *be*.

With him? a little voice asked deep inside her chest.

Only, said another little voice, that she suspected was her. And for a second she worried she'd said the blasphemy out loud.

Then Griffin was pulling down out of her, lancing shocks of sweet sensation up through her, goosepimpling her flesh, making her nipples ache. And *into* her again, the motion building like a steam engine. He went faster and faster until her whole body was shuddering.

Oh God, all of him. Her fingers clutched and racked over his back. Her hands found the sides of his head to do something she'd never once done with any of the johns she'd had the four years she'd spent on the street. She grabbed the sides of his head, slick with sweat already, and forced him to look at her, right in the eyes.

See me, she wanted to shout. *I'm actually here now. All of me. See all of me.*

And despite the glaze she saw in his eyes, she chose to believe they did see, and she craned her lips forward to his, trying to tell him with her lips what this meant. What all this fucking, all her anxiety and hysterical behavior around him—what it really meant. That she was his. That all he had to do was say the word and she'd give up everything. She'd give up her fears, her hangups, her driving needs, everything.

All she needed was a word.

What he gave her, as she pulled back, dragging her tongue along the roof of his mouth—oregano, garlic—around his lips, and free, was a grunt.

He was building inside her, his hips bucking faster and faster. She could feel the swell of him and tried to picture it filling her completely, wishing insanely for a second that she wasn't on birth control even as she imagined the agony of finding she was pregnant with Griffin's child and Griffin gone from her life.

Then he thrust deep into her, clenched tightly, and exploded.

~~~~

Griffin's orgasm turned every muscle in his body to steel, clenched and shaking. He felt his sinews would burst, his head explode.

But it was his middle doing that, and it seemed to suck everything with it. His vital force rushing from him into her, the socket he'd pinned to the wall, a connection to the *world*.

It went on, softened, clenched again, softened, again.

Finally his steel became just muscle again, quaking and ready to collapse.

He pulled out of her, staggered back and stared at her. She collapsed down from her tiptoes, but remained splayed against the wall, arms spread back, head tilted up to the right, eyes closed.

Holy..., he found himself thinking again, in multiple senses of the word. Time was still.

Then he became aware of a banging from somewhere. Banging on a door? He turned around, blinking. The storeroom door. Wallace. His voice coming in, muffled. "Mr. Walsh? Griffin? Are you okay? Is there someone in there with you? What's going on? Are you hurt?"

Griffin turned back to Sharon with a confused half-smile and saw her watching him. Her face was stripped of its earlier seduction or lust or despair. Now her eyes just tried to hold his in a kind of needful lock.

"We need to get dressed," he said.

She nodded, and they both did, her faster than him because she had so much less to put on. There was a fumbling sound of a key in a lock just as he finished, sweaty but done. Even his tie knotted.

Wallace came bursting through the door, tripped over Sharon's coat, then stopped as he saw Griffin, Sharon standing behind him, the scattered and crushed Happy Flap merchandise on the floor all around.

Griffin indicated the mess. "Sorry about this, Wallace. Something... unexpected happened."

Wallace's gaze shot from the mess, to Griffin's sweaty face, to the equally flushed face of Sharon behind him. "No shit," he said slowly.

"Excuse us," said Griffin, taking Sharon's hand and pushing past him, scooping Sharon's coat as he went. "We're going to have to go over the business stuff another day."

As he and Sharon cleared the front door, he heard Wallace say, "I *knew* the meeting was supposed to be next week."

~~~~

Sitting in the close leather confines of Griffin's car, the doors closed, engine off, Griffin could feel Sharon's dread. Over *what*?

"Explain," he said without preamble.

Sharon nodded. She sat simply, like a young girl, her face bowed, her hands crossed loosely in her lap. She'd donned her coat again, which was good. Griffin wasn't sure he would have been able to concentrate if she hadn't.

"I was hiding out," she said.

"From me?"

She shook her head. Stopped mid-shake. "Not completely. But I couldn't tell you where I was. I didn't know if you were still...if you were working with the group from Kelowna."

Griffin shook his head. "Tanaka's investigation showed they were another biker gang, like the ones here that were trying to buy the Red Owl. I dropped them as clients and alerted the police and real estate people about them. It doesn't mean they can't buy the Red Owl now, but they'll have to try to do it under a different name."

Sharon looked at him and chewed her lips. "Oh."

"Was that who you were hiding from?" Griffin pressed. "Was it something to do with the time you spent in Kelowna?"

She nodded, chewed her lips some more, then looked out the window. "I'm amazed you haven't heard. Tighe...?"

"He hasn't shown up since last Thursday. No one's heard from him."

"Ah." Sharon gave a painful little huff. She turned to him and her face screwed up in despair. Fought it. She finally said, "It's going to come out sooner or later. It has to."

"What?"

"My past."

"In Kelowna? When you lived on the street?"

She tore her face away, tears starting to come even though she was gritting her teeth angrily against them. "When I left you last Thursday, I got a call from one of the prostitutes I've been trying to help...."

And she told him, in halts and rushes, of everything that had happened that night, right up until the point that Tighe had run out of the room screaming and Micky and Rose had followed.

"But this 'admissions file' they stole from you," Griffin said when her voice seemed to choke and stop. "What did it have in it that was so deadly?"

"Oh God." Sharon was staring up at the low-sloped ceiling of the car. Tears poured out of her eyes now, and Griffin wished he could just hold her and wipe them away. But he had to know.

"*What?*"

~~~~

Sharon swallowed and took a deep breath. She had to tell. It was bursting inside her. It was bursting inside *him*, in a way. She could hear it in his voice. If she didn't tell, she might as well not have come back to him.

If she didn't tell, he couldn't know her.

And when he found out from somewhere else...

But she wouldn't even be in his life by then, would she? Because there would have been no trust, no chance for anything beyond fucking. Nothing real.

She had to tell.

She swallowed once more and turned towards him...

34

W HEN TIGHE WAS GONE," Sharon said as if she was answering, "Bhoja took me out to Tighe's car. We broke into it, took out all the copies he'd made, and stashed them in a nearby dumpster. I went back later and got them. Burned them."

"But then...." Griffin was confused. She'd said earlier that it was the file that was so damning. Now it was gone. Why had Sharon gone into hiding?

"Before we stole back the file," Sharon said, "Bhoja also told me he knew the leader of the Kelowna motorcycle gang, the ones who were going to come and run the Red Owl."

Griffin frowned. "David? No, Daryl something."

"Daryl Polson. He was just a pimp six years ago. A mean, dangerous, vindictive pimp who'd love to find out that my name is now Sharon Dekker and I'm living in Vancouver."

"Because?"

Sharon's eyes looked out the windows, down at her lap, anywhere but at Griffin. She swiped at her eyes. "I...lived with him. For a time."

Griffin could feel the tension creeping in across his shoulders, tickling the back of his neck like a danger signal, warning him to stop. But he couldn't stop.

"How long?" he said.

"Four years."

"Four...years." He tried to imagining her, a runaway from home, all of what? Seventeen? "And you must have seen...during that time..."

"Yes."

"You did drugs."

She stuck out her lower lip. "Never!"

Griffin felt a mini-shock of relief at that, but it vanished the instant he really heard what she was saying. "Four years, living with a pimp," he said slowly, carefully. "Do you want to tell me what you were doing during that time?"

She found his eyes and he saw her own were filling again, though she was blinking hard to clear them. "You know," she said.

But he didn't know. His mind wouldn't accept it. It had to be spelled out clearly. "You were a prostitute."

"Yes."

"You walked the streets?"

"Yes."

"Got into cars with men. Sucked them off. Or let them feel you up and...fuck you."

"Yes."

The tears were flowing rapidly down her face now but she wasn't looking away from him. Griffin could hardly see her, though. The world was becoming a big buzzing gray thing he had to push through to stay focused. Get it *clear*.

"Every night? 24/7?"

"We had Monday nights off. Monday nights were slow nights. And when we were really sick."

"Did you...make a lot of money?"

"For Daryl? Yeah. I was good. You know that. You've seen that. Don't you think I'm good?"

"You're very good." It was punch in own gut as Griffin flashed through all the times she'd been with him, every move she'd made, ever moan, every trick that had driven him crazy. Even that distance in her eyes sometimes. Like he could have been this Daryl Polson, or the legion of faceless men cruising the streets and choosing *her* panties to crawl into—Colm Tighe, for example. Was that how she had been going to shut him up?

Or...or even...

"Jamal Bhoja," Griffin blurted. "He helped you. Why?"

She said nothing.

"Because you paid him, didn't you? With the one thing you have that you've always been very good at?"

"He...offered to help me if I had sex with him. Yes."

"And *did* you?" Griffin's heart was racing now. The gray buzz had turned red. He couldn't sit still. "No! Don't answer that! Don't!"

He needed air. He burst out through his driver's side door and stood gasping in the rain that was coming down harder now. He moved his arms back and forth, wider and wider, trying to catch his breath.

The passenger-side door opened and thunked shut. He turned to see Sharon looking at him across the top of the car, her face as stricken as it had been in that photograph of her and Tighe. But now he knew why. He knew *why*.

"So why do you think Polson's after you now?" he snapped at her.

"I think Bhoja would have told him where to find me after I refused to...give him what he wanted."

"Refused. Right. Protecting your *honor*, right? And he just let you walk away."

"I pepper-sprayed him. He ran away. Screaming."

Griffin looked at her through the rain, his mouth open in a grimace, wanting to believe her, hang onto this much at least. As if it made some kind of difference.

"And Polson *beat* me into working for him, Griffin," Sharon said. "You can't know what it's like. You...you with your family wanting you to succeed. Even as an 'accident' they wanted you. Mine didn't. My dad, my natural dad? He walked out on us when I was ten years old. Just left. My mother said it was because he was too tired of all the responsibility. Meaning me!"

"Stop," Griffin said.

She shook her head. "So my mother tried just ignoring me, maybe figuring if she pretended I wasn't there, then I wouldn't be and some new guy would come and save her from working her ass off in the Safeway. And he did. My stepdad. Which is when you mostly knew me, right? High school?"

"We all have our challenges," Griffin said coldly, hating himself for it, but needing something, anything hard to hold onto.

It made her bust out in a choke of tears but she slapped the top of the car and brought herself back. "Yeah? Well my 'challenge' in high school was the fact my mom got leukemia and died. And my stepdad figured that maybe I was a good replacement for her after she'd gone."

She stopped there for a minute, quivering. Griffin couldn't say anything. What was there to say? He'd known even in high school that they couldn't fit. That they were from two different worlds. He just hadn't known *how* different.

"Hello?" she said.

Griffin said nothing.

"So that's it?" she said. She wiped back the rain from her forehead, slicking back her short hair.

Griffin's tongue was stuck, his jaw locked.

"All the beatings Daryl gave me, the one that finally ripped open my nose here and made me get help, get out, finish my high school and go to university. They don't count for anything?"

Nothing. Griffin couldn't move. His hair was plastered down around his ears and it was probably steaming because his ears were so hot. Burning. His thousand-dollar suit was getting drenched. Water was getting into his Beamer and all over the leather because, unlike Sharon, he hadn't had the presence of mind to close his door when he got out.

He did now. And he stared coldly across the roof of his car at this woman whom he thought he'd known, whom he'd been ready to give his heart to.

But he didn't know her. He never had. She'd lied to him from the start. She'd pretended to be...honest. And strong. And smart. And caring. He wouldn't even think about the sexual attraction they'd had. How much had been...like a *job* to her?

"Okay," Sharon said shakily. "Okay."

Without another word, she turned from him and began walking down the rainy street towards Oak. Griffin watched her go, her long coat wrapped around her all the way down to her calves. Her feet splashed through puddles she didn't seem to see. Then she was just a blur through the rain. She reached the corner and turned. Vanished.

And Griffin stared at where she'd been. Where she'd vanished.

Then, slowly, like the rain had rusted all his joints, he reached down into the car and took his keys out of the ignition. He locked all the doors, stepped back, and gently slammed the door.

Turning in the opposite direction from where Sharon had gone, he turned up the collar of his drenched suit jacket and began to walk.

35

A RAIN-SLOSHED STREET WITH TAXI CABS honks loudly when Griffin crosses, unseeing.

~~~~

The Oak Street bus, with Sharon heading downtown out of habit, even though her hideout is way out in Richmond. The middle-aged woman sitting beside her, tries to start a conversation.

Sharon has no more words.

~~~~

Griffin's phone jingles in his pocket like the door of the Red Owl. He answers in monosyllables as Majo verbally pushes him around about his attitude. About what he and Brent did to Sharon.

Griffin interrupts. "She told me she used to be a hooker."

A pause, then, "So what? You used to be a stiff-necked drone. Where is she?"

Griffin hangs up.

~~~~

Where is she going? Why does it matter?

Boobo needs her, yes. But not for one night. For one night Julia Morrow's sister out in Richmond, where Sharon hid this last week, can look after Boobo. Right now it is Sharon who is needy. For peace. Familiarity.

She will go back home to her apartment on Pandora, Sharon decides. For just one night.

~~~~

Griffin's cell jingles again when he is standing under the awning of a laundromat. The rain is still pouring down. He has no idea where he is.

"What?" he says into the phone.

"You're being an asshole," says Majo. "I'm coming to your office at five-thirty. You going to be there?"

Griffin considers. "If I can find my way back to my car," he says.

"Oh, Christ," says Majo.

~~~~

Almost an hour and a half later, Sharon is home.

She finds her building and apartment keys in the pocket of her coat and goes inside. Up.

All the lights are off as she goes in but there is enough gray light from outside to find her bedroom. She takes off her coat, lies down on her bed and, though it's not even five yet, falls instantly asleep.

36

S HARON DREAMT WHILE SHE SLEPT about all the things that had gone wrong in her life—her father leaving, her mother dying, her stepfather, Daryl.

But somewhere in the middle of it, a ray of sun shone down on her from above and she dreamt of her and Griffin walking a sandy shore on Lake Okanagan. They laughed and talked about the Ogopogo, and Griffin said he'd ride it if he ever saw it. Then he playfully swatted her bum.

"Stop it," she said.

But he swatted her harder, so it stung.

"Please," she begged him.

And he swatted still harder, so that....

Sharon's eyes jerked open. For real. Her apartment on Pandora. Her bum hurt from being slapped and her bedside light was shining directly into her eyes, directed by someone sitting on the side of the bed who smelled like burnt licorice.

The person leaned down and she looked into a face that sent instant icicles shooting through her veins. The rusty red hair. The mustache. The bright eyes that she knew sparkled most when he was hitting someone weak.

"Hi, darlin'," Daryl Polson said. "Long time no see."

~~~~

They'd been watching her place for almost four days now, he told her as he dragged her out to the hallway and towards the elevator. He'd slapped a piece of silver duct tape over her mouth and bound her hands behind her and her ankles together with thin rope, but Sharon managed to squeal and thump loudly enough coming out that someone heard. She saw the door of Mrs. Dewdney's apartment open a crack and the youngest Dewdney boy, six, stuck his head out.

Daryl turned and snarled at him. The boy popped his head back in again.

It was dark by the time they were outside. Six-thirty? Seven?

Daryl threw her over his shoulder and carried her, bouncing and struggling, to his car. A Crown Victoria. Daryl waved at the shadow from the front seat to pop the trunk. The shadow did, then hurried back with that distinctive sideways gate and burnt lip to help throw Sharon in.

The trunk lid closed her into darkness.

~~~~

She didn't know where they were when the lid opened again. Some back alley. Vaguely familiar from the brief view of the dark roof lines. Why?

Then a man she didn't recognize pulled a black hood over her head and wrapped his arms around her upper torso pinning her arms tight to her body as he lifted her out, sideways to the ground. Another set of hands got her legs. Together, they carried her in lurching discomfort through the thump and creak of what must have a been a heavy metal door, into a place as dark, dank, and moldy as the crawlspace where her father had stored all their old clothes and Christmas ornaments and where she'd been stuck once when she'd crawled in to hide in a game of hide-and-seek gone too far.

Someone hit a switch and a light came on so she could see

shadows through her hood—three figures, outlines of a door.

"Take her all the way up," said Daryl's voice. The tallest figure? She was sideways to everything. Disoriented. "The back, right room. Keep her tied up. Give her water. Watch her. Hit her if she gets noisy."

Then the lurching ride continued, climbing stairs, past the sound of cars, other footsteps, passing shadows, music and female giggle, clinking glass, an electric saw and banging (construction?), and finally the sound of muted conversations she could almost make out, before she was thrown roughly down on a creaking mattress that had a sheet over it but smelled of old sweat and dust.

"We leave the hood on?" said one of the men who'd carried her up.

"I guess," said the other and they both stood there for a moment, not moving.

But Sharon could feel their eyes on her and wished now she'd changed into something else, anything else, when she'd stupidly gone to her old place to sleep. She was still in her fuck-me clothes, the ones she'd worn to hijack Griffin with. The too-short red shorts, the black half-tee with no bra. Both still damp and bunched around her body in her crotch and armpits, the shirt clinging tightly to her breasts.

"*Mm*-mph!" she said through the tape over her mouth, careful not to wriggle so they would see her as talking, not just trying to escape. "*Mm*-mph!"

"You want to?" "You want me to?" "Sure. Go on." "I'm going."

One of the two shadows bent over her, lifted the bottom of her hood, scrabbled blunt fingers around the edges of the tape, and ripped it off.

"Aaaah!" she cried.

"Shut up!" the man said.

"Water," Sharon said quickly. "He said give me water."

One of the men went out. Sharon rolled on the bed, the other man watching the show, until she managed to get her tied-together legs over the edge. She swung them down hard to sit up. It took her four creaking, leg-bruising tries. When she made it, the man watching clapped slowly.

"Mother-a-God," he said, "would I like to–"

The other man returned and he shut up. But when number two had finished feeding Sharon water, the first man pulled him over and the men whispered together. Grunted. Kept stopping and turning their shadowy heads in a way Sharon was sure meant they were looking at her.

The last silence was the longest. As Sharon felt her breath getting shallower and panic rising, she saw one shadow walk to the door, lean out, then back in, pulling the door closed after him.

Click.

Think.

There was the clinking sound that might have been a belt loosening. A zipper came down.

No! Think back! Survival!

"You first, dude." "Yeah." "Alright."

What would she have...?

"So!" Sharon said cheerily. "How well do you guys know Daryl anyway?"

"What?" The first man. The instigator.

"I mean, you've been with him now for what? A few years? You ever actually been with him around his women? Because I was one of them, you know. Four years."

"What the–?"

"And I saw him once," Sharon chirped, "with a guy who tried to take one of us without paying. Without permission. You know what he did to him?"

"Holy crap, dude." The second man.

"It was great," said Sharon. "He twisted the guy's nuts right off him. Guy bled to death trying to get to a hospital. True story." It was, actually.

There was a choking sound and one of the shadowy figures backed off to the other side of the room.

"But go ahead and touch me, guys. I'm sure Daryl's mellowed with age, right?"

They didn't come near her after that.

~~~

Nighttime.

Colder.

The construction noise and music finally died out downstairs. She heard a number of motorbikes roar off in the distance, the sounds of shuffling boots on wooden floors below. How many flights had she come up? Was it three or four?

Daryl hadn't come up. Probably wasn't coming tonight, Sharon guessed. He had her. He was in no rush now.

The two guys watching her decided to take shifts. Number One clumped out and left Number Two to sit in the chair by the corner. And fall asleep.

If she'd been Wonder Woman, she would have found a way to saw these ropes off her and escape. As it was, the best she managed was to get rid of the hood. Which only showed her a plain box room with a single window too grimy to see through. It had the one bed she now lay on, which was a mattress on a kind of metal, spider-web frame, and one wooden chair. A low-wattage bulb hung from the center of the ceiling. The door looked locked, even if she managed to hop to it and turn the knob with both her hands and feet tied.

She might as well have kept her hood on.

Sharon shivered. The one good thing about the cold was how it focused the mind. She was no longer zapped and depressed that Griffin had rejected her...again. At least this time she'd managed to show him who she was. All of her. If she never saw him again (which sure looked likely right now) at least it would be *her* he remembered. Not some figment she'd created, but all of her, good and bad.

That was important somehow.

It was key.

A strength.

If she could just figure out some way to use it to cut her ropes and get her out of this place.

Think.

37

GRIFFIN'S SATURDAY MORNING found him sitting in his condo's mini-sun room, looking southeast over English Bay as the sun struggled to come up behind a heavy, soggy gray sky.

He was still dressed in his ruined clothes from the day before. He hadn't slept. Instead he'd played the sex and melodrama he'd shared with Sharon over and over in his head, looking for something he'd missed, some hidden camera that was supposed to have jumped out and told him it was all a joke.

But it hadn't been. It wasn't.

And every time *that* truth klunked into place, his brain skipped through his meeting with Majo later, where he'd told his friend about everything that had happened and had Majo roar at him, call him an idiot, and vow to make him watch *Pretty Woman* over and over until Griffin realized he'd just let Julia Roberts walk away into the rain by herself.

"Sharon is prettier," Griffin had said.

"See?" Majo had shouted, tearing at his tie. "Idiot."

But that was Majo. For him the idea of commitment was calling a woman for a second date. For him, none of this was real life. For Majo, almost nothing was fully real. Because it took responsibility and commitment to make things real. You had to be willing to make your choices and live with them. That was character. That was how you built a life.

And yet...

Griffin stood and stepped up to the floor-to-ceiling window. He pressed his head against it.

Wasn't that what Sharon was doing? Living with her choices? Trying to be better? To build her life?

The first joggers and bikers were hitting Beach Avenue now, heading for Stanley Park. Griffin should be down there instead of sitting here in a sticky, smelly shirt and tie and pants from yesterday.

But the shirt still had some of *her* smell on it. As would his underwear, his hands, his body.

He suddenly realized that he hadn't changed mainly because it would be stripping away the last bit of Sharon that he still held close to him. He needed her that badly.

Yet he was prepared to let her walk away because life had kicked her around so badly that she'd made some bad choices when she was younger?

Hey, he'd basically snubbed her in high school when she offered herself the first time because he thought she'd mess up his career. *That* had been a stupid choice. Because if he hadn't rejected her then, she wouldn't have ended up in Kelowna with—he remembered now from Ken Tanaka's report—"a big mustached red-headed guy who likes to beat up women." And Griffin wouldn't have ended up here, feeling stupid and alone.

It was time to do better.

Pushing away from the window, he went to his home office and opened up his filing cabinet where he'd put Tanaka's report. He flipped through it to the brief findings about Sharon, then known as Breeze. And this time, reading it with new eyes, the name Julia Morrow jumped out at him. Tanaka had noted that Morrow, a social worker, considered herself Sharon's friend. Putting two and two together, Griffin guessed that meant she was the one who'd helped Sharon break free from Daryl Polson the first time. Didn't it make sense that when Polson threatened again, that was who Sharon would turn to?

He grabbed his phone and dialed the number Tanaka's sub-contracted detective in Kelowna had noted for Julia Morrow. She answered after two rings, with a voice so full of sunshine that Griffin found himself grinning and picturing her and Wallace Lester doing a happy dance together.

"Ms. Morrow," Griffin said, "My name's Griffin Walsh and–"

"You're looking for Sharon, I bet! I'm so glad! You know she told me to contact you if anything happened and I lost your number!"

"If anything happened?" he prompted.

"She didn't go back to my sister's house in Richmond last night and she's always there by eight o'clock," Morrow said in a rush. "Something's happened. Something bad, or she would have called at least. You know that a man named Daryl Polson may be after her? He's—"

"I know who he is," Griffin said.

"All of it?" she said, surprised. "How they...know each other?"

"All of it."

There was a beat as the social worker took that in. "Then you know what would happen to Sharon if he found her again," she said finally. "He *owned* her for four years. You can't imagine how that scars someone, Mr. Walsh. Griffin. If he gets his hands on her again, even with everything she's done, she could go right back to that place she was. Or worse."

Griffin felt a chill at the words and a horrible stab of guilt in his chest. If he was the one who'd inadvertently sent her back... *Bad choices.*

"Did she tell you anything about her routine now?" asked Griffin. "Something that would help me find her?"

He could almost hear her thinking hard and shaking her head. "She'd planned to stick close to my sister until I could help her move somewhere else. It's hard to imagine what would lure her away."

Only seeing him. "Okay. Look, I'll try to find her. I'll go to Polson himself if I have to. Don't worry."

Some of the perkiness returned to the woman's voice. "I feel better just hearing that. I'm so glad Sharon found you, Griffin. You sound like a nice man. She deserves a nice man."

She did. But if all she could count on right now was him, he'd have to do.

"Goodbye, Ms. Morrow. Julia. I'll keep you informed."

"*Please* do."

He hung up. And just like that knew where Sharon had gone. Because he was starting, he realized, to get into her skin, to understand how she thought. She *wasn't* a Breeze that just wafted away. She'd struggled hard to put down roots. And where would she go when it seemed all her world was being ripped away from her?

Her Vancouver home. Her apartment.

Griffin hurried to the bathroom to shower and change. This Saturday, at least, was not going to be spent in the office.

~~~~~

Awake!

Sharon jerked her head up from the dirty sheet where she'd obviously fallen asleep. Her tied legs were stretched out on the bed and she couldn't feel her left arm, the one she lay on. Her neck had the mother of all cricks.

Wiggling painfully, the metal frame squeaking and rattling below her, she turned onto her back and tried to move her left arm to regain its feeling. After what seemed like forever, it started tingling and coming back, thank God. Part of her had been afraid that somehow they'd come to her while she slept and cut the tendons and nerves or something.

Now...

Straining to look around she saw that dull, silver light was pushing through the grime of her room's window. Despite the noise she'd been making, furthermore, no one was looking in on her. The chair where man Number Two had sat to guard her was empty.

The door was closed.

She let herself lie back on the sheets and gently roll her head around to work out the kink. Her position sucked. Whatever Daryl planned for her.... Well he'd had almost six years to think about it, and he wasn't as stupid as he let people think.

But she wasn't about to fall into reliving her nightmares about him—all the beatings, the manipulation, the simple stark fear. Because she'd figured out late last night exactly what strength her confession to Griffin had given her. It had cleansed her of the hold her past had on her. Not because Griffin had absolved her somehow. But just because he'd listened. Because she'd put it out there on the roof of the car between them in the rain, and she herself had finally been able to look at it clearly.

It had happened. She'd been fucked over. Her punishment had outweighed her bad choices and she'd paid the price for them twenty times over.

She wasn't going to pay them anymore!

Which, she thought with a rueful laugh, was fine in principle, but she had to get busy. She'd given up trying to work her hands or feet free of the knots late last night. All her efforts just made the cords cut deeper and she had bad welts and lacerations around them now.

Daryl had obviously learned good bondage skills over the years.

At least there were no sounds of stirring yet from anywhere she could hear. Rolling to the edge of the bed, she swung her tied legs over the side, then leaned her weight way forward and hopped to her feet.

It was time to explore.

~~~~

No one answered either Griffin's buzzes at Sharon's apartment building. Nor, after he'd waited and slipped in while someone left, had he heard anything at her door.

A few hard raps at Mrs. Dewdney's door, however, brought the plump woman to open it and stand before him.

"I haven't sold the computer," she said before he could say anything. "I'm still holding it."

Griffin smiled. "Good, because Sharon hasn't left town. I saw her yesterday afternoon. In fact, I thought she said she was coming back here. You haven't seen her?"

An odd, worried look flashed over the woman's face. "I...um...*I* haven't seen her."

"But?"

She brushed back one of many stray hairs. "My youngest, Nick. I thought he was just making up stories. What with all the excitement. You know."

"Uh-hunh. Could I talk to Nick?"

"He's due at school in twenty minutes, but...I guess."

She let him in.

~~~

The door was locked from the outside.

All Sharon had found in her room was a pen, two paperclips, an old bolt of some moldy cloth under the bed, and a loose screw she'd managed to pull out of a rotting floorboard.

Plus, of course, a few bruises and scrapes from the times she fell as she hopped and scrabbled about. And a whole lot of sweat and frustration.

She lay panting on the floor by the chair, listening to what sounded like construction starting up again on the floor below her—saws, hammering, some incredible whamming and rubble sounds like someone was trying to break down a wall.

Before that there'd only been the clumping of footsteps below her, only two or three guys. Maybe only the two left to guard Sharon, in fact. This had been borne out by the fact that the two times the footsteps had clumped upstairs, and sent her rushing back to her bed, it was Guy One or Guy Two.

Both were ugly sons-of-bitches with scraggly beards and tattoos. The idea they'd almost raped her yesterday had made her want to kick them in the crotches of their worn jeans. Guy One, the uglier of the two, with a long ponytail that he probably thought looked great under one of those little motorcycle skull-cap helmets, had dragged her, hopping, to the washroom down the featureless hall.

Guy Two had brought her some breakfast—an Egg McMuffin from McDonald's and an orange juice.

That last visit had been, Sharon estimated, almost two hours ago. Since then, she'd heard the sounds of more traffic outside, including some no-muffler roaring she figured was probably from motorbikes, and more clumping around inside.

She'd done a second whole search of the room, tried the locked door a few times, even tried to rub enough grime from the window to see out and try for a location.

No luck on all fronts.

Now she was just tired and sore and feeling vaguely nauseous from the greasy breakfast.

Clumping sounds in the hallway!

The instant adrenaline got her rolling up to her feet and hopping back to the bed. She fell onto it, wriggling around to slide the pen and paperclips, her only potentially useful finds, under the crumpled top sheet. Then she swung her feet back over the edge and managed to sit up just as she heard a key turn in the door lock.

The door swung wide with a bang she was sure was supposed to terrify her.

Instead she smiled a sardonic hello as Daryl-the-Dink Polson swaggered into the room. Jamie Bhoja sidled in behind him, wearing a sly smile that said he was looking forward to what was going to happen next.

38

As Griffin stood uncertainly in front of the run-down bungalow on this gray Saturday, he knew he'd reached a turning point.

Polson had Sharon. Griffin had no doubt of that. But the evidence of a six-year-old wasn't going to get the police involved. Especially when the only other evidence were the claims of an admitted former prostitute, the worried call of a Kelowna social worker, and the lack of known whereabouts of the supposed abductor.

Besides which, Griffin had no direction to point them in. Yet.

Which was why he was here, in front of the Port Coquitlam home of Peter W. Thompson. It had taken pumping Majo and, finally, the reluctant barkeep/owner of the Red Owl, to get the Hard Rider's full name. This was "Pete", of Sharon's recounted stories of Pete and Digger.

Getting help from a member of a motorcycle gang to locate the head of another biker gang was definitely not something Griffin had ever seen in his career path.

Until Sharon.

Shaking his head uncertainly, he strode up the front walkway and banged on the front door. Waited. Banged again. Nothing. Then he heard some clanking that sounded like it was coming from behind the house. He ducked quickly around the side and saw a back-lane-access garage. Someone was working inside it.

"Peter Thompson?" Griffin called, walking that way.

"Wh-what is it?" a voice answered.

Griffin rounded the back wall of the garage and looked in to see a bearded man with huge girth, sitting on a stool beside a beautiful Harley Davidson Fatboy.

"Hey, I remember you," Griffin said. "B-b-b-boobies! Right?"

The guy blinked at Griffin, took in the clothes Griffin was wearing—loafers, dress pants, polo shirt and leather jacket—and ducked his head suspiciously. "Wh-what do you w-w-want?"

Dropping his bad "hearty friends" routine, Griffin walked in, pulled up an old crate that sat against the wall, and sat on it, hands spread in front of him.

"It's like this, Pete. Sharon Dekker has been taken, kidnaped, by a guy named Daryl Polson. You know him?"

The biker shook his head and Griffin would have sworn the name indeed meant nothing to him.

"What about his friends Jackson Kilhenny? Or Andre Malovet?"

"Y-yeah." He said it slowly, something behind it.

"What?"

Pete wiped his nose with a greasy-black finger and his head began a worried little weave back and forth. "Kilhenny's j-j-j-just got a price on his head. F-For selling H. And s-s-stealing a sh-shitload of money from us."

"A price on his head? By who? Jean Calibeau?"

Pete's head jerked like he'd been caught talking too much and he pursed his lips together.

"Which means you don't know where I can find Kilhenny either, I assume," said Griffin.

"N-no."

"Shit," Griffin muttered and started to turn away.

"B-b-b-but...it'll be somewhere easy. He's not as s-s-smart as he looks."

"Right," Griffin said in frustration. He started to go again, but this time stopped himself. "If I find Kilhenny," he said slowly, thinking hard, "would Mr. Calibeau want to know?"

Pete licked his lips and tugged at his beard. Finally he nodded his head.

"Can you give me a number to call?" said Griffin.

~~~~

"My little Breeze darlin'," Daryl said. He ran his hand down her cheek and beyond, stopped at the tip of her breast, and used the back of his finger to lightly rub her nipple through her shirt.

"Name's Sharon," she said thickly. She willed her nipple to stay flat, not respond.

"I told you she calls herself that," sang the high voice of Bhoja from behind Daryl somewhere.

"Shut up," said Daryl. Then to Sharon, "You know I would have found you soon anyway. Some P.I. came snooping all over downtown Kelowna, asking for info about Sharon Neal, or maybe Sharon Dekker as she goes by now."

So Bhoja hadn't even mattered. Sharon was glad she'd pepper-sprayed him.

"Dekker is my legal name now," she said. "I had it changed."

"Hell," Daryl said, now rubbing her other nipple with his other hand, "you can call yourself anything you want, girl. You're still mine."

"You think so, *Dink?*"

His fingers suddenly gripped her swelling nipples and twisted them hard. The pain made her scream, then she whipped her head up and spat full in Daryl's face.

He slapped her hard across the face so she flew back onto the bed, face aflame.

And Sharon started laughing. "You bastard! You pussy! Dinky-dick Polson! That's what we all used to call you behind your back, you know."

She saw him coming down at her, his face red, like so many times before. And thought, in that instant, how she would normally just go quiet at this point, let him beat her, whimper and cry out like he seemed to want, hope it would stop sooner that way.

This time Sharon whipped her body hard to the side at the last second, so that Daryl's whole clutching mass crashed into the mattress where she wasn't, driving the rickety bedframe hard down against the wall with a metal-tearing sound.

Sharon laughed again. "Beating on tied-up women and little girls! That's your style, isn't it, Dink?" She squirmed around on the bed to face him, drawing up her tied feet to kick him once...tw–

He grabbed her feet and rose up off the damaged bed with them.

"Oh, that's good, Dink," Sharon taunted, fighting a gagging fear even as she readied for another quick twist. "Now you can show Bee-hoja here how it's done. He likes to beat up women too. Come on, big guy! Come *on!*"

Maybe it was the crazy light she put into her eyes or Bhoja's girlish scream of rage that did it, but Daryl suddenly stopped and dropped her feet to the floor. Turning, he gave Bhoja a stiff-armed shove that threw the skinny pimp back towards the door. Bhoja stumbled and fell before he reached it.

When Daryl turned back towards Sharon, his face still flushed, but his smile back on. "I'll be back for you later, darlin'. We got all the time in the world."

No, Sharon thought as she watched the two men leave and lock the door behind them. *She* didn't have all the time in the world. She had to figure out exactly where in hell this building was, then she had to get out of here.

She rolled all the way off the bed to land with a painful on the floor. She had to see if the metal frame had broken in any useful way. She just needed a ragged edge, something...

~~~~

Griffin just needed a clue, something. His body was thrumming with a sense of running out of time. He'd tried all the business contact numbers that he'd had for the Coogan Group.

Nothing.

He'd tried directory assistance on all the names, been referred back to Andre Malovet's office, of course, duh, and been unsurprised to learn that Mr. Malovet was not in the office and no, the secretary didn't know when he would be back.

Nothing.

Griffin stomped around his small office at Greene McNamara, literally beating his head with his fist. Come *on*. Pete Thompson had said Kilhenny was not very smart, that he wouldn't be hard to find. So where would a renegade biker guy who'd been swinging deals with a Kelowna biker gang boss go to hide? And what had pushed him to steal from someone like Jean Calibeau? Kicks? Cash flow?

He stopped hitting himself and pacing as the craggy figure of Burt Lester stuck his head into Griffin's office.

"Griff," he said like it was a secret handshake. "Got a minute."

No, he didn't. "Come on in, Burt."

The ex-football player did, looking around like he'd never been in there before, and Griffin wondered if the man had early Alzheimer's.

"What is it?" Griffin said.

"Wally likes you," Lester said, still looking around. "Thinks you're very cool for some reason." He winked nonsensically at Griffin. "But this other deal I've heard you making calls about, this Coogan Group?"

"They're not a client any more."

"No. Ah," said Lester. "Why is that exactly?"

"How about the fact they were criminals who wanted to buy property in the AIDS-ridden downtown east side just..."

He let it trail off. *The AIDS-ridden east side*. Where Pete had told Sharon that Calibeau would never go. *Wanted to buy property...*

Kilhenny couldn't be that simple, could he?

Ignoring whatever it was Lester was asking now, Griffin pushed the elder partner out of his office, shut the door, and picked up the phone to a friend of his in the Land Titles Office. Ten minutes later the friend called back.

There had been inquiries lately on three attached properties that stood side-by-side in a run-down part of Pender Street (which just happened to have easy access to all the drug and prostitution trade of both Chinatown and the downtown east side). One of those properties, the Red Owl, was now a heritage building and apparently no longer of interest.

But the one just to the east of it, a deserted garment factory, had been sold just that week.

"The name on the title?" Griffin asked.

"Andre Malovet."

Griffin hung up the phone with his heart pounding. They'd managed to buy, all Griffin's efforts to the contrary.

And Clara Dewdney's boy claimed he'd seen Sharon taken away from her apartment just after dinnertime last night. That meant that Sharon had been with Daryl Polson for almost twenty-three hours. She was still alive. Griffin had to believe that. But how much time would it take before, as Julia Morrow had put it, she went back to how she'd once been? Or worse?

He *had* to get the police out there. How?

Blinking with a spurt of creative thought that wasn't his usual bent, he reached into the pocket for the phone number for the number Pete Thompson had written down for him. Stared at it.

For a second he considered calling Majo and getting his advice. Criminals were *his* specialty, after all. Or even Brent or Rotty, respectively, for their talents in bullying and bluffing.

But Griffin's plan, ironically, was probably too far over the line for any of them. You had to be as committed as Lillian and as blindly desperate as Griffin to consider what he was about to do.

As Sharon might say, fuck it.

He put the phone number for Jean Calibeau on the desk in front of him and picked up the phone to dial.

39

Under the bed, Sharon gave another grunting push to grate the rope holding her hands against the jagged metal end of the torn bedframe.

She was on her stomach on the floor to do it, eating dust and getting splinters in her knees, feeling like the hammering and sawing below was going to cut straight up into her it sounded so close. But she was almost there. She could feel the rope loosening.

Or was that just her wrists going numb?

She pushed again, but jerked as the crazy whamming sounds started again and felt the metal gash her forearm. "Ahh!" She bit down on her tongue. Damn it! This was why she'd slid the old pen in between her wrists and rope—it was supposed to be a buffer between her flesh and her improvised saw.

Try again.

With three more careful pushes, the ropes suddenly loosened and Sharon twisted and turned her hands until they were...free! She swung them down and around her body, coughed at the cloud of dust that brought, and fought back tears over the sharp pains shooting through her shoulders.

Using her free arms, she pulled herself out and went to work on her feet.

~~~~

From the south side of the street, Griffin stared at the front of the garment factory and felt his hands sweating. Unlike the stately old Red Owl to its left, the blank poured concrete of the factory was obviously undergoing a major face lift. Two broken windows were being replaced on the second floor. Griffin could hear buzz-saws going inside, and what sounded like someone taking down an inside wall with sledgehammer. *Bam! Bam!*

And it was so obviously for bikers—Griffin counted five motorcycles parked on the street out front and another two in the alley on the building's right side—that it drove Griffin crazy Calibeau hadn't agreed up front to sweep in and shut it down.

But just like Griffin couldn't prove to the police that Sharon Dekker was being held captive in there, neither could he prove that Kilhenny was around. What if it was just Polson and company? What if, in fact, they'd taken Sharon somewhere else—or simply killed her?

Well there was just one way to find out.

He double-checked his watch, looked nervously around for the backup he hoped was there somewhere, then sucked up his courage and crossed the street to the factory's front door.

~~~~~

Feet clumping in the hallway!

Jumping back up onto the bed, Sharon looped the ropes she'd removed from her feet back around them, tugging them just tight enough to look convincing. She did the same over her wrists behind her back.

The door swung open. This time it was just Daryl. No witnesses to embarrass himself in front of.

"Hey, Dinky!" she called brightly so he'd look at her face, not her wrists and feet.

"Boy, you've gotten cocky, ain't you?" he said, not coming closer but just standing across the room, looking at her. Did he see the dust all down her black tee shirt? Did he see the loose way the ropes hung around her ankles?

"You've just gotten older," Sharon threw back. "More wrinkles. Hanging out with more guys like Bhoja. Thinking maybe the queer side's more your thing?"

Come on! Come closer!

~~~~

"Whaddya want?"

The mountainous blond speaker blocked Griffin from the doorway. Unlike the tee-shirted beer drinkers (no Kilhenny or tall redheads with mustaches) whom Griffin saw going in and out of what looked like a kitchen deep behind the man, the blond had sideburns but no beard or mustache. He probably didn't need them with all that muscle.

Griffin blinked up at him innocently. "I'm the fire inspector. We were informed of the recent purchase of this building for mixed use and we need to see what's being done."

The blond blinked down at him, probably trying to figure out what, exactly, Griffin had just said.

"Stay here," he said finally and turned to go find someone smarter inside.

Griffin stepped in and ducked left through a doorway, looping through what looked like a lot of deserted, connected rooms until he came at to the stairs he'd seen to the left of the kitchen. He dashed up them quickly, hoping no one had seen.

~~~~

Sharon saw a flush creeping across Daryl's face and his hairy hands clenched into fists. It pricked all the old fear memories, but those memories weren't the ones in control anymore. The ones that counted were how crazy-sloppy Daryl got when he was totally out of control. That and surprise just might get her by him.

"Because we always thought that about you, you know," Sharon said. "Me and the girls. Every time you beat us, we figured it was because you really wanted to suck dick."

"You...fucking...cunt," he said. He kicked the door closed behind him then stalked towards her with his jaw and fists clenched, his body shaking.

Sharon, dry-mouthed, got ready to move.

~~~~

Griffin reached the second floor with no one shouting at him from below, but there looked to be nothing there. One huge, empty space. Three long rows of tables upon which sewing machines had probably sat. A drop shaft over at the east side of the room that looked like it went from at least the third floor all the way down. It must have been used to cast down bales of completed clothing. Or crank up materials to the upper floors?

This was avoidance thinking.

Or an escape route?

But he wasn't there yet. He hadn't found Sharon and he hadn't found Kilhenny or Polson. Sharon and at least one of the latter two had better be in the building.

He could hear all the work going on up on the third floor. He turned the corner of the stairs and went *up*.

~~~~

As Daryl reached for her, she jerked right, but he'd been expecting that and grabbed her by the left arm.

What he hadn't expected was to have her right hand swing around at his chest with a pen clutched like a knife. He turned instinctively and the pen drove into his shoulder, ripping up Sharon's right hand but hurting him more.

He shouted with pain and released her arm. She pushed him back just enough to get a clear kick at his groin that he didn't even see coming.

He collapsed in with a whuff, curled up on himself.

Sharon ran for the door.

~~~~

My God, Griffin thought as he stopped, stunned, on the third floor landing. There had to be thirty guys, all wearing boots, work gloves, and earplugs. Some also had bandanas tied around their heads or mouths and there were a disproportionate number of beards and beer bellies, but otherwise it could have been a home make-over show.

In a haze. Because immediately to Griffin's right, two squinting guys with safety goggles and sledgehammers were pounding out the walls of a little hive of narrow rooms situated just right of the staircase landing between there and the building's front wall. Dust was a cloud around the crunching walls, the sledgehammers, and now around Griffin. It was probably laced with asbestos.

Beyond all that, towards the building's back wall, another set of guys with workhorses and chop saws were squealing through two-by-fours and banging together walls as fast as the sledgehammer team was whamming them down.

"Walsh!" said a thin figure in leather by the further group.

He was wearing a dust mask, but as he came closer, he tugged it down. Kilhenny!

Griffin would have been happier about the discovery if the former Hard Rider hadn't signaled one of this new gang's goons to walk over with him. And if Kilhenny himself hadn't been pulling out a gun.

There was a new window that had just been put in a ways along the wall past the sledgehammered walls. Now if Griffin just had a stone...

~~~~

Sharon ripped open the door, gasping, her heart pounding triple-time staccato in her chest.

To the left the hallway did an L-turn around where she'd been held. To the right it ran the length of the floor with a tee-branch halfway.

Which way? Which *way?*

She heard Daryl stagger up to his feet behind her.

~~~~

"What the fuck do you think you're doing here, Walsh?" Kilhenny said as he came.

Griffin, keeping the dust and crashing rubble between him and the gun, shrugged his shoulder, watching his feet. He mustn't trip.

Losing patience, Kilhenny signaled for one of his goons to circle around the other way to catch him.

Taking the distraction as a last-chance cue, Griffin grabbed up a four foot piece of downed lumber, braced it like a spear in front of him, and ran with a roar for the window.

40

THE ANGLE WAS TOO INDIRECT and the wood just bounced off, ripping it out of Griffin's hands and leaving momentum to carry him crashing into the wall beside it.

Shit!

A broken window or something thrown out of one was to be the sign he'd found Kilhenny! Sign for the backup troops to arrive! Now he had nothing!

"Walsh! What the fuck!"

He was cornered now. Kilhenny was to his left, coughing and stepping around the hive of half-demolished walls with his gun raised. His goon was closing from the right.

Suddenly a thumping of footsteps behind Kilhenny made all three of them turn. And there, stopped on the stair landing, momentarily frozen in shock as she saw them, was Sharon.

"Griffin?" she called.

Then a roar behind her made her run down the stairs.

Griffin dove past the goon to his right and drove left into one of the sledgehammer guys who had finally clued in something was going down. As the man stumbled, Griffin grabbed his sledgehammer, stumbled with shock at the weight of the thing as he hefted it up to his shoulder, then turned and roared towards Kilhenny's goon. The man held up his hands in horror and darted to the side. The hammer whomped against the glass, shivering it into a million fine cracks, tearing out the top of its frame so it hung by a blasted shard.

But not pushing it out.

"God*damn* safety glass!" Griffin roared, lifting the hammer again.

A gunshot whizzed past his shoulder. It hit the window, which detached and fell to the pavement in a tinkling crash.

"Thanks," said Griffin at Kilhenny's enraged face, then sprinted away from the stairs on an erratic course for the far side of the room.

"Get him! GET HIM!" Kilhenny screamed to his adopted gang.

~~~~

A floor down, as she backed away from Daryl and two guys from downstairs, passing the rows of long-abandoned sewing tables, Sharon heard the shot, cried out, then shouted, "Go!" as she heard Griffin's voice and running feet.

"Forget him, darlin'," crooned Daryl with a crazy edge to his voice. "I just want to show you I ain't playing for the wrong side."

Sharon almost stumbled on a rotten floorboard, regained her balance, and looked back over her shoulder. There was a hole in the ceiling there and the floor below it, maybe six-by-six. But it had to be too far to drop. If she broke her foot or even sprained it, it was the end.

The chase upstairs sounded like a herd of rhinos through the old wooden floors, weaving back and forth across the room. As it seemed to bear down right over them, Daryl and the other bikers looked up.

Sharon dropped down to rip up the rotted floorboard she'd tripped over. She held it like a three-foot baseball bat in front of her.

"Come on!" she shouted at Daryl over the thumping. "Come on!"

"Ho-lee shi-i-i-it!" sounded out of the stampeding above and Sharon jerked her face up to see a man in a dusty business suit come down backwards through the hole, catch the edge of that hole with his outstretched hands, and swing onto the floor beside her, landing in a stumbling hop step, his arms windmilling.

"Griffin!"

"Hi," he said as he caught his balance. Then he turned and kicked at a young biker who was jump-swinging down like a copycat. The youngster lost his balance and went screaming down the bottom hole.

"This is your boyfriend?" sneered Daryl, jerking her attention back that way. He was about to charge.

But everything changed in an instant as the sound of hundreds of engines—big, throaty, no muffler, chopper engines—suddenly filled the room, pouring in through the smashed out window at the far side and back, surrounding the building.

"What?" said Daryl and Sharon at the same time.

"The cavalry," said Griffin.

"Fuck that," said Daryl and rushed them.

Sharon swung her board and Griffin tried to grab and swing Daryl down the hole, but the former pimp was too strong for both of them. He took the board on his shoulder and grappled with Griffin, tearing at his suit and trying to slam his head into the floor.

With a grunt of effort, Griffin grabbed Daryl by *his* shirt and rolled him sideways so they both plunged into the hole.

Sharon swung around to the other two bikers, saw the men in Hard Riders' jackets pouring up from below, and put up her hands in mock surrender as they rushed to grab the two from the Mean Machine.

"I give up," she said.

41

THE SOUND MADE BY TWO MEN FALLING TWENTY-FIVE FEET onto a prostrate third man is a thud that shakes through your bones and whips your head back, clacking your teeth together and cracking your ribs.

One rib, as Griffin found out later.

The sound made by a bullet fired as an execution shot into someone's head two floors above you, where you can't actually see them, is something like a loud *pop!*

That's how Griffin would remember it.

And when he picked himself up off Daryl Polson, who'd been unfortunate enough to land *under* Griffin when they hit, the main thing Griffin felt was...unclean. The feeling was so intense that the only thing he could do to set it right was lift up Polson's head by his rust-red hair and wallop him one as hard as he knew how across his jaw.

The first time Griffin had ever punched a man. And the last, he hoped.

After that, it was just a matter of staggering out through the chaos—Hard Riders ripping up the place, tossing tools and furniture out the third story window, spray painting the walls, boarding up the doors.

Griffin passed one Hard Rider who looked considerably older than the others—small, bald, shriveled, and mean-looking. He was walking towards the bottom of the drop to where Daryl Polson lay.

"Wait," Griffin said, turning to stop this man.

But before he could see or do more, two Hard Riders grabbed him by the arms and gave him a painful bum's rush to the door. There he found Sharon, shivering, her arms clutching each other, a Hard Riders jean jacket wrapped around her.

She grinned up at him with a manic look that said she was going into shock. "You came for me!" she said. He held her and she scrabbled her hands against his chest. "And they said Daryl wouldn't bother me anymore. You know what that means?"

She made a sound that could have been laughing or crying.

Griffin swallowed. "We have to go. The police will be here any minute." His chest hurt as he raised his wrist to check his watch. "In fact they're late."

Sharon shivered harder, but he took the biker jacket off her anyway and threw it on the ground.

"Next door," she said.

"Okay," he said.

~~~~

Sharon let him walk her to the Red Owl because his right arm around her was the only thing keeping her from breaking down into a puddle of tears on the ground.

This time Griffin got the key from Henry and led her upstairs to the top room where they'd made love before. They both had showers then lay on the bed together, wrapped in towels. And even though his whole left side seemed to be in pain, she could sense him wanting her, on fire for her.

But not yet. First was talk.

She told him roughly what had happened to her, leaving out the most graphic parts because he was vibrating even worse than she had been, and *he* didn't have his own protective Griffin Walsh to calm him.

Then he told her how he'd tried to locate her through Julia, found she'd been kidnapped, and tracked down Pete, then the place. Also about phoning Calibeau, thinking he would arrive and then the police could arrive and arrest everyone.

He finished with, "Should we have stayed for the police?"

"They didn't even come," Sharon said.

But as she said it, the sirens and lights began arriving *en masse*. Soon the entire area was swarming with them and the light pulsed a weird, syncopated rhythm across the ceiling of their room.

On Sharon's insistence she and Griffin kept the room lights off and nobody bothered them.

When the television crews appeared, Griffin lowered the shade, pulled the curtains, and put the room's small TV on the floor to watch the live report.

"A gang war is said to have occurred here," said a beautifully-coiffed Asian reporter. "And detectives have confirmed they've found as many as six blood spatters, but so far no bodies. Witnesses say the former garment factory building was recently taken over by an out-of-town motorcycle gang, the Mean Machine, but that the Hard Riders had been planning to evict them as early as three days ago."

Griffin rolled painfully out of bed and switched off the TV so that the room was plunged into blackness. Almost. As her eyes adjusted, she could see him turned towards her. She could feel how his face screwed up tightly. "'Witnesses say?'" he said. "What witnesses?"

"Can you be sure it wasn't that way?" Sharon said.

"No."

"Then?"

"What about what I believe happened? Shouldn't I tell them?"

She held his eyes. Griffin Walsh, Boy Scout. Despite coming to rescue her, risking his life for her, all he could think about was his not telling the whole truth and nothing but the truth. She couldn't help but love him for that. Wasn't it the truth that had recently set Sharon herself free? But...

"It would only be speculation," she said.

"We were there!"

"And saw what, Griffin? I spent most of my time kicking at people and running away. How about you?"

"I called in the Hard Riders! I told them where to go!"

"Says you. Pete and Digger are always at the Red Owl. Downstairs. Right next door to where everything happened. You don't think they've noticed the bikers showing up there all week? The noise? The work? Didn't you say it was Pete who gave you the main clue on how to find me?"

Griffin frowned and she could see his mind whirring.

"It's hard for you, isn't it?" she said, going up on her knees on the end of the bed and taking his hands. "When nothing's as clean as you want it to be. No one's as perfect as you wish they were."

"Like me," Griffin mumbled.

Sharon gave a short laugh, though she felt like sobbing. She grabbed his hand and pulled him gently down on the bedspread beside her, careful of his left ribs. "I meant me."

He lay beside her and pressed his forehead to hers. "I haven't forgotten."

"But...you've decided you can live with it?" She held her breath and suddenly realized she could hear her own heart booming in her ears.

Then the fingers of his free hand were running back through her hair, pausing over her ears as if *he* could feel her heart beat, too. Which was only right, because this moment he figuratively held it in his hand. No, he could never destroy it completely. She'd learned that much. But oh please, all powers of forgiveness and redemption, how she yearned to just once find out at last how much he could make her heart *grow*.

"When you told me? I could only think of how ugly it was to have other people touching you, people like Daryl Polson, and all the nameless. It took two hours of walking around in the rain before it even occurred to me that your life back then, or now, or ever—it's not all about me. It's you!"

"And you can...live with it?" Sharon repeated. "Just tell me."

He reached for her chin and lifted it so that she could see his eyes, even in the dark. "Your life in Kelowna and your escape, your struggle to overcome it, to deal with it and use what you learned—they've all made you what you are now. The beauty, the strength, the compassion. How could I not 'live with it'?

"Besides," he said and kissed her once, gently, on the mouth, "what choice do I have? I don't think I can live without you. I love you. Do y—?"

"*Yes.*"

She shut him up with a kiss and he kissed her back, grew hotter.

She pulled back. "Can you? With your ribs?"

"Just be gentle," he said and let his hand slip to where she'd rolled the bath towel together just above her breasts. She moaned with pleasure as his hand pulled the towel apart and slipped smoothly around her breast, her hot nipple.

Because now it *was* time for this. The vise grip of her past had died while she had survived. As had Griffin. As had their love.

It was time to go forward.

42

IN MID-FEBRUARY, when Griffin escorted Sharon to the left rear corner of the Red Owl to stand at the head of what was quickly becoming "their" table, all the others were already sitting with their coats over the back of their chairs and the wooden blinds pushed down tight against the wet cold outside.

Majo shot his "I told you so" grin up at Griffin, something he did now every time he saw Griffin and Sharon together. He also could no longer say the word "stiff" in Griffin's presence without cracking himself up.

Lillian shared a secret smile with Sharon. The buzz was that all the problems with the Red Owl had vanished at about the time of the mysterious biker gang war next door. And while Griffin wouldn't take credit for it, Sharon had shared with Lillian how Griffin had helped her use her corporate sponsors to set up a permanent lease of just *one* Red Owl room to be a guarded "safe room" for prostitutes trying to leave that life for good. It currently had Micky and Rose in it. Bhoja had vanished, along with Angel.

Rotty had brought along his own date today, a gorgeous nineteen-year-old who made Lillian roll her eyes every time she spoke, but whom Sharon found charming. Her attempts at crude humor reminded Sharon she owed Lisa Doigis a call. If nothing else, to tell her that little Danny's father had finally shown up asking for her—almost reluctantly, Sharon thought—and then just left. He hadn't been back.

And Brent. He reached up to grab Griffin's arm the second Sharon went to talk to Henry. "Is your woman still crazy?" he whispered.

"Right out of her head," Griffin whispered back.

"Excellent. Tighe resigned finally, by the way. He sent Sharon a check to cover the cost of the course."

As if on cue, Sharon returned with a huge smile. "I am happy to announce," she said grandly, "that in exactly one minute the Red Owl is donating one round of draft to this table in celebration of this auspicious occasion!"

There were cheers and table thumping, growing in volume until the waitress of the day, Jenny Lind, had brought two full trays of beer and passed them around to everyone.

Then Rotty said, "What special occasion?"

The others leaned forward, equally clueless.

Griffin smiled and felt Sharon smiling with him, her hands around his arm. "It's a celebration of two announcements, actually," he said. "The first is that Sharon and I are engaged."

A round of cheers broke out, with Majo pumping up a fist in triumph and Brent drolly announcing over the hubbub, "Oh, *that's* a surprise."

When it died down, Griffin set his beer momentarily on the end of the table. "The second announcement!" He reached into his inside sports jacket pocket and drew out a thick sheaf of papers folded in half lengthways.

"The lease to our new offices in Yaletown, my friends. Walsh, Cruz, Major, Lee & Rothschild, Partners in Law, is now officially open for business!"

He threw it onto the table and Majo hoisted his glass of beer simultaneously. "To freedom and adventure!" he offered.

Lillian sang out, "Truth and compassion!"

Brent said, "High billings supported by endlessly long work hours and don't tell your hubby I said that, Sharon!"

Rotty waved them all down, turned to Griffin and Sharon, stood, and said simply, "To love."

Which was promptly booed and huzzahed until he sat down with an elaborate shrug.

Griffin picked up his mug and they all grew silent, looking and waiting. "To everything you all have mentioned, with the possible exception of Mr. Major's stupidity, and to all of you."

They all rose their glasses and drank, save for Griffin and Sharon, who turned towards each other, licked their lips simultaneously, and laughed.

"To us," Sharon said.

And the kiss they shared outdid any toast in the Red Owl or beyond.

About the Author

Terri Darling lives with her family in the Pacific Northwest, where she writes sensual, suspenseful, and sweet romance. You can find more about her and her work at www.terridarling.com.

Want more?

Read on for a sample from her romantic suspense novel *Downhill Rush*.

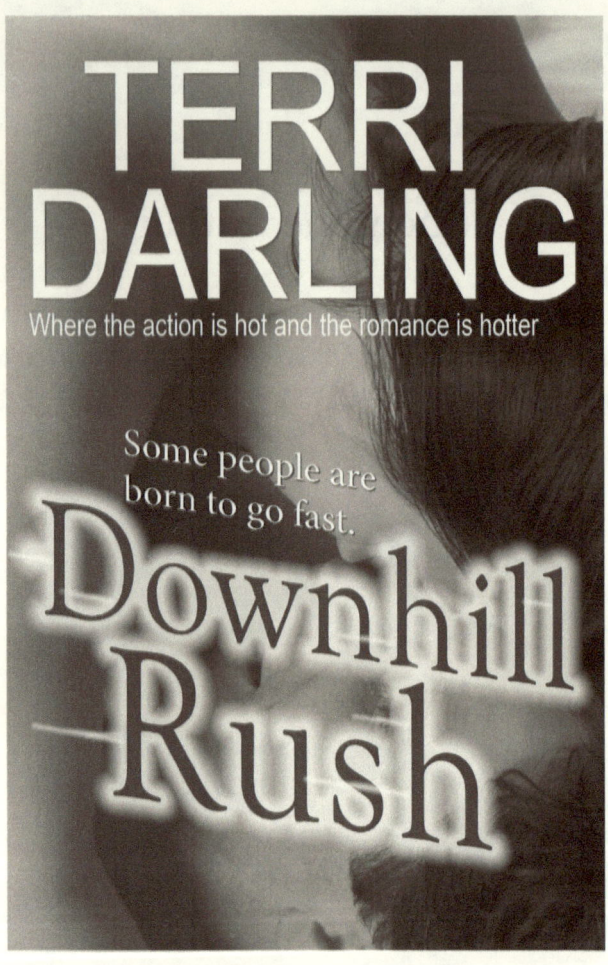

At a new ski resort in B.C.'s Coast Mountains, Kylie Michaelson is desperately trying to find her sister, last seen with a Russian playboy who just may be involved in human trafficking.

Against her will, Kylie accepts the help of a failed lawyer/ski bum. But how can she trust him when he's clearly got dark secrets, she's already falling for him, and the people they're hunting together may have started hunting them?

DOWNHILL RUSH

Terri Darling

PROLOGUE

WHEN THE MAN KNOCKED ON THE DOOR of the downtown hotel room, his partner opened it. The man led in his latest conquest.

Without a word, the partner looked the dazed young woman over and grabbed her by the round chin to open her lips and check her teeth. The blond hair was next—it was tugged, the roots checked. Then the rear and breasts, squeezed to ensure they were natural.

"Okay," the partner said at last and stepped back. "She'll be the sixth."

The man who'd brought her in flipped back his own long hair and spoke with a Russian accent. "Good. Do you know how hard it is to find American girls who fit our requirements?"

The partner gave a crude laugh. "So taxing, I'm sure. You still don't think this is necessary, do you."

"If it works...." The Russian shrugged.

"It will. You watch. In three days we suddenly get the power you've been looking for. The girls are the key."

"We will see."

"And you?" the partner asked his blond captive, who had been blinking around with a dull expression since being led in. "Do you believe you will get everything you've ever wanted?"

The girl blinked hard, trying to focus on where the voice had

1

come from. "Home?" she said wistfully.

Even the Russian laughed at that. "Not just yet, little *kroshka*," he said.

"Let's get her to the hills," said the partner.

The Russian nodded and took the girl's arm. But just before they left the room, the girl seemed to clear her head for a brief moment of lucid analysis. "Kylie?" she whimpered. "Kylie? Take me home."

1

THERE SHE WAS! The flash of dark blond hair. The small willowy body carving back and forth between the trees off the side of the ski hill beneath her. Samantha! It had to be. Maybe was?

Squinting down and backwards, Kylie Michaelson almost missed getting off the chairlift. Luckily one of the two snowboarders riding up with her elbowed her. She looked and jerked up her ski tips just in time. They hit the exit ramp and the boarders zipped down to the right to each strap in their free foot. Kylie slid, arms and ski poles waving madly, straight down the ramp and promptly fell over.

Blushing madly, she dragged herself quickly out of the exit path and managed to get to her feet. Okay, she thought, trying to steady her heart as she tugged up her gloves. Okay. Frosty morning air, overcast skies, crunchy snow. She remembered these from her childhood. She'd always hated them, but she remembered them. And skiing was like riding a bike. You never forgot.

Besides, she had no choice now. If that was truly Sam down there....

"Yo?" called one of the two snowboarders who'd come up the lift with her. He'd just finished strapping his free boot to his board and had rolled to his feet over to Kylie's right.

His companion answered with a whoop and they slid, faster and faster down the narrow trail that curved to the right.

Oh, jeez.

She brushed back her chestnut hair—it hadn't been cold enough to need a ski hat—and bent down to quickly double-check her bindings. Which is when one of skiers or snowboarders who'd come up the lift after her bumped her from behind and she started to slide forwards.

"Oh, no. No, no, no," she said as she waggled upright, her arms windmilling for balance.

Just like riding a bike. Really.

She was picking up speed, fighting to remember what she'd once known, when she noticed that as the lead-in trail approached the main slope, a small orange rope marked the out-of-bounds area along the left. Kylie was headed straight for it.

She was going to die.

Ensuring this, boarders and skiers who'd come up the lift behind her all seemed to be heading down at once, whooshing by her in sprays of powder. One clipped her on the left elbow and Kylie's left ski tip came up. Furiously she tried to compensate by pushing down with her right ski, but that just made the ski turn to the left underneath her. With a suppressed howl of frustration, she realized she was falling. Right into the path of a two more skiers.

Then suddenly she wasn't.

A hand had caught her by her right arm and swung it forward while an arm shot around her waist to bring her to an abrupt halt. She was panting, wild-eyed, in the intimate embrace of a tall drink of a man wearing a light, green-and-white ski jacket. He wore a Sherpa-style hat that wrapped around his face. All Kylie seemed to see was a chiseled, deep-tanned face that needed a shave, and eyes that were deep and hidden, but probing hers with an intensity that made her feel suddenly naked.

"Whoah," he said.

She wasn't sure whether her legs were holding her or only his hard body. And the air around them—it seemed to crackle and go very thin. Or was it just that she'd stopped breathing? It was hard to look at anything but the man's dark eyes.

Then he began to smile at her, a mocking smile, and she found her breath again. She pushed at him furiously. He kept his hands on her elbow but skidded just enough downslope from her so she could see he was on a snowboard.

A snowboard! Her parents had always told her that boards were for kids and snooty teens. They were totally uncontrollable, a hazard to the more responsible skiers, death to powder slopes, rebels and druggies all.

Of course, those were her parents' thoughts from the early days of snowboards at Telluride where Kylie's parents had taken Kylie and Sam learn to ski, but still.

She shook the elbow. "Let go of me!"

"You're sure?" He was definitely mocking her.

"Please." She made it colder than the mountain.

"All right."

He released his hold, and the sudden weightlessness she felt unbalanced her again so she began sliding forward to the lip of the narrow trail. Beyond its orange rope, she saw now, was a gully of tumbled, snow-covered boulders before the pine trees.

Her rescuer hopped like a spread-legged bunny up the hill to grab her a second time, but by this time some of her childhood ski legs had come back to her and she'd dug her downhill ski in hard, coming to an ungainly-but-effective halt.

"Good," said the man, his hand steady on her arm, tingling and annoying. "Now if you just bring the back of your left ski down a—"

"I've got it," Kylie said. Her face was red with humiliation.

Even worse, she suddenly realized, this man, this...overgrown rescue hero, had so distracted her from her missions that shed completely lost her chance to catch Samantha on this run. Who knew where Sam would be by the time Kylie reached the bottom? Maybe this was just a quick morning ski for her, and now she'd be walking to some nearby hotel. Or driving out of this little ski development altogether; maybe driving back to Vancouver.

"I said I've got it," she said peevishly. "Thank you for your help. You can go."

"I can go?" he said. Laughing at her. But he released her arm and slid down a foot from her, not skiing away. Watching her.

"I mean it," she said, digging in her poles and pushing, sweating, back from the drop-off.

"Yes'm." Imitating something from *Gone with the Wind* now. He wasn't leaving.

Fine. Not only had he blown her chance to catch Samantha, now he needed proof that she could get down the hill without killing herself or taking out a dozen other people? With her teeth clenched and poles planted hard, Kylie, strained her way back to a downhill position. There she thrust her jaw forward, hunched her shoulders, and placed her skis into an ungainly-but-determined snowplow. Slowly, ever so slowly, she began a controlled descent around the curve of the trail.

Boarders and skiers, including two who looked to be about six years old, steered as far around her as they could, but she still felt a grim sense of pride. There was nothing, ever, that she hadn't been able to do when she set her mind to it.

"See?" she called back to her snowboarding rescue man.

With a swoosh, he was down beside her, sideslipping on his snowboard to exactly match her descent. His lips still had their mocking curve. His eyes watched her with fascination. But there were squint wrinkles around the eyes that put him at least into his thirties or even early forties. And snowboarding! A mid-life thing then. Probably married with kids. Seeking a little thrill in his life. Kylie had met enough of those in her job as a buyer down in Portland. Men eager for a quick fling to make them feel young and important. Kylie had actually fallen for one of them a few years ago. She'd let Richard string her along for almost three years, believed all his lies about getting a divorce, let him twist her heart into knots, before she'd finally found the internal resources to pull back.

Only to find that her baby sister had been getting into even worse trouble while Kylie had been messed up.

What was it about the Michaelson sisters that attracted such jerks? And why, so soon after she'd gained a more mature perspective on romance, was she once again feeling a tug of attraction here? Looks and snowboarding skill did not a good catch make. Especially when they distracted her from her mission.

She looked away from him, thrust out her jaw, and concentrated on getting down the hill.

"You're welcome," he said.

"What?" Kylie started at the nearness of his voice as he'd slid right up beside her, but kept her eyes determinedly ahead.

He laughed. "Macaulay Rush," he said and began sliding away from her.

"What?" she repeated, turning to watch, mortified by her sudden lack of verbal skills.

"My name!" he called back to her. "Take it slow and have a good time!"

Then he was onto the main slope and bulleting down the hill.

~~~~

Mac shook his head and wished he could smack it hard against something as he boarded away from Miss Fancy Pants. What in hell was he thinking? It was like his old rescue complex had jumped up from its grave the second he'd seen her struggling to get her rental skis on.

Something about the childlike jump of her nose married to a distinctly womanly body. Where had she gotten a ski suit these days that clung to her curves like that? Deep red, no less. And the determination in her eyes battling the fear.... When he'd followed, then saved her from skiing into the gully, he'd been doubly hooked by the perfume she'd been wearing—light and breezy, expensive, as if she'd chosen it for the occasion. As if she'd carefully put together everything about herself.

She was trying so hard. For what? For whom? She looked like she'd been skiing alone, which was why he'd tried approaching her. But then she'd rebuffed him, something he wasn't used to.

Married, then? Attached? Lesbian? Work obsessed?

Mac shook his head hard a second time. Regardless, if there was one thing he was not going to do, it was get all wrapped up in a difficult woman. He'd been there, done that, had chosen a different course for his life that was working out just fine, thank you very much.

Oh, yeah? nagged a little voice inside him. *You're going to be blind to this too?* His head twitched backwards as he rode, pretending to follow the flight of the resort's sightseeing helicopter swooping back to its pad on the other mountain. Yes, Miss Fancy Pants was still there, stopped halfway up the hill from him.

I'm surviving.

Case closed. He had a snowboarding class to teach.

~~~~

Kylie saw her rescuer look back at her, then turn his lean body downhill and lean forward to pick up speed, jump moguls, and carve quickly around the trail's switchback down through the trees.

She chewed her upper lip and inwardly checked off all the errors she'd already made on this foray today. The most glaring one after overestimating her skiing ability was not asking her rescuer for information. He was obviously a regular at the hill, probably knew all the hills and maybe even a few of the people who came out here all the time. He should have been the first person she asked about Samantha.

But she'd been too proud and too wary of his interest in her. She'd behaved like a defensive schoolgirl or beauty queen. That might be acceptable behavior for a Nieman Marcus buyer, but it wasn't going to help her find her sister. She had to go back to the mode she'd been consciously developing since her search began. Think *open-minded*, *charming*, *questioning*.

Yet at the same time, *tough*. The man who her parents said had seduced Samantha away from university sounded dangerous. It had taken Kylie almost three days of asking around the University of Wisconsin where Sam had met the man to get his name, Mark Roskov. He apparently was sleek and gorgeous, with a hawk-like nose and jet black hair worn down to his shoulders.

Another day of asking turned up someone who thought Roskov had only been visiting Wisconsin; he'd originally come from BC, Canada. Kylie got on the internet to hire a private eye in Vancouver who discovered Mark Roskov did not exist. But someone matching his description had taken a business trip to Madison on the very days Roskov had been there. His name was Tibor Balakirev, the playboy scion of a wealthy Russian-Canadian family in the Vancouver Ports shipping industry.

"Traveling in secret?" Kylie had said. "Who does that sort of thing?"

She'd almost been able to hear the man's shrug over the phone line. "Russian mafia."

"Really," she'd insisted.

"Serious," he'd said. "So if you want me to probe any more, it's gonna cost."

Instead, over her parents' protests, Kylie had taken an indefinite sabbatical from work, bought a plane ticket, and flown to Vancouver in person. She'd gone to the elder Balakirev's offices to ask after the son but she'd gotten nowhere. A quick check through the white pages, though, had turned up Tibor's condo address. And though Tibor hadn't been there, one of his neighbors told her that through most of February Tibor could often be found at his "second home" in the mountains just north of Vancouver. It was an exclusive new ski village he was helping to develop, more extensive and self-contained than the local hills but closer than Whistler. Balakirev's consortium had named it Milaya Ridge.

Which was why Kylie was here now.

"Shit!" some kid yelled as he skidded a sharp turn on his snowboard just above her and missed her by inches.

Kylie took it as a cue to get moving.

She snowplowed carefully down this hill, designed to be the introductory run, and decided she had to relearn to ski before she went looking further for her sister. If the man she'd met near Tibor's Vancouver condo was right, Tibor came out here for days at a time. Loved to ski. All Kylie had to do was learn to maneuver these slopes, ask enough questions, and she'd at least find this possible mobster. Hopefully her sister would still be with him.

Kylie therefore headed for the same chairlift she'd first come up and flashed a dazzling smile at the young liftie who operated it. He was a few years older than the average liftie here, maybe all of twenty-two. Still too young for her, but hunky in a soap opera kind of way. Windswept blond hair he'd obviously spent some time on, but a refreshingly open country boy manner, with the strong thighs of a regular skier or boarder.

"Made it down okay?" he asked as she slid into one of the four loading tracks, alone this time since the line had become less crowded.

She laughed and read his name tag. "Barely, Bo!"

"Well you keep right on trying," he said with what she guessed was meant to be his killer smile. His eyes ran obviously down and up her body.

Good. Kylie smiled to herself as the chair swung under her and she was away. She wasn't above flirting a bit to get an ally. She'd ask him about Samantha soon. But first she had to relearn to ski!

And so she did.

For the next three hours she pushed herself relentlessly. She studied other skiers. She found ways to ride the chairlift up with the good ones and pumped them with questions on technique. She even accepted the offer of one older gentleman who skied down with her twice from the top and gave her pointers all the way.

Crouch, plant pole, spring up and swish around...

She passed Macaulay Rush a few times, surprised to see he was a snowboard instructor teaching a group of teens half his age, both boys and girls. Even from a distance, Kylie was struck again by the man's incredible sense of self-assurance, but even more by his apparent patience. Yet when he came close to each kid to point out how they could improve, joking where needed, or serious and supporting, she saw no trace of mockery. Just caring.

Hm.

The third time, she caught his eye as she skied past to show him there were no hard feelings. He looked away like she didn't exist.

Of course. Of course. She deserved that. She'd been rude. Downright nasty. But *he* hadn't exactly been patient and caring with *her* now, had he?

Distracted by how mean he was being to her now, she missed a mogul, had it buck her suddenly, and went sprawling and spinning in a snowy mess down twenty feet of hill.

Thank you, Mr. Rush, she thought when she'd stopped. She wiped snow from her eyes and mouth. *Thank you very much.*

By noon, she'd progressed enough to try a few blue runs and came down them feeling pretty good. Yes, her thighs and bum ached from the unexpected demands and her feet were cramping from the ill-fitting rental boots, but the satisfaction of being able to actually look *good* from her imaginary bird's eye view, pushed all the aches away. She hoped Macaulay had noticed.

No. Wipe that thought.

How about—even her mother and father would be impressed? Sure. She decided against one more run up the beginner's chairlift and poled her way to the sprawling lodge for some lunch. Of course, if her parents had been impressed, it would have meant they'd seen her, which meant they'd have been up here looking for Samantha themselves. And that would have been too time consuming for them, wouldn't it. Too inconvenient.

The thought made her mood take a sudden dive and everything became harder. She reached the front of the lodge and skied awkwardly to the ski racks. A line of perspiration trickled down her temple as she looked down to stab her ski poles at her bindings to make them release.

Face it, she thought. So far all she'd really accomplished today was prove once again that she could do anything Samantha could by dint of sheer hard work. But she hadn't found Sam herself. There'd been no sign of her on the hills after all. The people on the chairlifts, mostly visitors, many German and Asian tourists, didn't recognize Samantha's picture. Bo-the-liftie swore he'd never seen Sam here but sure would have remembered if he had. "Almost as pretty as you," he'd gushed.

And now her bindings were not releasing.

"Argh!" she grunted and rammed her ski pole tips together into the snow. One stuck. The other fell over.

Forcing herself to ignore it, she bent over double to try releasing the right binding with her hands. It only unbalanced her so she began sliding. She hopped, skipped sideways, grabbed at the ski rack, missed....

Strong hands caught her under the arms from behind and pulled her upright. She didn't have to turn to know it was Macaulay's face she'd see smirking at her. It was like her whole body had somehow become sensitized to his touch and thrilled with eagerness to get more, even as her pride bristled. What? He only came to her when she was weak? She stared straight ahead, her face burning.

"Let me give you a hand," came his voice, warm and gravelly. His boot—he obviously had his snowboard off now—stomped down on the back of her right binding, springing her ski boot free. He still held her as he did the other one and she stepped completely free of the skis.

"You can let me go now," she said.

"You're sure?" With incredible audacity, he'd stepped closer to her and slid his hands forward under her arms so his own arms wrapped around her from behind. She didn't let men *do* that sort of thing. Other than her one mistake with Richard, it was always Kylie who was in control and calling the shots.

But through her jacket now Macaulay's arms pressed the undersides of her breasts and sent little shocks through her. Then his grizzled cheek trapped a wave of her hair against the left side of her face. She could feel his breath, hot and smelling like sweet coffee, and the rustle of his ski jacket, open and rubbing the sides of her own.

Kylie felt her knees shake and heart race so hard that her scalp tingled. She forced coolness into her voice. "I've been able to stand on my own two feet since I was a year old."

"I bet."

His hands suddenly released her and her body felt an urge to turn and grab them back again, an impulse that was so out of character it almost made her cry out.

He saved her by stepping fully away and to one side so she could see his face. That half smile, mocking her. It slapped Kylie's weakness away and she arched a brow at him.

"Are you trolling for business?" she asked.

"What?"

"You're a ski instructor, right? Or do you only do snowboarding? Do you get a commission if you bring a new student into the school for lessons?" She jabbed her ski pole toward the rental shop building just left of the lodge. A sign across the peak of it also announced it as the meeting place for ski or snowboarding lessons.

Macaulay's tan face flushed red. "This isn't my usual mountain. I'm only up here filling in as a favor to someone. So no, I don't get a 'commission' for bringing in new students."

Kylie was flustered by his anger but fought not to show it. "You're here as a favor? For whom? Tibor Balakirev?"

His face froze and his eyes tightened. "What do you know about Tibor?"

"Um...he's...a friend," she said.

"A friend."

"That's right." She licked her lips. Her mouth had gone very dry under his narrowed gaze. "Do you...uh...know where I can find him?"

A part of her hoped he'd burst out protectively that Tibor was a dangerous man and she had to stay away from him, but he didn't. Rush just stared at her a beat longer then tossed his head towards the second story of the ski lodge. The lodge looked like a high-end log cabin that had been stretched lengthwise double tiered at the northern end, far down from the main entrance where skiers and snowboarders stomped in and out. The steeply-sloped roofs were covered with snow that was melting back from the eves. Where Macaulay Rush was indicating was the second story at the northern end.

"I understand Tibor's got a private club up there," Rush said, "for all his girls."

The slight accent he put on the last word, the way his eyes flicked dismissively over Kylie's body as he said it, made Kylie blush. She recalled the descriptions of Tibor as a Russian lothario and her blush grew hot with indignation. She wanted to whip out her picture of her sister, show it to this man, and tell him *that* was who she was really looking for.

But two things suddenly struck her. First, this man obviously thought she'd be safe talking to Tibor so Tibor likely wasn't the Russian mobster her p.i. had believed. Second, if Rush thought, however rudely, that she was somehow the type who could be on of Tibor's "girls", then maybe others would too. It might ease her way to seeing Tibor himself. And that mission was more important than her pride right now.

So Kylie smiled tightly, nodded, and simply said, "Thank you."

Her answer made Rush's face go dark and he stepped definitively back from her.

He made no move to leave or walk with her into the lodge, so Kylie said, "What's good to eat in there?"

"Ask Tibor."

"Maybe I will," she snapped and clumped in that direction without looking back.

~~~~

As she entered the lodge, a man reluctantly cracked open his cell phone, touched a speed-dial number, and said, "The woman you asked me to watch? She's on her way into the lodge."

"For lunch?" snapped the voice of Tibor's shadowy partner.

The man sighed. "I think she's going to try for the upstairs rooms."

The cursing that came through the phone was so guttural that the man held the cell phone away from his ear. When it finished, he quickly held the phone close again and heard his boss say, "Follow her. If she tries to go upstairs, stop her."

"How do—"

"Whatever it takes. She's a small woman. Surely you can handle that much."

To keep reading, look for the novel at your favorite retailer in e-book or trade paperback editions.